Provided

by

Measure B

which was approved

by the voters in

November, 1998

ellipsis

A John Marshall Tanner Novel

STEPHEN GREENLEAF

SCRIBNER

NEW YORK LONDON TORONTO SYDNEY SINGAPORE

SCRIBNER
1230 Avenue of the Americas
New York, NY 10020

SCRIBNER and design are trademarks of Macmillan Library Reference USA, Inc., used under license by Simon & Schuster, the publisher of this work.

Designed by Colin Joh
Text set in Aldus

Manufactured in the United States of America

1 2 3 4 5 6 7 8 9 10

Library of Congress Cataloging-in-Publication Data
Greenleaf, Stephen.
Ellipsis: a John Marshall Tanner novel/Stephen Greenleaf.
p. cm.
1. Tanner, John Marshall (Fictitious character)—Fiction.
2. Private investigators—California—San Francisco—Fiction.
3. Women novelists—Fiction.
4. San Francisco (Calif.)—Fiction. I. Title.

PS3557.R3957 E45 2000
813'.54—dc21   99–087721

ISBN 0-684-84955-0

To Ann,
first and last

ellipsis

chapter 1

I've been in the business a long time, so these days I make them come to me.

They don't like it much, the lawyers and their satraps, and they like it even less when they compare the pedestrian decor of my office to their own palatial work environments, but if they want me, they put up with it for as long as it takes to hire me. Sometimes it takes quite a while. Like this time, for instance.

Her brown hair was flecked with gray and crimped into a Brillo bun that reminded me of my grandmother, the one on my father's side who always made me take off my shoes before coming indoors, the one I didn't like very much. Her powder blue blouse buttoned to the throat with mother-of-pearl, her navy blue suit jacket covered the entire topology of her torso, and her matching straight skirt was hemmed well below the knee, at the point of maximum frumpiness. Her shoes were as sensible as snow tires; the eyeglasses on her nose made her look like a jungle bird on the brink of capture. Some people think women lawyers are like Ally McBeal. Those people have never met one.

She didn't have an ounce of fat or of irony either. Whatever had brought her to my place of business was deadly serious, in fact, or so I was urged to believe by her demeanor.

We faced each other like bookends in the reference section. "Mr. Tanner?"

I glanced at the calendar, the one labeled HARD BOILED. "Ms. Sundstrom?"

"I'm pleased to meet you," she said without meaning it, and extended a ringless hand.

"Same here," I said as we shook. Her flesh was as cold as custard. Her knuckles were as faceted as fine jewelry. "And please call me Marsh."

"Karla."

"With a *K*?"

"Yes."

"I'll bet your father was Karl and you were an only child."

"How did you know?"

"Elementary, my dear Ms. Sundstrom."

After a twitch of indecision that no doubt questioned my sobriety, she gestured toward a chair. "May I sit?"

I'm nothing if not magnanimous. "Of course." I gave her credit for not trying to dust it off.

She squirmed this way and that, trying to find a comfortable angle of repose, but it would have been easier to find a four-leaf clover in the carpet. Her focus on her own contentment was such that she didn't even respond to the painting on the wall at my back. It was just as well. She probably viewed Klee as random and racy and therefore profane.

She clasped her hands and launched her pitch. "Before we get into details, I should mention that the engagement I'm going to describe will occupy virtually all of your time, at least periodically. Are you in a position to take on such a task, assuming we formalize the arrangement?"

My mind glided across my active case list the way a seagull glides across a landfill. "As it happens, I'm between projects at the moment."

"Good."

"Not according to my accountant."

She frowned until she deciphered it. "Yes. Of course. Well, I'm sure the hiatus is only temporary. What are your rates, if I may ask?"

I employed the fudge factor I use when the job seems tedious or the client obnoxious. "Sixty dollars an hour plus expenses."

She raised a well-penciled black brow. "That seems rather high."

I crossed my arms and propped my feet on the desk, assuming my own favorite angle of repose. "You're a lawyer and you're here on behalf of a client, am I right?"

"That's correct."

"So your meter is running, as they say."

"I . . . yes. If you want to put it that way."

"Then I'll charge whatever you're charging."

She colored and looked away. "That wouldn't be at all appropriate."

"Why not? I'm the one loaded with free time. Seems to me it's a seller's market."

She readjusted her position and recrossed her shapeless legs. When she was adequately arranged, she tugged so hard on her skirt I was afraid she was going to rip it off. "You seem rather out of sorts this morning, Mr. Tanner."

"And you seem rather dour and reluctant, Ms. Sundstrom."

We locked sight lines until we decided to mutually disengage. "I find a certain reserve helps me be more effective in my work," Ms. Sundstrom acknowledged finally, though not without embarrassment.

"As do I," I countered.

"Plus my expertise is in personal services contracts and intellectual-property issues. I've never dealt with a potentially violent situation before."

"Whereas I deal with such situations all the time," I exaggerated.

She took the bait. "I suppose that's why I'm here."

"And I suppose that's why I charge sixty bucks an hour."

After a philosophical struggle that seemed to be unique to her experience, Ms. Sundstrom bowed in homage to my trump. Then she consulted a watch that was thinner than her wrist but not much. Then she looked up. "Shall I proceed, or have we decided we're terminally incompatible?"

I laughed because I assumed she'd made a joke. "You tell me."

"I'm prepared to go forward."

"So am I. Though not necessarily all the way, since this is our first date."

Her lips wrinkled and her nose lifted. "Men frequently assume I'll be undone by double entendre. I have four older brothers; I've yet to hear a scurrile reference that wasn't inflicted upon me with regularity from about the age of nine."

Now I was the one who blushed. "I apologize."

"What for?"

"For being like all the other men in your life."

"I have no men in my life."

"I guess that's what four brothers will do for you. Shall we get down to business?"

"Please." She retrieved her briefcase from the floor and extracted what looked like a contract. "I have a client who's in danger, Mr. Tanner."

"What kind of danger?"

"Her life has been threatened. Several times."

"Threatened by whom?"

"The threats were anonymous."

"Have there been actual attempts to harm her?"

"Not yet. Thank God."

"But you take the threats seriously."

She nodded. "More important, so does my client."

"Who is?"

"Chandelier Wells."

Now my brow was the one that elevated. "The writer?"

"Yes."

"My hourly rate just tripled."

I finally provoked an infinitesimal grin. "I take it you're familiar with her work."

"Not her work; just her reputation."

"Yes, well, whatever you may have read or heard about her, shall we say, personal peccadilloes, Chandelier Wells is the most successful novelist in San Francisco, Danielle Steel and Richard North Patterson not excluded."

"Good for her."

"But I'm afraid success comes at a price."

"I wouldn't know."

"The price in this instance is danger."

For some reason I looked at my sagging couch and my faded carpet and my peeling paint and wondered how long it would be till I could stop taking on troubles for a living. "What does Ms. Wells want from me, exactly?" I asked before I'd answered my question.

Like all good lawyers, Ms. Sundstrom was ready with a succinct answer to a predictable inquiry. "She wants you to serve as her bodyguard until the source of the threats is identified and neutralized. The precise nature of the relationship is spelled out in this document I've prepared for your signature."

As Ms. Sundstrom placed the document on the desk, I pushed back my chair and stood up. "Sorry to disappoint you, but I don't do that kind of work. I don't even go to those kinds of movies."

Ms. Sundstrom stayed seated. "Please hear me out."

"Why should I?"

"Because Chandelier asked for you by name. And because she doesn't take no for an answer."

I did a partial pirouette. "Take a look, Ms. Sundstrom. I don't have enough muscles to make anyone think twice, I have only one gun and I'm not sure where it is at the moment, I've never attended defensive-driving school or counterinsurgency training or even learned CPR, and I don't like being cooped up with strangers even on a bus ride. You'd better get a new boy."

She shook her head. "That's not an option, I'm afraid."

"But why me?" I asked, more plaintively than I intended. "There are all kinds of mammoth security firms that can guard Ms. Wells day and night and she won't even know it's happening. I can give you names if you want. I'll even make you an appointment."

She was shaking her head before I finished my screed. "Sorry, Mr. Tanner. I don't want names, I want you."

"I still don't understand why."

"Because you come highly recommended."

"By whom?"

"Millicent Colbert."

I sank back to my chair, heavily and disconsolately, and propped my head with my hands. "How does Ms. Wells know Mrs. Colbert?"

"They have children in the same preschool."

"Laurel Hill."

"I believe that's the one."

"And Millicent told Chandelier I could take care of her problem."

"Yes, she did."

I sighed and closed my eyes. It began to look like I was about to guard a body.

chapter 2

I asked Karla Sundstrom for more details about the anonymous threats to her client, but she told me that would have to wait until I met Chandelier Wells in person—apparently Ms. Wells was not about to buy a pig in a poke no matter how effusively I came recommended at preschool. We set an appointment for eight that evening at Ms. Wells's Pacific Heights home, then Ms. Sundstrom went back to her law firm, where the bad mood she'd brought to my office would undoubtedly be fully restored.

After a trip to the bank to deposit the $123.42 I'd earned last week and an early lunch of patty melt and American fries at Zorba's, I spent the rest of the day clearing the slate of old business and warding off a platoon of second thoughts. The old business had to do with bunko—my client had been ripped off by a time-share scam up at Tahoe; luckily, the scam was widespread enough that the attorney general had shut it down and filed suit for recision and restitution. The second thoughts were of going to work for Chandelier Wells.

All I knew of her had come from the media, which of course made it suspect by definition. Almost daily, it seemed, the *Chronicle* contained a feature piece on her doings in sections ranging from style to society to business to the gossip column. Almost as often, the local talk shows throbbed with praise of her prose or her sales records. What I knew for sure was that Ms. Sundstrom had not exaggerated—Chandelier Wells was a fabulously successful writer, one of those whose glossy fat paperbacks overflow the racks and shelves to rise like stalagmites from the floors of bookstores and supermarkets, to say nothing of Costco and Walgreens and S. F. International. According to snippets of reviews I vaguely remembered, what she wrote was romantic suspense of a sort, wherein the heroine runs afoul not only of a roguish male and a recalcitrant private life but also of one or another brand of social injustice that she always manages to set right in the penultimate chapter.

Each book was part of a series that featured a middle-aged newspaper columnist named Maggie Katz. Apparently to millions of women, Maggie was the embodiment of their fears and desires and hopes and frustrations, an irresistible mix of their real lives and their feminist fantasies in which all always came out right in the end. An hour with Maggie Katz was better than an hour with Newman or Redford or even Oprah, or so Chandelier's sales levels suggested. It was an idolatrous phenomenon I understood myself, at least partially—during my college and army years, it had done me worlds of good to hang out with Lew Archer and Philip Marlowe on a regular basis and pretend their triumphs were somehow my own. In fact, Raymond Chandler and Ross Macdonald were to blame more than anyone else for my becoming a private eye.

My problem with Chandelier Wells was not with her work, my problem was with her person. First, she was a celebrity, and most celebrities inhabit nothing beyond the universe of their own desires, which is a swell definition of boring. Second, she was vastly wealthy, her income exceeded among her peers only by Grisham, Crichton, and King, and I had a genetic aversion to the upper crust. She was also, if you could believe the papers, opinionated, arrogant, and autocratic. Which is to say, she was like most of the titans of industry in the city. Also, like the most notorious of those titans, she had somehow managed to convince the struggling middle class that she was on their side, nonetheless.

Her personal life was off-putting as well. Divorced for many years from a youthful marriage to a ne'er-do-well, she had dated and discarded most of the city's eligible bachelors, several of whom were as rich and famous in their own sphere as she was in hers, and the details of the denouements always made it into the press. Worse, at least in my view, she was a public mother, exhibiting her sloe-eyed daughter at all the right social and charitable events when she wasn't being photographed romping with her child at the zoo or on the Marina Green, the quality time coincidentally captured in some flattering media profile. Admittedly, she donated lots of time and money to good causes, always generously but always publicly as well. She was also rumored to have political ambitions of the moralistic bent that is so predominant in the Southern reaches of the nation. In sum, I wasn't sure I could endure fifteen minutes of her time over a fast-food lunch, let alone guard her person for eighteen hours at a stretch.

Nevertheless, I rang her bell at 8 P.M. Behind me, the grounds of the estate stretched toward Pacific Avenue like a cleverly built quilt abundant with botanical appliqués. Above me, the house rose like an advancing glacier, its white stone facade broken by narrow slits of windows, pebbled with ornamentation of a medieval motif, and topped by a gray slate roof rising beyond a row of battlements that in the gloom of a late winter evening resembled a derelict's teeth. Thanks to her bankroll and her architect, Chandelier was ready to repel invaders—all she lacked was a moat and a drawbridge and a knight in shining armor. Or maybe that was me.

The bell was answered by a young woman who gave me a smile full of bright teeth and pink gums and told me her name was Lark McLaren and that she was Ms. Wells's executive assistant. She wore brown slacks over flat heels and below a beige cable-knit sweater that advertised a trim figure and an understated sense of style, which was the only understated object I'd seen since I'd parked my car.

When we shook hands, hers was warm and agreeable, in contrast to Karla Sundstrom's clammy clasp. She told me Ms. Wells was waiting in the sunroom. Since this part of the city hadn't seen the sun since Christmas, I figured Chandelier had borrowed one from an adjacent solar system. Rich people can do anything when they set their mind to it.

The sunroom was off the dining room, which was beyond the great room flanking the foyer—I've taken shorter hikes in search of a loaf of bread. When we reached a massive walnut door, Lark asked me to take a seat on the adjacent oak bench, its contours as rigid and unsettling as if it had been stolen from Chartres. "She's on the phone with her Japanese publisher," Lark added. "Certain errors in the translation of her last book need to be corrected before the soft-cover version comes out."

"Chandelier speaks Japanese?"

"No, but for comparison purposes she has her foreign editions translated for her by some professors down at Stanford. Chandelier is extremely diligent about protecting the integrity of her prose," Lark added when she saw my expression, which was a mix of wonder and dismay.

"Does that smile contain a dash of sarcasm, Ms. McLaren?" I asked.

She blinked with genuine surprise. "Why would it?"

With that succinct and justifiable rebuttal, Lark McLaren disappeared inside the sunroom, leaving me waiting my turn on the bench like a donor at the local blood bank.

I looked up and down the hall. At one end, I heard the clatter of crockery and culinary gear—someone was cleaning up after dinner. At the other, a massive staircase led to the second floor and conceivably on up to the clouds. Between the extremes were various arts and crafts in the manner of the French baroque, which oddly were a fit to my mood—I was as antsy as if I were waiting for Louis Quatorze.

The door beside me finally opened, but instead of Lark McLaren, a little girl emerged. She was four or five, black-haired and -eyed, dressed in a light blue pinafore and patent leather shoes that were far too nice to play in. Her hand was held by an older Hispanic woman I took to be her nanny.

"Night, Mommy," the girl called into the room. "Night, Mommy," she repeated, this time more sternly.

Mommy said something I couldn't hear.

"I love you, Mommy."

I bet Mommy loved her, too.

"Come, Violet," the nanny said, tugging the girl's slender arm to add some muscle to her instruction.

As flighty as a colt, the little girl pulled away from the older woman and twirled to look at me. "Hi," she said happily, clearly at ease with strangers, even ones who looked mean and ugly.

"Hi, there."

"My name's Violet."

"Mine's Marsh."

"Are you here to see my mommy?"

"Yes, I am."

"Are you a fan?"

"I . . . sort of, I guess. Sure."

"Mommy has lots of fans. Millions, even."

"So I hear. I also hear you know a girl named Eleanor."

Violet frowned in concentration. "I know two Eleanors." She held up the appropriate fingers. "Eleanor Colbert at Laurel Hill and Eleanor Mitchell at church."

"I know Eleanor Colbert, too. She's a nice girl, isn't she?"

"She's all right," Violet said carefully.

"Is she your friend?"

"Yes."

"Do you go play at her house sometimes?"

"No."

"Does Eleanor play over here?"

"No."

I knew better but I couldn't help myself. "Why not?"

"She's too messy." Violet glanced at the sunroom door. "You better go in, or Mommy will be mad."

"Does Mommy get mad very often?"

"Mommy gets mad every day," she said with journalistic precision, then strolled down the hall with her nanny, heading for the stairway that would take her away from me and from her mommy's moods and into a world much closer to heaven. Eleanor Colbert was messy, huh? I needed to have a talk with her mother.

As I watched Violet hop her way up the stairs, Lark McLaren poked her head out the door and motioned for me to join her. After I gulped back my reservations, I did as I was told.

The room was large and rectangular, with an entire wall of leaded windows bisected by a set of French doors. Another wall was a fireplace, and the third and fourth were shelves containing everything from books and magazines to photographs and bite-sized arts and crafts. Some of the books looked rare; most of the photographs looked new; all of the art looked expensive. A tawny cowhide couch faced a giant stone fireplace that blazed tastefully and soundlessly, indicating the logs on the andirons weren't real. A leather-covered library table backed up to one section of the bookshelves supported a computer, printer, fax machine, and telephone console, an array of multimedia weaponry potent enough to direct-dial Pluto or e-mail the pope.

Sitting behind the Queen Anne desk was the woman I had been summoned to see. She wore a black cashmere cardigan sweater over a white silk camisole, a double strand of perfect pearls, rings on at least four of her fingers, and an expression that was a mix of impatience and curiosity. Beneath her auburn hair, her face was as serene and imperial as a courtesan's—without uttering a word, she seemed aristocratic and omnipotent, elegant and expert, certain of her aims and of her ability of achieve them, hobbled by neither doubt nor etiquette. I paid her a silent tribute. I hadn't possessed as much self-confidence for one minute of my entire life.

She gestured toward a white slipcovered chair that was draped with a colorful afghan and positioned in front of the desk. "Please sit down, Mr. Tanner."

"Thank you." Unlike poor Karla Sundstrom, I was comfortable the second my butt hit the cushion.

"May I offer you a refreshment?"

I started to politely decline, then figured what the hell. "Beer, if you have it."

"I have pilsner and lager, both imported."

"I'll take the pilsner."

"Lark?"

Lark McLaren picked up the phone on the table at the end of the couch, pressed a black button, and whispered my order with the hush of a state secret. When I looked back at Chandelier

Wells, she was inspecting me the way she would inspect a royalty statement.

"I assume Karla Sundstrom has told you what this unfortunate circumstance is all about," she began in a cultivated voice that was both melodic and hypnotic. She hadn't the slightest doubt that Karla had done just that.

"In outline, but not in detail," I confirmed.

"That will come later."

"Fine."

"Assuming you are available to assist me immediately."

"I can be."

"Good. Have you done this type of work before?"

"Not precisely."

Her expression firmed from frustration; she wasn't used to people who nitpicked or lacked enthusiasm and she had trouble knowing how to react to the combination. "But I understood you are accustomed to violence and to subduing the people who commit it."

"Only psychopaths are accustomed to violence, Ms. Wells. But I run into it from time to time. When I haven't been able to get out of the way."

She pursed her lips and nodded, apparently believing she had won a battle only she was fighting.

A tap on the door brought my beer, courtesy of a young Hispanic who looked enough like Violet's nanny to be her offspring. He placed the beer on the corner of the desk, then bowed and retreated, all without saying a word. His servility made me wince. As an antidote, I took a sip of beer. In its frosty mug and with minimal head, it was as cold as beer gets without freezing.

"Perhaps I should outline the arrangement I have in mind," Ms. Wells was saying officiously.

"I read the contract Ms. Sundstrom drew up."

"Contracts seldom tell the whole story."

"I suppose they'd call them novels if they did that."

My lurch toward literacy provoked a frown. She leaned back in her chair the way I do when the positions are reversed and I'm the one being courted.

Her voice was a strong contralto, her hair was carefully coiffed in a ragged fringe at her neck, her lips were precisely defined with crimson, her cheeks were rosy with blush, and her eyes seemed to be augmented by a set of tinted contact lenses. When she relaxed, Chandelier Wells was far more attractive than in her pictures in the paper, but when she didn't, she wasn't.

"Let me tell you a little about my situation, Mr. Tanner," she said after a moment. "My professional situation, that is."

"You think the threats were provoked by your writing?"

"I'm certain of it."

"That's a bit premature, isn't it?"

Her smile was condescending and maternal. "As I was saying, when I begin to write a book, I lock myself up in this house for three months. No trips abroad, no cocktail parties or gallery openings, no plays or concerts or charity balls. I write fourteen hours a day, seven days a week, till it's done. When I've finished the book, I send it off to my editor, then go out to promote my last one, which according to plan is just being released. I spend four months on promotion, then four months relaxing, then a month of research on my next book, which I've been conceiving and structuring in my mind the whole time, then three more months in seclusion in my study, writing the next magnum opus. I've followed that schedule for twelve years."

"How did you work before that?" I asked, but only because I was curious.

"Before that, I wrote four books in a year and the only place I relaxed was the bathtub. Thankfully I don't have to live that way."

"I don't either," I said. "But not for the same reason."

Her eyes narrowed with yet another tic of annoyance. "If you go to work for me, I'll require your total attention and effort, Mr. Tanner."

"You'll get it, Ms. Wells. Just like all my clients."

"Good."

"So where are we in this schedule of yours?"

"I've just finished a book. It's called *Ship Shape*. Next week I'll send it off to New York. Tomorrow afternoon is my launch party for the last one—it's called *Shalloon*, if you're interested. The next four days are readings and signings at local stores, plus media appearances and chat-room stuff, then I'm off to L.A. and environs, then up to Seattle and Portland, then off to the East Coast to do national television, then the Midwest and South, then back here for a rest in the middle of next month before I set off again for the second tier."

"Second tier?"

"The smaller cities. Reno, Wichita, Des Moines, Columbus. Twenty-eight in all. Actually, I tend to draw larger crowds in the smaller cities than I do in the big ones."

"Less competition, I imagine."

She scowled. "I prefer to think it has to do with taste—that readers in the hinterlands are less prone to the winds of intellectual incest and political correctness that prevail in more metropolitan areas."

"Could be," I said, to be agreeable. "Or maybe they're just bored."

Chandelier looked out the windows at the ancient cypress trees that bordered a backyard that fell away toward the bay like a ski slope. "They hate me, of course," she murmured in a non sequitur.

"Who? The folks in Des Moines?"

She shook her head. "The aesthetes, I call them. The reviewers in *The New York Times* and their ilk in Chicago and L.A. and the newsmagazines. Mostly male, of course. But not all, sad to say. They flatter themselves that they're the literary vanguard, entitled by birth and education to dictate the reading habits of the country. To them I'm a joke, an insult to their impeccable taste, but what I *really* am is proof of their impotence. I sell a hundred times more units than their precious geniuses do, and they can neither understand nor acknowledge it. Deep down, they would prefer that I stop writing, but what they *really* don't get is that at this point they are what keeps me going. And the fans, of course." Her eyes grew as moist as fresh melons. "My fans are wonderful, Mr. Tanner. Truly. They send me the most amazing gifts, handcrafted work of immense skill and even greater hours of labor and of love. I'm humbled by it. Truly."

"Except that one of them sent you a death threat."

She shook her head vigorously. "Not a fan. Never."

"Then who?"

"I don't know. If I did, you wouldn't be here."

She looked out over the grounds, as if to confirm her fortress was still impregnable. "Tell me about them," I said to her back. "The threats, not the fans."

She waved away my request as a nuisance. "Lark will take care of that."

"Do you have any idea at all who might want to harm you?"

She spun back toward me with vigor, the antique chair squeaking under the centrifugal strain. "I have several suspects in mind, but I have neither the time nor the inclination to narrow down the list myself. Lark can give you those names as well. It is a sobering thought when the list of people who want you done away with approaches double digits."

Before I could comment, she shrugged off the circumstance and looked at her watch. "Now you really must excuse me. *The Sacramento Bee* is calling for an interview at nine, then I'm on-line with AOL for an hour, then I have books to sign for my media people, then I need to review my notes for my talk after the readings. If you need anything at all, Lark is the one to talk to."

She pushed back her chair and stood up. When I did the same, I noted she was nearly as tall as I was.

She came to my side and put her hand on my arm in the only affectionate gesture I would ever see her make. "I find you a satisfactory choice as my guardian angel, Mr. Tanner. If it's agreeable to you to take on the task of my protection, you should be here at four tomorrow. We go to the launch party, then to dinner afterward with my editor and publicist and agent. It shouldn't be a long night— we've done this, let's see, twelve times in the past ten years. We're getting pretty good at it."

"What about here at the house?" I asked quickly. "Don't you need someone on duty while you're home? If you'd be uncomfortable with me clomping around, I know a woman who would be perfect for—"

Chandelier shook her head. "This house has the best security system money can buy. Primarily to guard the valuables, of course, but to safeguard my work in progress as well. Also, one member of my staff is a former FBI agent who has been trained in weaponry and counterintelligence. For various reasons he is not amenable to public appearances. You need only report for duty when I'm going out—Lark will provide you with a schedule. Do we have a deal, Mr. Tanner?"

Prodded primarily by my debt to Millicent Colbert, I stemmed an urge to abstain. "Yes, we do."

"Good. I assume you've signed Karla's contract."

I nodded.

"I will sign it this evening as well, and you'll get a confirmed copy tomorrow. In the meantime, Lark will make arrangements for payment of a small advance, just to get things going."

"Thanks."

She took two steps toward the door, then turned back. "Have you ever read one of my books, Mr. Tanner?"

"I'm afraid not."

"Do you plan to?"

"I don't know. Is it a requirement of the job?"

"Not at all. But you might enjoy it. They're not nearly as bad as you've heard."

chapter 3

Lark and I looked at each other, then sighed and smiled simultaneously. The tension in the room had dropped by a factor of
five.

"Quite a woman," I said.

"Definitely."

"Tough boss?"

"At times."

"Good pay though, probably."

She shrugged. "Good enough. For now."

"What did you do before this?"

"Editor." She blushed. "Well, editorial assistant."

"Where?"

"New York. Madison House. Chandelier's publisher."

"How long have you been on staff with Ms. Wells?"

She squirmed uncomfortably. "This is beginning to sound like
you're interrogating me. Are you?"

I grinned. "Sure."

"Am I a suspect?"

"Not yet."

"If I wanted to do something to Chandelier, I'd just . . ."

"What?"

Her back straightened and her nerve firmed. "Never mind. I've
been on Chandelier's staff almost four years."

"You edit her work?"

She hesitated. "I read it and tell her what she wants to hear."

"Which is what?"

"That it's her best book ever."

"Is that a genuine response?"

Her smile was thin and resigned, as though it answered a question she'd asked herself too many times. "No comment."

"Do you want to be a writer yourself?"

She chuckled without amusement. "Not anymore."

"Why not?"

"If you hang around here very long, you'll know."

I walked to the couch and took a seat beside her. "Okay, Ms. McLaren. Let's get down to brass tacks. Why am I here?"

"That's easy."

She stood up, walked to the bookcase nearest the desk, swung open a hinged panel disguised as a matched set of Thackeray, opened the wall safe that was secreted behind the panel, extracted a manila folder, and brought it to me. I opened the folder and looked at the contents. Six sheets of white bond paper were inside, each sheet protected by a transparent plastic sleeve and each containing a message, handwritten in black block print with a Magic Marker or a Sharpie. All six messages were essentially the same as the one on top: IF YOU DON'T STOP, YOU WILL DIE!

I put the sheets back in the folder and looked at Lark. "I don't suppose it's as simple as she's poached the property of an irate wife. Or husband, for that matter."

She shook her head. "Nothing like that, I'm sure. Chandelier dates quite a lot when she's not writing, but she doesn't date married men." She grinned. "Or women. Chandelier is relentlessly heterosexual, if it makes any difference."

"It usually doesn't." I gestured toward the notes. "I take it you provided the plastic."

"Yes."

"Have the sheets been dusted for prints?"

"Yes."

"So the cops are in on this?"

She shook her head. "The testing was done privately by an independent forensics lab in Sacramento. At this point, the authorities have not been consulted about anything. I'm sure Chandelier wants to keep it that way."

"Why?"

Lark took a deep breath. "For years, Chandelier was both unhappy and unpublished. Her marriage was a mess, her first book didn't sell, she weighed well over two hundred pounds, she couldn't have children, and she couldn't afford to do what you have to do to make a splash in the business, such as hire a publicity person, mail out expensive promotional materials, and travel to stores and book conventions all over the country. But she saved her pennies and made a plan and slowly but surely it worked. She got where she is by taking total control of her life, both professionally and personally. As much as is humanly possible, nothing happens in Chandelier's world unless she wants it to. Among other things, she has created a marvelously potent image of herself. She feels if the police are brought in, if she's seen as incapable of responding to and resolving a crisis in her life, she'll risk undermining that image to a degree. At this point, she's not willing to take that chance."

I'd heard Baptist sermons less fervent. Clearly Lark looked on Ms. Wells as something more than a boss. "If these notes are serious and someone takes a pop at her," I said easily, "she'll wish she hadn't been so worried about image."

"At that point, if it comes, I'm sure she'll do the sensible thing and inform the police. In the meantime, we're hoping you can put the matter to rest unofficially."

I didn't bother to temper her tribute to my expertise. "When did the first note show up?"

"Three weeks ago."

"How?"

"In the mailbox. In an envelope. But not postmarked so not mailed."

"The writer wants her to stop something. Stop what?"

"Writing, I assume."

"Why would her writing put someone on edge?"

"I'm not sure, but she sets all of her books in a realistic context. *Shalloon* is about fraud in the cosmetics industry—substituting cheap imitations for the real thing. Shalloon is the name of the fictitious perfume in the book. The novel she's just finished is called *Ship Shape*. It takes place on a luxury cruise where the sponsors prey on customers both physically and financially."

"These books are based on actual practices in those industries?"

"By some companies. Yes."

"Have there been any repercussions from outraged corporate flacks or their counsel?"

"Not that I know of."

"What's she working on next?"

Lark shook her head. "I don't know. She probably doesn't either. I never know till she's finished the first draft. No one does."

"You're sure about that?"

"Yes."

"So presumably not many people know what *Ship Shape*'s about either."

"Not for another week, when it will hit New York City. And then it will only be Madison House and book club and chain-store people till the bound galleys are ready. Of course TV and the film studios often share the same corporate parent as the major publishing houses, or they have moles inside the smaller publishers to alert them to hot properties, so confidentiality is never assured."

"Ms. Wells doesn't have some sort of critique group of other writers who read her stuff as she goes along?"

Lark shook her head. "Chandelier doesn't feel anyone knows nearly as much about what she's trying to do in her fiction as she does herself."

"Sounds a little egotistic."

Lark made a face. "In my experience, writers are all egotistic. How else would they keep going?"

I laughed because I guessed she was right and because at one point in my life, I'd wanted to write a novel, which made me an egotist myself. "Are her agent and editor both in New York?"

"Their offices are there, but at the moment they're here in San Francisco. Ever since Chandelier became a bestseller, they always come out for the launch party."

"I'd like to meet them before this show goes on the road."

Lark nodded. "I thought we could do that tomorrow. Chandelier's hairdresser and personal shopper are coming to the house at noon to get her ready for the party. I won't be needed, and Sally and Amber are free as well. I thought we could all meet for lunch."

"Sure."

"Where?"

"Wherever."

"You're near North Beach, right?"

"Yep."

"How about the Black Cat? Or Tavolino?"

"They're a little steep for my budget."

She looked away to avoid augmenting my embarrassment. "We'd be paying the tab, of course."

"Still."

She frowned in thought. "Enrico's?"

"Fine."

"One o'clock?"

"One it is."

I handed back the manila folder. "You won't need it?" Lark asked.

"Not until I have a suspect. Speaking of which, Ms. Wells suggested that she'd given you some ideas along that line."

The shift in focus seemed to discomfit her. "Oh. Yes. Well, I wouldn't go so far as to call them suspects."

"Then what would you call them?"

"Possibilities, is all."

I got out my notebook. "Give me a rundown."

Lark leaned back on the couch. Although she put up a good front, at bottom she seemed exhausted, or bored, or exasperated, but something definitely less than chipper. I had a feeling that a day tending Chandelier Wells could do that to a person. After four years of it, well, I'd be surprised if Lark remained unmedicated.

She held up her index finger. "First and foremost, there's the ex-husband."

"Name?"

"Mickey Strunt."

"Address?"

She consulted a Rolodex beside the phone and read off a number on Judah Street.

"Where's that? Out near the ocean?"

She nodded. "A block away, I believe. Mickey used to be a surfer."

"Other than the obvious, why does Mickey lead the list?"

"They've been divorced for twelve years but he still comes around and asks for money and threatens to make trouble if he doesn't get it, which he does, usually, though in smaller amounts than he claims to need."

"What kind of money are we talking about?"

"Last year, twenty-four thousand dollars. Two thousand a month."

"That's a lot."

"Not to Chandelier."

"And now he wants more?"

"He always wants more. And lots of it."

"How much?"

"Half. Of her assets."

I blinked. "On what basis?"

"That back in the early days he worked like a dog to give Chandelier the time and the inspiration to write. That she would still be nothing if he hadn't urged her to write that first book. That she took the basic character sketches from him and ran with them."

"Is any of that true?"

"Not according to Chandelier. She started to write so she could afford to leave him, basically."

"What's Mickey do for a living?"

She laughed. "Nothing discernible."

"Is he violent?"

"Not so far."

"A drunk? A doper? A nut?"

"According to Chandelier, he's been all of those at one time or another. Plus a surf bum."

"Police record?"

"I think so, but nothing major. Public intoxication. That kind of thing."

"I'll check him out. Who else makes the list?"

Again, Lark seemed uncomfortable with casting a net of suspicion. Which made me like her even more than I did already, which was a lot.

"Well, there's Viveca Dane, I suppose," she said grudgingly.

"The name's familiar."

"She's a writer, too. Or was. Queen of the field, until Chandelier came along."

"Why's she a suspect?"

"Thanks to Chandelier's success, Viveca's career has been pretty much obliterated. She's not happy about it, understandably."

"She's said so?"

Lark nodded. "Often and in print. At her most vehement, she accuses Chandelier of plagiarism. If she wasn't so pathetic, Chandelier would probably sue her."

"Where can I find her?"

She consulted her list and read off an address on Francisco Street.

"Nice neighborhood."

"Viveca made lots of money in her heyday. I guess she managed to hang on to most of it."

"If she's rich, why the ire?"

Lark met my look. "They don't do it for the money, Mr. Tanner."

I was about to ask Lark what they *did* do it for when the phone beside her buzzed. She picked it up and listened, then quickly replaced the receiver. "Sorry. I have to go."

"Home?"

She pointed at the ceiling. "She needs me to take some dictation."

"You live here in the house?"

"Yes."

"Any private life at all?"

She grinned. "Thursdays, if I'm lucky."

"What do you do on Thursdays?"

"I go to the library to get good books and go to the museums and see good art."

"What sort of books?"

She shrugged. "It varies. Currently I'm quite enamored of William Trevor and Francine Prose."

She stood up and I did, too. "That's it for suspects?" I asked quickly.

She closed her eyes to think. "There's also Thurston Buckley."

"The real estate guy? He owns half the city. If you believe what Herb Caen used to say about him, he could have any woman he wanted just by snapping his fingers."

"Well, he couldn't have Chandelier Wells and that seemed to upset him."

"How bad did he want her?"

"A lot. He gave her a diamond as big as the Ritz-Carlton."

"They were engaged?"

"He thought he was; she knew she wasn't."

Lark took two steps toward the door. "One more thing," I said to stop her.

"What?"

"Be honest with me."

She blinked. "Of course."

"It's occurred to me that this whole thing could be phony. A fake death threat that leaks to the press and becomes a publicity ploy to sell the new book. Plucky author under siege and all that. Any chance of that being the case, Ms. McLaren?"

Her arm swept the room as her eyes chastened mine. "Does it *look* like she needs more publicity, Mr. Tanner? Or more of anything, for that matter?"

I had to admit that it didn't. On the other hand, if her life were truly without need, Chandelier Wells would be the first person in my experience of whom that was true.

chapter 4

She leaned forward to fit her breasts in her bra, then arced her back to fasten the hooks, then tugged her Levi's up over her hips and pulled her sweatshirt down over her head. When her sneakers were on and tied and her hair was pressed into some semblance of style, she was ready to hit the road. As for me, I was still naked, though covered demurely by a sheet, less out of modesty than in an effort to mask my flab, as though she hadn't seen every inch of it ten minutes earlier.

"If you're not going to stay, at least let me walk you to your car," I said as I tossed the sheet aside.

She gestured toward my milky torso. "Only if you do it like that."

"The neighbors couldn't stand the excitement."

She laughed. "That's a tad more self-esteem than you're entitled to, dude."

I love it when she calls me dude. "Oh, yeah? Well, this doughy body seemed to stir *your* nether regions a few moments ago, counselor. Those didn't sound like objections you were voicing."

She colored nicely and shot me a hip. "So I'm easily aroused. So sue me."

I raised a brow. "Was that sue me or screw me?"

"Now you're *really* dreaming," she said, then clipped her holstered .38 to her belt, leaned over to give me a kiss on the forehead, waved good-bye, and was gone. Leaving me to wonder and worry whether I was finally and truly in love. And if so, whether that was good or bad, all things considered, in the long run, given the situation. Maybe I had commitment issues.

Her name is Jill Coppelia. She's an assistant district attorney and she's tall, dark, and almost lovely, with blue eyes that glow like morning glories, brown hair that gleams like a walnut burl, a nose that's as elegantly arced as a saber, and a mouth that can turn from insolent to inviting in an instant. When I was with her, I felt like I could whip a bully or write an epic. When I was without her, I wanted to be with her. When we made love, I wanted to wallow in her warmth and wetness, then surrender every last grain of my being to show her how grateful I was for being privy to her body and her mind and her spirit. Okay, I was in love, no question about it.

So sue me.

We met when Jill was assigned to look into the circumstances surrounding the death of my best friend, Charley Sleet, detective lieutenant SFPD. The crucial facts weren't in dispute, at least not from my point of view—Charley was dead because I shot him to keep him from killing any more cops than he already had, which was three, but mostly to keep him from killing himself. He'd killed the cops because they'd deserved it, at least in Charley's view, because they were part of a group of rogues called the Triad, which had been serving itself rather than the city for years, committing far more serious crimes than most of the crooks it was supposed to be locking up. I'm not sure that's the way Jill saw it yet, but she was working on it—the grand jury investigation was still under way.

Since I was conceivably a witness and even a potential indictee, and since grand jury testimony is secret to begin with, Jill was careful not to confide in me. I didn't know the particulars of the case outside the lines of my own involvement and the rumors that were batted about in the media, but I wasn't pressing her on the point because I didn't want to compromise Jill's independence any more than I was already doing by taking her to bed and occasionally to breakfast.

All I knew was what I read in the papers, which was that a grand jury had been charged with looking into the entire spectrum of police corruption in the city, which presumably encompassed many more individuals than were on hand the night Charley had shot me at the precise moment I killed him. All Jill had said about it of late was that it would help if they could find themselves a Serpico who would deliver the Triad on a silver platter. What I still thought about on a daily basis was how much I missed the cop I'd shot and killed myself.

I looked at my clock radio: 11:15. I could stay in bed and try to sleep, which meant I would wake at five if successful or toss and turn till two if I wasn't. Or I could get up and read the Ward Just novel I'd just started, or watch Letterman or Leno on TV, or eat something or drink something or more than one but less than all of the above. I opted for option four. But what I did after I poured two fingers of Ballantine's over two cubes of ice and curled up on the couch with a half-eaten bag of Oreos within reach was think about my birthday.

I was going to be fifty in two weeks. I don't think anyone knew it—I hoped they didn't, anyway—but I knew it the way I knew I was in love with Jill—in the stem of my brain and the core of my soul and the sting on my skin when I thought about her. Try as I might to evade the issue, the impending anniversary had rocked me back on my heels like an overmatched middleweight dreading the inevitable big blow.

What do you think about when you're two weeks from fifty? You think about your life. And if you're a borderline depressive like me, you don't think about what you've enjoyed and achieved along the way, not a minute of that. What fills your mind like garbage fills a plastic bag is the long list of what you haven't accomplished. Goals not met. Dreams not realized. Potential untapped. Fantasies unfulfilled. It's no barrel of laughs, let me tell you. Maybe it's time for Prozac.

For example. When I was ten, I wanted to be Lash LaRue. When I was twenty, I wanted to be Perry Mason. When I was thirty, I wanted to be Clarence Darrow. When I was forty, I wanted to be Ralph Nader. But I was never any of those guys, not even close. Whenever the subject came up, which fortunately was always internally, I tried to tell myself it didn't matter, all that mattered was if I was happy, and if I was, how I got there was irrelevant. I tried to believe that as long as I treated people with sympathy and respect, and asked no more of life than what I was willing to give to it, I was as valuable as the next guy. The problem was, it didn't often work.

When my mental masochism became epidemic a few years back, I began a process of self-medication. I drank to forget, I ate to feel better, I took silly risks to agitate my adrenaline, I made love to strange women to elevate my ego. Still not enough. So I tried Saint-John's-wort, but that only made me exhausted. And I read some self-help books, but that only made me mad. And I saw a shrink for two weeks, but that only made me insolvent. So I make do with Centrum Silver and a C and E supplement and I've cut back TV to three nights a week and don't do anything at all on the Internet, and I'd been feeling pretty decent till this birthday nonsense came along. But the only time I feel great is when I'm with Jill.

Will we stay together? I don't know. I think I know I want to. And I think I know she enjoys her time with me as well. But I also know for a fact that we never discuss our future, whether joint or separate or somewhere in between, and never pledge undying love or extrapolate the mathematics of our alliance much beyond the end of the week.

There are a lot of reasons for her to move on. She's a dozen years younger than I am. And a lot more attractive. And earns more money. And has medical and dental and PERS for retirement while I'm barely hanging on to Blue Cross. She likes doing things actively and outdoors and she's stylish and social and sophisticated. At times her energy is a lightning bolt that threatens to give me a heart attack. But at other times, her incessant buoyancy approaches the transcendental and promises to be my salvation. At times like those, it's easy to see my future happiness as entirely dependent on her continued presence in my life. Which, among other things, is terrifying.

I read Ward Just for a while, and drank the Scotch and ate the cookies. Then I looked at my watch and did what I had wanted to do in the first place, which was pick up the phone.

"Hi," I said when she answered.

"Hi, yourself."

"Just checking to make sure you made it home okay."

"I always make it home okay."

"I wish you'd let me drive you."

"I'm armed, I'm paranoid, I drive a fast car. What could possibly happen to me between your place and mine?"

Since I'm more than current on crime in the city, I chose not to answer the question. "What I really wish is that you'd spend the night."

"Not during the week, remember? It throws off my biorhythms or something. We've been through that, ad nauseam."

"Then I wish you'd move in," I said before I knew I wanted to say it.

She treated it as the caprice it was. "And do what with my stuff? My *cat* has a larger closet than you do."

"So we get a new place somewhere else."

She hesitated. "Not yet."

"Then when?"

"I don't know."

"Jill?"

"What?"

"I'm sorry. It's too soon. I know that. I just get . . ."

"I know."

"I like waking up with you."

"I know."

"I think I love you."

"I know."

"Shouldn't we do something about it?"

"We are, aren't we?"

"What are we doing?"

"We're talking on the phone in our jammies."

I was back in bed and under the covers before I realized that in response to the flood of feeling I'd spilled so abjectly, Jill hadn't said a word of reciprocity. Not for the first time in my dealings with women, I felt like a blithering idiot.

chapter 5

Although the ex-husband seemed the most likely prospect to be harassing Chandelier Wells, I decided to spend the morning probing the jealous rival. Jealousy is always a fertile field, and after a late night contemplating Jill and my birthday, I didn't have enough energy to go up against domestic outrage.

Viveca Dane lived on Francisco Street a block west of Columbus. The house was a tidy two-story stucco number typical of the city's residential districts, although this one possessed some grass and some shrubbery in contrast to its more barren brethren out in the avenues. I should probably have called first, but people are more likely to be helpful if they're knocked a bit off-balance when I show up at the door like a Mormon.

I had rung the bell four times and made ready to retreat down the stairs when the door squeaked open at my back. "What do you want?" a husky voice demanded in the middle of an audible yawn. After it coughed to clear itself of a stew of congestion, it swore like a trucker in traffic. "Nothing happens in here before noon."

I turned to see a small woman, wiry and wired, age well over sixty, hair spectacularly awry, skin creased and crisscrossed with wrinkles but untouched by anything other than age. Her hair was artificially blonde, her eyes chocolate truffles afloat in a dish of sour cream, her fingers a fistful of knotted twigs curled in arthritic arcs. She wore a royal blue housecoat that looked to be in its second decade of use and white silk slippers she could have worn to a ball. She was obviously irritated at being disturbed at that hour, even though it was after ten o'clock.

"I said what do you want?" she repeated in a sandpaper voice that had seen a lot of smoke and a lot of straight booze during a lot of late nights in a lot of dark bars.

I tried to look charming but it's not my best guise. "My name is Tanner. I'm a private investigator. I'd like to—"

Her frown turned from surly to thoughtful. "I've heard of you, haven't I?"

"Could be."

"You got shot a year or so back. Along with some policemen."

"That's right."

"You killed a policeman yourself that night, as I remember."

I felt myself color. "Yes, I did."

"So why aren't you in jail?"

There was a lot I could have said to that, but what I chose to say was, "It was self-defense."

"Says who?"

"The district attorney."

She cocked her head in the universal mark of the skeptic. "Lucky you."

I remembered my best friend's body, its last seconds of life leaching toward death in a scruffy, vacant lot down by the bay from the bullet I'd put in his chest. And I remembered precisely how it felt to have done it. "Lucky me."

She folded her arms across her wool-wrapped chest. "So why are you here? Am I being investigated for something?"

I raised a brow. "Should you be?"

Her eyes twinkled and blinked and squinted. "Only for my fantasies these days, I'm sorry to say."

"I hear your fantasies have made you lots of money over the years. And lots of fans as well."

She was pleasantly surprised and showed it. "You know my work, Mr. Tanner?"

She seemed likely to quiz me about it, so I stemmed the urge to lie. "I know your reputation."

Her laugh was brassy and sarcastic. "You're twenty years too late for my best moves, big boy—my reputation has mellowed to the consistency of tapioca. But in my prime, well, you could have burned your tongue on my reputation, don't think you couldn't. And a few other items as well."

I smiled. "Too hot to handle, I guess."

She tossed me a hip with the panache of a New Orleans stripper. "When I choose to be. But once in a while, if the right man comes along and treats me the way I like to be treated, I can be as smooth as Baileys Irish Cream—the best little tonic in the world." Her look was mischievous enough to make me believe her.

Viveca Dane was a pistol and I was having fun. I began to wish she was my client instead of her more illustrious peer.

I gestured toward the foyer at her back. "Would you mind if I come in for a minute?"

"To do what?"

I opted for candor. "Talk about Chandelier Wells."

Her mood darkened to the color of peat. "That bloated old bitch. What do you want to know that you couldn't read in the *Enquirer*?"

"Whatever you've got to tell me."

"How long have you got?"

I looked at my watch. "Two hours."

"Hellfire, big boy. That won't even get me through the third Bloody Mary."

She backed into the building and motioned for me to join her. The house was silent and dark, an obedient ox waiting for permission to stir. We ambled through a narrow hallway and into a sitting room that seemed to serve as a public parlor. Viveca Dane flipped on a ceiling light and asked if I wanted some coffee. I said I did if it was no trouble. As reflexively as a blink, she said she was too old for most kinds of trouble, invited me to make myself at home, and said she'd return in five minutes after she'd slipped into something more comfortable. Among her other attributes, Viveca Dane had a graduate degree in Mae West.

"The flowers are real, by the way," she said on her way out, referring to the spectacular floral arrangements sprouting out of ornate glass vases on three different occasional tables. "Courtesy of an anonymous admirer." With that little hint of lubricity, she disappeared down the hall.

The room was low-ceilinged and the heavy velvet shades were drawn tight across the light, but it was somehow quite cozy nonetheless, a hive of memorabilia and art deco furnishings. The former included a row of framed book jackets above the sooty face of the mantel, most in the style of a risqué Norman Rockwell, and a host of framed photos of Viveca arm in arm with a variety of local luminaries, from Joe Alioto to Carol Doda to Jerry Garcia. A baroque frame displayed a letter from a famous New York publisher accepting what must have been her first book; another framed a fan letter from Erma Bombeck; a third held a portion of a page from a review in the August 22, 1979, *Seattle Times* that compared her work to Colette's.

The furnishings were as assertive as the mementos. At least five lamps were in evidence, with shades ranging from fringed damask to stained glass. The tables were shiny with lacquer, each bearing a slightly different hue, rendering the light in the room subtle and elusive and no doubt flattering to Viveca Dane's complexion. The couch and the chairs were tufted and tucked, the wall sconces were of brass and colored glass, and the hearth was tiled in a purple-and-black motif that resembled a sign of the zodiac. The overall sense was of flair once-removed, a museum rather than a homestead, a relic that had slipped from stylish to passé without the owner's notice. But the aura of obsolescence vanished the minute Viveca Dane returned to the room.

She'd been gone fifteen minutes, not five, and the transformation was remarkable. Her hair was now a sculpted crown, courtesy of an indiscernible wig. Her face was as unmarred as a bust of white marble, her figure was petite and even provocative in snug slacks and a sweater of a dusky gray that offered a vale of décolletage. Her eyes gleamed like the cut glass in the lighting fixture that was twinkling above her head. In a quarter of an hour, Viveca Dane had dropped twenty years off her age and added two tons to her gravitas. I wondered if she gave lessons. Past her prime or not, she was clearly a force to be reckoned with. I began to take her seriously as a suspect.

She sat on the couch across from me and crossed her shapely legs. Her slippers had been replaced by boots of such soft leather they seemed to have melted around her ankles. "Coffee will be ready in a minute," she said. "Do you take cream?"

"No, thanks."

"I could make a Bloody Mary if you want one."

"Not while I'm on duty. But thanks."

"Is that chair comfortable enough for you?"

"It's fine."

"The reason I ask is that you seem ill at ease all of a sudden, Mr. Tanner."

I laughed uneasily. "I think it's because I have a feeling I'm not going to get the job done this morning."

"What job is that?"

"Tricking you into revealing your deep-seated animosity toward Chandelier Wells."

"Ha," she cackled gleefully. "My animosity's as deep-seated as Dolly Parton's boobs."

I felt myself blush. I tried and failed to remember whether any other sexagenarian had ever prompted a similar reaction. "I just meant that—"

"Chandelier is a lying, cheating, thieving bitch," she surged on. "And that's when she's on her good behavior. Is that up-front enough for you, or should I elaborate?"

I grinned. "I really hate people who mask their true feelings. Come on, Ms. Dane. Tell me what you really think."

She giggled. "You're on to me, you rascal. I've hated the woman for more than a decade. Let me get the coffee."

She left and returned after some rattling around in the kitchen. In her absence, the smell of lavender threatened to overload my olfactory nerves. After my first sip of coffee, I realized she'd laced it with whiskey. Not suppressing a smile, I asked her what had happened between her and Chandelier more than a decade ago.

"That's when she wrote her first book."

"You didn't like it?"

"That's putting it mildly."

"On aesthetic grounds or something else?"

"Chandelier Wells stole my literary creation, which is to say my life's work, lock, stock, and barrel."

"How so?"

"My first book was set in Carmel and hers was in Monterey. My heroine was a lawyer, hers is a newswoman. My heroine's sidekick was a cabbie; hers is a bus driver. My first plot involved the fashion industry; hers delved into the diamond business. My first title was *Spike Heel*; hers was *Pendant*. I could go on, but it will only depress me."

"When was your first book published?"

"Nineteen seventy-seven. It was a national bestseller."

"And Chandelier's?"

"Ten years later."

"Same publisher?"

"Don't be ridiculous. *My* publisher has been in existence since the Civil War. It doesn't print trash; not even profitable trash."

"If she stole from you, did you ever think of suing her?"

"I not only thought of it, I did it. Copyright infringement, theft of intellectual property, passing off, intentional infliction of emotional distress—I sued the bitch for everything my lawyer could think of, and when he couldn't think of enough, I got another lawyer."

"And?"

Her nose wrinkled and her lip curled. "I got tossed out of court on my tight little ass. It didn't even get to trial. I was sleeping with my lawyer at the time, which I think was part of the problem—he was more interested in the after hours than the nine-to-five. Ended up costing me fifty grand for an empty gesture. But, hell. It was fun while it lasted. I got to see her sweat, at least."

"So after that her career flourished and yours declined?"

"In a nutshell."

"Do you publish at all anymore?"

"Only in France. Two books a year. The French are the only people in the Western world who still possess a modicum of good taste."

I waved at the room and its contents. "You don't seem exactly hard up."

"I invested my money wisely, mostly in real estate. I bought houses out in the avenues for fifty thousand bucks, cash, and now I rent them for three thousand a month. Also cash. Plus the French contracts provide me with thirty thousand a year in mad money. And I've known some generous men in my time." She laughed dryly. "Though not lately, except for the poor addled idiot who sends all these flowers."

I adjusted my position. "I have to ask you something, I'm afraid," I said with a surprising degree of embarrassment.

"What is it?"

"Have you been making threats against Chandelier Wells?"

Her brow peaked like an alp. "What kind of threats are you talking about?"

"Bodily harm. Violent death. Murder and mayhem and assorted misfortunes."

She looked at me more closely. "You're serious, I believe."

"Afraid so."

"Well, I can't say I'm sorry that Chandelier has some terror on her plate at the moment. But, no. I'm not making threats. To her or to anyone else."

"Can you think of someone who might be?"

"You mean except the poor schmucks who pay hard-earned money to read her wretched prose?"

I grinned. "Except them."

"Well, she's gone through lots of men, and she's made a ton of money, and she's backed some fairly extreme political causes, plus she's a sour, evil person." She reconsidered her list and smiled. "But I suppose you were speaking specifically."

"Yes, I was."

"Then no. I'm the likeliest suspect I know, but I have an alibi."

"Which is?"

"My revenge against Chandelier is reserved for my memoirs."

"Really?"

"Oh, yes."

"Which will be published when?"

"When I'm dead and buried, Mr. Tanner. Which will be well into the next century if I have anything to say about it. And I believe I'll have quite a bit to say, don't you?"

chapter 6

T he women were there when I arrived at the restaurant and had managed to commandeer the best table in the place— I guess that's the sort of skill you develop by dining out in New York on a regular basis. Enrico's was loud and lively as always, and chichi and clean and efficient as not often of late until the recent makeover by the new management.

The weather had cooperated, so it was as good a day as occurs in the city in February, warm enough to dine alfresco, sunny enough to wear shades, and clear enough for the bay to sparkle like a blue bank of snow and the hills to be observed lurking on all sides like kindly chaperons. The complex smells from the kitchen and the carefree banter from the throng strolling by on the sidewalk added to the sense of perfection.

The only one of the women I'd met previously was Lark McLaren, but even if I hadn't seen her at Chandelier's, I'd have known she was the one who was local. Garbed in black from head to toe not excluding lips and fingernails, sheathed in long-sleeved and floor-length dresses that flattened every contour below the jawline, draped with capes and scarves of similar tints and functions, the two New Yorkers looked as if they had just come from a funeral of someone who didn't matter very much. My faded corduroys and threadbare tweeds looked cutting edge in comparison to the East-erners' monochromatic garb, which made me wonder why such high-powered women would choose to dress as similarly as sheep.

As for Lark, she looked swell in a bright print dress that didn't try to erase all evidence of her gender.

Although their outfits suggested they were twins, beneath their macabre couture the New Yorkers were distinctly different. Amber Adams, the agent, was large, buxom, and brash and wasn't bashful about any of it. In contrast, Sally Rinehart, the editor, was slim to the point of emaciation, with chalk-white skin and straight, dark hair drawn back in a bun that made her look three times her age, which I guessed to be no more than thirty. Her skittish black eyes never seemed to light on anything for more than an instant, and her manner suggested the outside world was as potentially damaging as a peptic ulcer. The idea of Sally Rinehart imposing an editorial judgment on the deathless prose of Chandelier Wells was one of those concepts around which my mind had difficulty wrapping itself.

Whatever the women had been discussing clanked to an immediate halt when they noticed me. It took a while, since there was wine to be drunk and shrimp to be nibbled, but when I made it onto their radar, the three of them looked up expectantly, as if I were bringing an advance copy of *Publishers Weekly*. I hated to disappoint them, but my most creative contribution to the meal was going to involve a meat-loaf sandwich.

Amber gripped my hand like a lady wrestler the moment Lark introduced us, and her eyes roamed over me like a Sotheby's appraiser's—I don't think I made the list for the next auction. Sally Rinehart made do with trying to pretend I was invisible.

After I took my seat, we exchanged small talk about the weather and the city. Amber found San Francisco a major disappointment on this trip, especially in the amenities at her hotel and the stock on hand in the new boutiques around Union Square. For her part, Sally loved every single thing about it, especially the new museum of modern art, which she'd visited the day before. Despite several provocations, I refrained from becoming either a jingoist or a cynic.

We placed our orders—the women each had a salad featuring various esoteric amendments and another eight-dollar glass of a

Sonoma chardonnay; I had a turkey sandwich and an Anchor Steam, meat loaf not being featured for some reason, probably involving longevity.

"I take it all of you know why I'm here," I began when we were comfy and cozy and slightly buzzed. Each of them nodded her head. "I haven't come up with anything helpful so far, so I'm going to need a history lesson, provided there is one."

The women exchanged looks. "History of what?" Amber Adams asked. "Or who?"

"Chandelier Wells," I said.

"Boswell himself couldn't do justice to that one," Amber muttered sardonically, though loudly enough for all to hear.

I tried to stay in front of the agenda. "Before the first of the threatening notes arrived, was there any sign that Ms. Wells was creating trouble for anyone? Threatening them? Embarrassing them? Complicating their lives? Anything like that at all?"

The women looked at one another once again and once again let Amber take the lead. "If you're talking about her books, then as far as I know the answer is no. If you're talking about personal relationships, it's an entirely different story."

"What story is that?"

Amber shrugged. "Chandelier is aggressive, demanding, and ambitious, both as a writer and a businesswoman. She drives people hard and demands nothing short of total perfection and absolute loyalty." Amber paused for a sip of wine. "What makes it tolerable for those of us on the receiving end, usually, is that Chandelier drives herself even harder than she does the rest of us."

Sally Rinehart nodded a meek concurrence. Lark McLaren didn't move a muscle. Apparently she had her own take on Chandelier and wasn't about to go public with it.

Just then a cell phone rang. Amber and Sally looked at each other. Amber took hers out of her purse, flipped it open, pressed a button, and said, "Adams."

I looked at Lark and Lark smiled indulgently. Just then another cell phone rang. This time Sally made the move for her purse, with the same result. And then it was Lark's turn. For the next five minutes I was in the middle of an Altman film, with two and three people talking simultaneously, in incomplete sentences and cryptic jargon, about subjects that were mostly foreign to me:

". . . Don't forget we have jacket approval. Yes, that includes flap copy, and blurbs, cover art, author bio, and the photo, too. The whole nine yards. . . . *Final* approval, that's right."

". . . First printing is definitely two point five million. Sandra approved it at sales conference."

". . . It's hard/soft or nothing, Max. . . . I know England isn't the U.S., but let's face it, you're all going to be owned by the Germans sooner or later, so what the hell difference does it make? . . . If Random House couldn't say no, what makes you think *you* can?"

". . . Pub date is February 14 because Chandelier's pub date is *always* February 14. . . . Valentine's Day. Right. . . . It's Chandelier's gift to her fans. . . . Of course she's serious. Chandelier is *always* serious. . . . No, adding Tucson to the schedule is not an option. I won't even bring it up with her."

". . . That's not what I hear, I hear she's jumping to Putnam and taking Johnson with her. . . . That's old news, Max. . . . No, dramatic rights went for a million five. . . . No, he didn't. I'm an *agent*. I'd *know* something like that."

". . . We want the Amazon reader reviews to start coming in now. . . . They don't *have* to use the ones we drafted and sent out, but if they improvise, it had better be an improvement. And there'd better be at least fifty of them."

". . . She brings her hairdresser with her. We'll fax them a menu a week before she arrives and we expect each item on it to be available from room service twenty-four hours a day during her stay. . . . If that's a problem, I understand there are one or two *other* hotels in Chicago, Mildred. . . . Oh, yes, she would."

". . . Our buyers will hit the stores on Monday. . . . I know, but last time we opened at number two behind Clancy. Jesus. I don't know how that happens. I've never met a single breathing soul who's ever read a word that guy's written."

"... Okay? See you Thursday."

"... Fine. Lunch on Friday. . . . Not Balthazar again. . . . Whatever."

"Let's get back to the threats for a minute," I said when the phones were back in the purses. "Ms. Rinehart, has the publisher received any complaints about the content of any of Chandelier's recent work?"

Sally Rinehart blanched as though I'd suggested we go back to her room and get naked. "I don't think you grasp the nature of the relationship Chandelier has with her public, Mr. Tanner," she managed finally in a voice the size of a gnat's. "We get thousands of letters about Chandelier. Most are addressed to her personally, of course, and those that are we forward to Lark without opening."

When I looked at Lark, she nodded. "We average close to a hundred pieces of mail a day."

"Jesus," I blurted.

Lark grinned. "Not one from Him as yet. I think I would have remembered."

"I'm sure He's a big fan," Amber said sourly. "Although the conceptions Chandelier portrays can hardly be termed immaculate."

"Which is why she sells," Sally Rinehart offered meekly.

Meanwhile, I was trying to imagine what would make me read a thousand pieces of correspondence unless each of them was a personal missive from the pen of Michelle Pfeiffer. "Does Chandelier read all her mail?" I asked.

Lark shook her head. "She can't. There's too much of it."

"She doesn't answer fan mail? Isn't that kind of an insult to her public?"

Lark sniffed. "Her public is well served."

"How?"

"I answer them in her name."

"You mean you forge her signature."

Lark glanced left and right. "Each of us does, from time to time. It's the only way to keep things running smoothly and leave Chandelier enough time to write. She reads much of the business corre-

spondence, of course, though only those items that contain proposals Amber or I feel she would be interested in."

"You're her filter, in other words."

Lark reddened. "Among other things."

I turned back to Sally Rinehart. "How about the letters you open
in New York? What are they about?"

She thought it over while she nibbled a crouton as if it constituted
her entire meal. "I would say the hostile ones are equally divided
among the religious zealots who feel Chandelier is an agent of the
devil in advocating immorality in one form or another, usually sex-
ual; the crazies who believe she speaks to them through their TVs or
their toothbrushes or their toenails; and those who believe she is
their long-lost mother, wife, daughter, or lover. Or son, as one of
them insisted. Or that she is Marilyn Monroe reincarnated. Or
Edith Wharton. Insert the name of your favorite ghost."

I looked at Lark. "You get this kind of stuff, too?"

"All the time."

"What else?"

Sally squinted to summon her mental list. "There are requests for
money, of course, and proposals of marriage, and ideas for new books
and new wardrobes, and hair and makeup and wellness advice, and
requests to promote products or services. And gifts of homemade
fudge and hand-knit sweaters and on and on and on. You wouldn't
believe what shows up in our mail. Drugs, even, once in a while. Pot,
usually. Homegrown."

I smiled. "Does Chandelier partake?"

Lark smiled back. "No comment."

I looked at Amber. "Do you get letters, too?"

"Tons. And faxes and e-mails and phone calls. I expect a carrier
pigeon any day. Most of them are from people who say they can
write as well as Chandelier so I should be their agent, too."

"Do you take any of them on?"

Her mouth made mincemeat of the question. "You must be kidding. I also get commercial proposals of various kinds, mostly offers
to option film rights from self-styled producers who think a thou-

sand bucks will lock up dramatic rights in Chandelier's work for life. God, there are a lot of morons in this world," Amber concluded bitterly. "And agents see them all."

I drank half my beer and ate half my sandwich and left the ladies to graze at their salads and talk New York talk. My plate was empty and I was wondering about dessert before their piles of greens had noticeably diminished.

"I take it none of these letters have threatened bodily harm," I said after a while.

"Some of the religious ones do," Sally said.

"What do you do in those cases?"

"Send the letter to the authorities."

"In New York or out here?"

"Both."

"Police or FBI?"

"Postal inspectors, actually," Lark said. "They've opened files on several of Chandelier's more imaginative antagonists. I think they've interrogated some of the more vociferous ones."

"But none of them have ever followed through?"

"No. Not until now."

"Does Chandelier see the stuff from the crazies?"

Lark shook her head. "She asked me to stop showing them to her when there got to be so many."

I laughed. "I have to say that being a successful author sounds like a depressing experience."

"Not totally," Lark said quickly. "Most of the letters are from fans. True fans, I mean; people who have enjoyed the books or have had their lives changed by Chandelier in some way."

"Literally?"

"Oh, yes. We have a whole folder full of letters from women who say Chandelier's work has encouraged them to persevere in the face of financial hardship, or keep fighting a debilitating disease, or take steps to end an abusive relationship. We're thinking of publishing a selection of them, in fact. I'm sure you find it surprising, but Chandelier is a spiritual icon for thousands of women all over the world."

"How many countries is she published in?"

"Twenty-eight, at last count."

At first blush, I found Chandelier's transcendent importance both surprising and sad. Surprising because she didn't seem particularly holy in person. Sad because so many people search so desperately for salvation.

"Spiritual icons get blame as well as credit sometimes," I said without voicing my skepticism. "Do you ever hear from women who feel Chandelier has let them down in some way? Caused even bigger problems than they had before?"

Lark nodded. "Once in a while. Some women interpret the books as encouraging them to leave their men, or stay with them, or turn them in to the police, or some such conduct that turns out to be a mistake. When it doesn't work out, they blame Chandelier, who had no idea what was going on in the first place and is not in the business of giving advice to the lovelorn in any event."

I looked at each of the women in turn. "You're not helping me narrow this down, ladies."

Amber Adams spoke up. "In her world, Chandelier is as big a celebrity as Julia Roberts and Madonna are in theirs. Even bigger, in some ways, since most women can relate to Chandelier a lot easier than they can to movie or rock stars. If you know any celebrities—"

"I don't," I interjected.

"—then you know they have the most bizarre love-hate relationship with the public you can possibly imagine. In fact, I'm sure you *can't* imagine how totally and pathetically some people attach themselves to the rich and famous. And how many truly disturbed people are walking around out there." Amber's wave encompassed the city and the entire world beyond it.

"That last part I've had some experience with," I said.

Sally Rinehart squeaked like a mouse. "One woman sent Chandelier a Tampax. Used. She wanted Chandelier to drink her menstrual blood."

Everyone but Sally shuddered. I began to see her more as a ghoul than a sprite.

"Then there're the critics," Lark piped up. "Some of them are so insulted by Chandelier's success they seem to become literally unhinged. One of them said there should be a federal law prohibiting her from writing any more books."

"Are you seriously suggesting that one of them might be a suspect?"

Lark hesitated. "Allen Goodhew, maybe. Allen's local—he writes the book column for an alternative weekly, the *Riff*. Allen seems to feel personally betrayed by Chandelier's work. It's as if he feels she's become some sort of Antichrist."

"I'll talk to him. Anyone else?"

"Only her entourage," Amber said with a sneer.

"What kind of entourage do you mean?"

"Copy editors, book designers, cover artists, publicists, store owners, talk show producers, various and sundry gofers and assistants. Everyone she comes in contact with, basically."

"You're saying she's difficult to deal with."

Amber laughed the way a hyena barks. "Has Cher had plastic surgery? All I'm saying is if you spend any time in her orbit, sooner or later Chandelier will accuse you of incompetence, treason, stupidity, or all of them, and not necessarily in that order. And the list of her victims includes all three of us."

I thought Amber might be exaggerating, or even have some personal vendetta she was pursuing, but when I looked at the other two women, they nodded. "Then why do you keep on?" I asked.

"Money," Amber Adams said gruffly. "Ten percent of a ten-million-dollar advance is hard to turn down."

"It's more than that, Amber," Lark insisted. "Chandelier is gigantic. She's one of the most successful women in the world. You just keep hoping that someday she will focus her energy and ambition on something larger than herself. Because when that happens, she'll do major things with her life."

"When pigs fly is when Chandelier will think of someone other than herself," Amber Adams muttered in the echo of Lark's encomium. Her bile was so obvious I decided to ask Lark about it the next time we were alone.

"She's not that bad," Lark protested. "She gives tons of money to charity."

"Tax dodge," Amber countered.

"She buys hundreds of books for the libraries."

"*Her* books, mostly. Which has the fully anticipated result of pushing her higher on the bestseller list."

"She's a good mom."

"When she's home."

"She's a good speller," Sally said, blushing.

I laughed. "I've known serial killers with fewer enemies."

"We're pretty sure the guy who wrote the notes is here in San Francisco," Lark McLaren said. "Aren't we?"

"Why?"

"The notes were hand-delivered, for one thing."

"If you can hire people to commit murder, you can certainly pay them to deliver an envelope."

"But this is where she lives. This is where most of her . . ."

"Victims live?" I offered.

"I suppose so."

"Besides," Sally interrupted, "I thought we were sure it's the ex-husband."

Lark shook her head. "I can't see Mickey going that far. I mean, if Chandelier died, what would he do for money?"

"What would any of us?" Amber added morosely.

I sighed and finished my beer. "That covers the bases, I guess. I'll see you all at the big party."

"That reminds me," Lark said. "Chandelier wants to make sure you scout out the place beforehand."

"Scout for what?"

"Bombs. Booby traps. Assassins. You'd know better than I would, I'm sure."

"Do you really think this is that serious?" I asked.

"Chandelier does," they said in unison.

I shrugged. "Okay. I'll take a look. Where is it again?"

"Jimbo's. She's had all her launch parties there for the past twelve years."

"How many people do you expect to show up?"

"Three to four hundred. And they'll be lining up by three at the latest, so you'd better get there early."

chapter 7

I went home to change clothes for the party, which meant switching from corduroy slacks to twills and replacing the old tweed jacket with the one that still had all the buttons. As I fixed a cup of coffee to help me stay awake through the festivities, I got an idea.

"Hey, Ruthie," I said when she answered the phone.

"Hey, yourself, Sugar Bear. How's life in the fast lane?"

"I'm still looking for the on-ramp and you know it."

Ruthie's laugh was a wheezy growl that a grizzly would envy. "Still loving up that assistant DA?"

"Whenever I get the chance."

"Time you tied the knot, is what I think, baby doll."

"I'll keep that in mind in case the issue comes up for a vote."

"This one's the one; I can feel it."

"Could be," I said, wondering how much Ruthie's judgment could be relied on. And if it would help to have someone to blame if I made the plunge, then things fell apart.

"What can I do you for, Sugar Bear?" Ruthie was asking as I was estimating eventualities.

"What're you doing at four o'clock?"

"Today?"

"Yeah."

She thought it over. "Same as usual, I guess—inching toward the liquor cabinet and trying to keep Conrad off me till nightfall."

I laughed because it was the truth and because I could picture it as vividly as if I were in the room.

Ruthie Spring was an old friend. Her first husband, Harry, had been my mentor in the investigations trade until he was murdered in a valley town named Oxtail more than twenty years ago. Her second husband, Conrad, is rich beyond calculus and spends his money on whatever Ruthie wants him to, which is usually one or another of Ruthie's favorite causes. She's a former army nurse and sheriff's deputy and is currently a private investigator carrying on for her fallen husband. She works when she wants to and doesn't when she doesn't, a state of nirvana I aspire to myself, although it's beginning to look as if I'll never get there unless I win the lottery, which is problematic since I don't play.

"What's happening at four o'clock?" Ruthie asked as I was scanning our recent history.

"Ever hear of Chandelier Wells?"

"The writer?"

"The very same."

"Sure. She's huge."

"Read any of her books?"

"I have to admit that when Conrad goes off on one of his quail shoots, she gets my juices flowing a night or two. Gets me wet as a sweat sock sometimes."

I was glad Ruthie couldn't see my blush.

"The lady writes a nice slice of erotica," she went on. "Not too gamy; not too tame. A sort of 'I think I'll try that myself next time' kind of thing. Why does it matter?"

"She's having a party celebrating her new book at Jimbo's at four. Thought you might want to go."

"You going to be there?"

"Yep."

She chuckled with a ribald nudge. "Big fan of bodice rippers, are you, Marsh?"

"I'll be working, actually," I said quickly. Not that there's anything wrong with bodice rippers. "And I could use some help."

"Doing what?"

"Keeping an eye out for anyone who might have something in mind other than literature."

"Something illegal, you mean."

"Yep."

"Even violent."

"Yep."

She paused. "Count me in, Sugar Bear. Might be a hoot, hobnobbing with the hoi polloi. What do I have to do?"

"Just keep your eyes open."

"We going together or separately?"

"I've got to be there early, so come on your own about four. And don't let on that we know each other, unless you need help shutting something down."

"Do I pack my piece?"

"I think so."

"No problem. I'll be the one in the lizard-skin boots," she added unnecessarily, then told me to be good and if I couldn't be good, to send her a copy of the videotape.

I got to Jimbo's a little after three. True to Lark McLaren's prediction, the devoted had already begun to assemble, most of them women, many of them lugging bulging canvas book bags and sporting sweatshirts emblazoned with one of Chandelier's book jackets, all of them surprisingly cheerful given the chill in the afternoon air and the length of the idolatrous line. I tried to remember if I'd ever gotten a book signed by its author and could only come up with the night I went to a reading by Mailer but didn't have the nerve to ask for an autograph even though I bought his book.

When I got inside the building, Lark was standing in the lobby with another woman at her side. "Long time, no see," I said. "And thanks for lunch, by the way."

"I wish I'd had what you had," she said.

"Hungry already?"

"Famished." She lowered her voice. "I took a quick look around and didn't see anything suspicious."

Just for fun, I lowered mine as well. "Good."

She made sure I wasn't mocking her, then placed her hand on the other woman's arm. "This is Meredith Dunne; she owns Dunne and Son Books on Upper Market. She and Chandelier are old friends— Meredith supplies all the books for these parties and there will be two of her staff here as well, sitting behind the table beneath the store banner."

Mrs. Dunne and I greeted each other minimally. She was big-boned and big-haired, compact and self-possessed, with a searching gaze that roamed my face so thoroughly it suggested she was writing my unauthorized biography. She was dressed in a chocolate brown pantsuit and toted a purse the size of a carpetbag that I bet contained everything she would need for the rest of the month because that's how far she planned ahead.

"I wanted Meredith to meet you," Lark was saying, "because she's been to all twelve of these launch parties, and if there's anything out of the ordinary going on, she might be able to spot it."

"Good," I said again, and turned my attention to Meredith. "If you see anything remotely suspicious, or even just odd, come find me right away. Don't try to do anything yourself."

"Fine. I guess." The words fluttered with worry before she brought them under control. "What do you think is likely to—"

"Nothing," I interrupted with false confidence. "I don't think anything at all unusual is going to happen this afternoon."

"Why not?"

"There are too many people around, for one. Plus the male of the species will stand out like a Republican at a union rally and this note business seems like a guy thing to me. So relax. Drink lots of wine; sell lots of books."

"Easy for you to say," Meredith said, and strolled off toward the table where her assistants were hanging her banner.

I turned my attention back to Lark McLaren. She had changed to a blue-striped blouse beneath a tailored gray business suit above blockish high heels that added two inches to her height and gave her thighs a provocative curve. She was calm, compelling, and comely. For just a moment, until thoughts of Jill made me shape up, I wished I were twenty years younger.

"What other outside elements will be here today?" I asked her. "Other than the fans."

"Well, there are Jimbo's people. A couple of guys to handle the heat and lights and chairs. They're easy to spot—they're wearing black satin shirts with *Jimbo's* in script on the breast. Makes me want to go bowling for some reason."

"I felt the same way at *The Big Lebowski.* Who else?"

She giggled. "I *loved* that film. The rug that tied the room together."

"I've got one of those myself, as it happens."

She looked at me. "I'll bet you do at that."

We exchanged smiles of confederacy. "Who else is here?" I asked.

"The food people. Red Riding Hood is the caterer we use. In keeping with the literary theme, don't you know."

"Are you implying your boss's books are for children?"

"I most certainly am not."

I couldn't tell if her anger was real or feigned. "You've dealt with Red Riding Hood before this?" I asked.

"Let's see." She counted fingers. "Four times. They're very reliable."

"Their employees must change pretty often, though."

She nodded. "I don't think serving cheese puffs and cheap Chablis has lots of upside potential."

I chuckled once again. "You're an amusing woman, Ms. McLaren."

"Thank you for noticing. Most men don't."

"How about your boss? Does she go in for witty repartee?"

"Not with me," Lark said, suddenly somber, then looked at her watch. "She'll be here in twenty minutes. I've got things to do."

As Lark hurried off toward the main room, I decided to check out the basement. The stairs were wide and plushly carpeted, but the rooms below street level were dark and dank and uninviting. Most of them seemed to be rarely used offices or overstocked storage areas full of stuff that had been stacked away for years. I looked in as many as I could get into, flipping on lights, poking and probing in likely spots and not very likely ones, too, then moving on. My search wasn't exhaustive nor could it be, given the timetable, but I had a feeling that when and if this guy made his move, it was going to be out in the open, a face-to-face showdown with Chandelier Wells, the settling of some long-festering grudge. Nonetheless, after I checked the rest rooms and boiler room and broom closet, I went back upstairs substantially less than confident that there was nothing dangerous down below.

Inside the ballroom, the caterers were setting out wine bottles and plastic glasses and trays full of finger foods, the Jimbo's boys were setting up folding chairs along the perimeter of the room, and the women from Dunne and Son were unpacking cardboard boxes filled with freshly minted copies of *Shalloon* with a meticulousness more common to archaeology than pop fiction.

I ambled over to Ms. Dunne. "What's the drill?" I asked. "They line up, get a book, have it signed, give you the money, then stay around to party if they want to?"

She nodded. "That's about it, except we make them buy the book first, then take it to Chandelier afterward. We've found if we do it otherwise, there are lots of personally inscribed books lying around after the party's over. Which makes Chandelier furious and costs me money since I can't send them back to the publisher."

"Sounds like there's some coercion involved in making up the guest list."

Ms. Dunne chuckled dryly. "I wouldn't call it coercion, at least not to her face, but Chandelier isn't happy when at least two hundred of her closest friends don't show up at her book parties. She lets them know it when they're no-shows, too."

"Who all gets invited?"

"Chandelier and Lark make telephone calls to a hundred people and we mail four hundred invitations to our customer list. The local chapters of Sisters in Crime and Romance Writers of America both get invited, as well as various reading and writing groups that Chandelier has spoken to over the years. The event is advertised on Chandelier's Web site and ours as well, of course. And in the local papers."

"Sounds like half the world will be here."

She laughed. "Not quite. But if fewer than two hundred people show up, Chandelier gets irritated. Since no one likes it when Chandelier gets irritated, we do what we can to fill the room."

"Do they have to have a written invitation to get in?"

She shook her head. "It's wide-open."

"Great," I said sarcastically, then tried to make nice. "How did you meet Chandelier, anyway?"

"We went to summer camp together. Up in the Sierras, near the Feather River. That was years ago, of course, but we were in the same cabin and we both liked to write poetry so we kept in touch."

"Do you know anyone who has reason to want her harmed?"

She took her time to answer, folding her arms across her chest, looking toward the pile of books that was materializing on the sale table. "Chandelier can be . . . difficult, at times. She's a proud woman and she doesn't forgive a slight very easily, so there have been several shattered friendships over the years. But none of it is life-and-death, I don't think. Except maybe for Thurston Buckley."

"The real estate guy?"

Meredith nodded. "He fell pretty hard when Chandelier dumped him. He even tried to get me to intervene at one point, but I know which side of my bread is buttered. And besides, he's a creep."

"Tell me about the butter and the bread."

She gestured toward the books piled high on the table. "Chandelier financed my start in the book business back in '92. Cosigned the loan. Took me to see a friend of hers at Wells Fargo. Everything. Things went great for a while, but what with Borders and Barnes and Noble opening stores on every corner, and the on-line services expanding as well, I'd be out of business if Chandelier hadn't been so supportive."

I looked at her table. "How many books did you bring?"

"Four hundred."

"Will you sell them all?"

"We've sold that many a time or two before, but anything over two is a bonanza for us. We double the average because Chandelier isn't happy if we run out of books."

I pointed toward the door. "Some of the fans seem to be bringing books with them."

"Not the new one they aren't—we're the only source in the city for *Shalloon* at this point. But lots of them bring her backlist to be signed as well. Fans, and collectors, too. But we try to set limits." She pointed at a small printed sign taped to the end of the book table: DUE TO TIME CONSTRAINTS, CHANDELIER CAN SIGN A MAXIMUM OF THREE BOOKS PER CUSTOMER AND CANNOT INSCRIBE PERSONAL MESSAGES. THANK YOU FOR UNDERSTANDING.

I pointed at the pile of papers next to the sign. "What's that?"

"Chandelier's newsletter. One to a customer."

"Free?"

"Free. It can be downloaded from our Web site, too, of course."

"Of course," I said as though I were a dot head myself. I looked at the banner tacked to the wall behind the book table. "Where's your son?"

It took her several seconds to answer. The starkly haunted expression on her face made me wish I hadn't asked the question.

"Jason's dead. Six months after he was born and three months before his father left me behind to grieve all by myself in the emptiest house there ever was. When I finally recovered, I decided this was a good way to remember and honor him and, thanks to Chandelier, his memorial won't be tainted by bankruptcy anytime soon."

Just then there was a noise outside, a rumble, then a buzz, then a swell of cheers and shouts in the nature of a hallelujah chorus. The queen must have entered the building.

chapter 8

Surrounded by a retinue of imposing women and followed by a knot of squealing, surging fans, Chandelier Wells swept into Jimbo's ballroom like Isabella returning to court after bidding Columbus bon voyage. She took a quick tour of the room to assess the arrangements, whispered something to the caterer and something else to Lark McLaren, then doffed her camel-colored cashmere coat and took her seat behind a pile of shiny books, chic and businesslike in a bright red dress with a low-cut bodice, ready to greet her public. As if in response to a cosmic prompt, the crowd, barely held in check by one of the Dunne and Son retainers, streamed toward the table cash in hand, clamoring to claim their prize. I heard the woman who was first in line tell Chandelier she had been waiting since 10 A.M.

As predicted, the file of fans snaked out of the building and down the block. Under the guise of a hall monitor on the lookout for cutters and rowdies and people not keeping their hands to themselves, I strolled its length looking for suspicious characters.

There were twenty women for every man, and twenty people over forty for every one under that. On the whole they seemed harmless enough, a cross-section of the city's Anglo-Saxon middle class, a surprisingly substantial number of people to whom Chandelier's prose was in the nature of a benign narcotic—addictive and pleasurable and productive of the self-possession so essential to getting through life in the big city. On the other hand, a few of the women's eyes glowed a little too brightly, and a few hands gripped book bags a little too tightly, and a few jaws were set in a brute determination that seemed far out of proportion to the occasion. For these, the experience was clearly more religious than literary, and those are always the ones you have to watch.

Given the makeup of the crowd, it was tempting to think the phenomenon of Chandelier and her ilk had mostly to do with gender, or educational shortcomings, or inferior self-regard, or debilitating socioeconomics. But my guess was that it was a complex mix of all of those and then some, a syndrome that claimed people of widely various backgrounds and belief systems, which made it far too dense for me to fathom. Whatever its social or psychic origins, the cult of Chandelier had produced a long line of people carrying bags and satchels that probably contained only books but could theoretically contain deadly weapons. Without mounting a body search of each and every fan, I wasn't sure what I could do about it but keep my fingers crossed.

I returned to the ballroom and decided to chat with Lark McLaren for reasons that didn't have much to do with the job. "Nice turnout," I said.

She shrugged. "About average."

"Chandelier seems edgy."

"She's always edgy when she's out in public."

"Even before the threats?"

She nodded. "Ever since I've known her."

"Why the nerves? She must do this kind of thing all the time."

"She's done over two hundred events since her last novel came out."

"And she's still nervous."

"She's gotten wary of the percentages, I think."

"Percentage of what?"

Lark's tone turned grave. "The percentage of serious mental illness afoot in the general populace. And the percentage of that percentage that feels compelled to prey upon celebrities."

Lark's dark mood was so uncharacteristic it made me wonder at its source. "Did anything happen after I left last night?"

She shook her head. "No. Nothing."

"You're sure?"

"Of course. If anything had happened, I would know it."

"Did Chandelier say anything about the security situation here?"

"No, but she's criticized everything but."

I looked around but failed to find a flaw. "She isn't satisfied with the arrangements?"

"She's *never* satisfied with the arrangements. In this instance, let's see—the wine's too warm, the food's too cold, the table's too rickety, and I forgot to bring her pillow and her footstool. Which I would have remembered if I didn't have to get two hundred boxes of perfume in the mail this morning."

"Perfume?"

"She's sending bottles of perfume to two hundred bookstores and media people to promote *Shalloon*. It's supposed to smell just like Contradiction at a fraction of the cost. That's the latest rage, in case you don't keep track."

"I don't."

"No wife? No girlfriend?"

"No wife; maybe a girlfriend. But we haven't gotten to the perfume stage."

"That's what you think."

I laughed.

"Shit," Lark said abruptly.

"What?"

"They don't have any bottled water. Chandelier insists we offer bottled water to the women who don't take alcohol."

Her agitation was such that I was moved to calm her down. "In the greater scheme of things, the water and the wine seem like minor irritants. I don't see any unhappy faces."

Lark's laugh was crimped and humorless. "In my job, the greater scheme of things doesn't extend beyond Chandelier's state of mind. And to Chandelier, there *are* no minor irritants, only flagrant errors committed by incompetent idiots." As Lark looked around the room, she wrinkled her nose as if the entire atmosphere reeked with imperfection. "As far as Chandelier's concerned, you're either a winner or a loser. Losers let things slide, don't sweat the details, leave their fate in the hands of others. Winners take charge of every aspect of their lives and make sure everything is always perfect."

"Your job isn't in danger because the canapés are cold, is it?"

"No, but Red Riding Hood may be left out in the woods at the next launch party. Jesus. What on earth is that?"

I looked where Lark was looking. The former orderly line had bunched into a cluster of women who had formed a circle around something on the floor. As I was on the way over, the cluster parted long enough for me to see that the disturbance had occurred because one of the women had fallen. Meredith Dunne was bending over her, fanning the air with her hand as though that were a proven form of ventilation. A second later, more professional relief arrived, in the person of Ruthie Spring, the former combat nurse.

As Ruthie issued instructions and began taking a pulse, I joined the crowd around the fallen fan. She was small and frail and as pale as my handkerchief, unremarkable in every aspect except her swoon. There was no blood or trauma in evidence, only a rather ragged outfit that suggested she had saved the money to buy a first edition of *Shalloon* by forgoing food for a week.

I was about to help Ruthie revive her when it occurred to me that the little drama could be in the nature of a diversion. I glanced toward the table where Chandelier had been signing books. Activity had come to a standstill and the featured players were locked in a frozen tableau of apprehension and uncertainty. Chandelier seemed to be hiding behind three two-foot stacks of books, and Lark McLaren seemed ready to throw herself between Chandelier and her assailant if that's what it took to save her. The confusion was such that I briefly envisioned the Marx Brothers, with me in the role of Groucho.

I walked to Chandelier's side and sat in a vacant chair. "What the hell's happened?" she demanded breathily. "What's that woman *doing* down there?"

"She's fainting, as far as I can tell. It's probably nothing to worry about. She was overwhelmed by the moment."

"What moment are you talking about?"

"You."

Chandelier blushed and adjusted her bodice. "Oh. Well. You're sure that's all it was?"

"Pretty sure."

After a last glance at the stricken fan, Chandelier looked at me the way she would look at a dog that had just soiled the rug. "I've been less than impressed with your competence, Mr. Tanner. As a matter of fact, that woman in cowboy boots looks more in charge of things than *you* are."

I decided not to tell her that Ruthie was working for me. "Lighten up, Ms. Wells. If someone takes a shot at you, it isn't going to happen in front of two hundred hysterical women."

"Three hundred at least. And not all of them are hysterical."

"They would be if someone pulled a gun."

Her scowl loomed large. "That's quite sexist of you, Mr. Tanner. I'm not sure I want someone with those attitudes on my payroll."

"Actually, it was more nasty than sexist. I tend to get that way when someone implies I'm not doing my job."

She lifted a blackened brow. "Well? Are you?"

"You're still breathing," I said, just to prove I was still nasty. Then I stood up. "Let me know if you're taking me off the clock. In the meantime, I'll be on the job." I started to walk away.

"Wait," she said at my back, in a voice I hadn't heard before, one that was scared and needy and even a little chagrined. "I'm sorry. I just ... those notes have gotten to me, I guess. I feel very vulnerable all of a sudden. Of course I want you to stay on the job. Definitely. Till we find out exactly what's going on."

"Up to you," I said nonchalantly, determined to be the only person in her life who didn't need the work. "How did you get here to Jimbo's?" I asked.

"My car. Driven by my driver."

"Where is he now?"

"With the car. Parked somewhere nearby. Why?"

"If someone's serious about taking you on, it's a lot more likely to happen en route than in some public place like this."

"As I mentioned last evening, my driver's highly trained."

"By the FBI."

She nodded. "He was a field agent here in the city. A friend in the U.S. attorney's office recommended him."

"What's his name?"

"Filson. Jed Filson."

"How long has he been with you?"

"Two years."

I looked back to where the woman had gone down. Thanks to Ruthie's ministrations, she was back on her feet and being comforted by her peers. "I'm going outside for a minute. Why don't you give that woman a free book?"

Once again, she bristled. "I don't need you to tell me how to do my job, Mr. Tanner."

"Ditto, Ms. Wells."

She started to say something that would remind me of my place, but I went looking for the driver before she had the chance.

I found him parked in a red zone a block away, wearing a gray fedora and sitting behind the wheel of a classic black Lincoln Continental of early-eighties vintage, looking less a federal agent than chauffeur to a minor mafioso. A uniformed cop was leaning on the window, talking to him. They both laughed, then they shook hands, then the cop strolled away down Columbus.

Filson was rolling up the window when I tapped on the glass. With a moan and a hum, the window reversed directions as Filson slid his right hand onto his belt holster.

"Sorry, Mac; I'm not for rent. This is a private car."

"I'm not in the market for transportation," I said.

"Then what can I do for you?" he asked, his eyes no doubt active behind his coal black shades.

"I'm Tanner. The inside man." I showed him my ticket.

He processed the information, then stuck his hand through the window. "Jed Filson. Heard you were on the job. Not that it amounts to much."

We shook. "Just wanted to introduce myself."

"Appreciate it."

"Cop giving you a bad time?"

"Not after he knew the situation."

"Good. See anything odd on the way over?"

"Only the usual. Which in this town is plenty."

"Any idea who might be behind the notes?"

"Nope."

"Take it seriously or is it just another nut?"

He shrugged. "Between you and me, I'm not losing sleep." His grin slid toward the salacious. "Not for this gig, anyway."

I nodded in deference to his estimate if not his ethic. "You packing anything but the side piece?"

He gestured toward a shotgun strapped to the opposite door. "There's some semiautomatic shit in the trunk. I got more firepower than the Third Marines."

"Good."

"Anything going down inside?"

"Only adulation."

He shrugged. "Typical Chandelier scene. Me, I don't get excited by anything but the ponies. Well, holler if you need me."

"Same here."

He smiled easily and professionally. "I imagine we'd both take a full-choke load of double aught before we'd ask the other for help."

I grinned to show he was right, then strolled back to the ballroom, wondering if Filson could be a plant in service to some thug. If so, it wouldn't be the first time a feeb had turned turncoat.

The crowd had thinned in my absence, and only a few people were still in line to buy books. Everyone else was eating and drinking, everyone except Ruthie Spring.

When she sidled my way, I spoke like a con, without moving my lips.

"Nice work with the swooner."

"Thanks."

"Just a case of the vapors?"

"Yep."

"See anything else of interest?"

"Nope. You?"

"Nope." I looked at my watch. "This is about over. You might as well take off."

"Fine."

"Buy a book?"

She patted her purse. "Damned right. It'll be on the expense account, too."

I walked Ruthie to the door and said good-bye. When I turned back toward the crowd, I noticed a small commotion around Chandelier's seat. As I hurried that way, Lark caught my eye and motioned me to join them.

"Look," Chandelier said tightly as I leaned over the table toward her. She shoved a copy of *Shalloon* toward me. "The title page."

I opened the book. Below the printed title and above Chandelier's printed name, in the space where she always autographed books, was a message, hand-printed in black ink: **SINCE YOU HAVE IGNORED OUR WARNING, YOU WILL DIE BEFORE SUNDAY. ENJOY YOUR WEEK—IT'LL BE YOUR LAST.**

chapter 9

A s silently as a contagion, the sneak attack on Chandelier Wells slowly infected the room. People milled around in worry and confusion, aware of the commotion and concern, wondering what could have happened, hoping Chandelier was all right and that she wasn't going to leave the premises before she signed their books. My guess was Chandelier was a trouper who would do her public proud, but given the extreme expressions that danced across her face, I wouldn't have bet the ranch on it.

After talking to everyone involved, which is to say to Chandelier's entourage and the people from Dunne and Son, I tentatively concluded that the message hadn't been written at Jimbo's, it had been written back at the bookstore. According to Meredith Dunne, the books had been in the store for five days. Most had remained in the boxes that had been shipped from the Madison House warehouse in New Jersey, but a few boxes had been opened so some copies could be displayed in various areas throughout the store, including a stack at the cash register. On the morning of the party, the display copies had been repacked and hauled to Jimbo's by the staff, then unpacked and stacked on the table, ready for purchase by Chandelier's fans. In the interim, there had been plenty of opportunity for someone to take a book off a stack at the store, scrawl the threat on the title page, put it back on the stack near the bottom, and be virtually certain that the next person to see it would be its author.

There was one flaw in that scenario. To maximize efficiency, Chandelier demanded that the jacket flap be placed in the book so that it would open to the title page, where she always signed her name. The woman who had that task was an employee of Dunne and

Son who was on duty at the event and who seemed as devastated as the rest of the retinue by what had occurred.

After I had traced the journey that *Shalloon* had taken, I pulled her aside. "I understand it was your job to go through every book before you sold it," I said.

She nodded.

"To fix the flap so it would open to the title page."

"Yes."

"Did you see any writing in any of the books?"

She shook her head vigorously. "Of course not. If I had, I would have said something. And I certainly wouldn't have sold the book." She rubbed her eyes then her nose, wetting her knuckles and smearing her eyeliner. "I've done the flap thing so many times I can do it blindfolded with one hand. If there was a tarantula in there, I wouldn't have noticed unless it bit me."

"Did you see anyone other than Chandelier writing in a book after you sold it?"

She shook her head.

"You're sure?"

"Yes, but I don't watch the customers, usually. I watch Chandelier or Meredith or . . . I mean, it never occurred to me that—"

"It didn't occur to me, either," I interrupted, and patted her on the shoulder. "It would help if you would ask the other employees if they saw anything odd around here this afternoon and let me know if they did."

"Sure."

"Or anyone fishy messing with the display books back in the store."

"Okay. Sure."

I held out a hand. "My name's Marsh Tanner."

We shook. "Andrea Lubitch."

I gave her a card. "If you learn anything, please give me a call. And thanks for your help."

"Okay," she said tentatively, not sure if it was okay at all. She glanced back at the book table as though she feared it would collapse under the weight of her distress. "Chandelier's so upset, I've probably already been fired."

I told her I was sure that wasn't the case, but both of us knew it was pablum.

The next person I talked to was the woman who had bought the book Chandelier had started to sign, only to be confronted by the addendum. The woman, Jessamyn Wallace, wore jeans and a sweatshirt with a picture of one of the Brontë sisters stenciled on the front. She was flushed and aflutter because she was, perhaps for the first time in her life, suspected of doing something wrong.

"But what did I *do*?" she kept saying. "Why is Chandelier so *upset* with me?"

I maneuvered her to where she couldn't see Chandelier. "Did you write anything in the book you bought?"

She blinked back a tear. "No. I . . . no. Nothing. I wanted *Chandelier* to write in it. I thought that's why we were here."

"Did you get the book off the stack yourself?"

"I think so. Yes."

"No one handed it to you?"

She replayed the purchase in her mind. "No. I picked it out myself. One of them had a torn cover so I passed it by for a better copy. Then I paid my money, got my change, and went to Chandelier to get her signature. It's for my niece. 'To Penny on her twenty-first birthday' is what I was hoping Chandelier would put in it. Even though it says she doesn't do personal messages, I hear sometimes she does." Jessamyn sniffed and trembled. "But now I guess I won't get anything."

"Stay here a minute, please."

I went over to Chandelier, waited till she had finished upbraiding her publicist for some shortcoming involving radio ads, then spoke softly in her ear. "I don't think this happened here. I think it happened while the books were on display in the store."

"Who's at fault, then?"

"No one, probably. Except the guy who wrote it." Then I grabbed a copy of *Shalloon* off the nearest stack. "In case I don't catch you before you leave, would you sign this for my niece? 'To Penny on her twenty-first birthday,' if you would."

She looked as if I'd asked her to lick me. "I don't usually do individual inscriptions."

"Just this once. Pretty please."

She started to take a stand on principle, but decided that whatever grace she granted me wouldn't set a precedent. "Very well."

She signed the book as requested and handed it back to me. When she was deep in conversation with Lark McLaren, I took the book to Jessamyn Wallace. "Here you go; signed as ordered. Chandelier's very sorry for the fuss. She hopes Penny enjoys the book."

"Thank you. And thank Chandelier especially. She's so wonderful."

"Yes, she is."

"If I did anything wrong, I apologize. Please tell her that, will you?"

"Of course."

As Ms. Wallace strolled off, I returned to the book table. Chandelier Wells was back on the throne, her minions duly chastised for events that were not of their making. My turn in the dock was next.

"Well?" she demanded as I approached. "What's your take on this, Mr. Security Expert?"

"My take is that no one could have prevented what happened unless they screened every book before you saw it. And that someone wants you to stop doing whatever you're doing."

"Signing books?"

"I doubt if it's that."

"Then what?"

"You'd know better than I would. How are you upsetting people these days?"

"I don't know."

"I think you do."

"I don't care what you think." She looked at me with cold composure. "Are you going to interrogate the people at the bookstore?"

"Not yet."

"Why not?"

"Because three of them are here and if they'd seen anything suspicious, they'd have said something already. I've asked one of them to nose around for me. If and when we get a suspect, I'll take a picture down and see if we get an ID."

"How do you suggest you find a suspect?"

"Step-by-step as always, Ms. Wells."

"I leave Friday on my tour. I'd like this to be solved by then."

"So would I."

She thought about issuing some orders, but decided I might not stick around till she finished. "So what's your next step?"

"I thought we were going to dinner with your people."

She shook her head. "I'm too upset to go out; I'm going home and have Ernie's send something to the house. Your presence will not be required the rest of the day. I'll see you tomorrow at noon at KXYZ. I have a TV appearance till one, then a reading at Steinway in Berkeley at two, then a drop-in at Baubles, Bangles & Books downtown at four. I'll want you at each event."

"All of these have been advertised?"

"Of course. There's no point in enduring this without publicity." She stood up and stretched, reminding me again how imposing she was. "Have you talked to Mickey?"

"Not yet."

"I assume you intend to."

"Of course."

"Quite soon."

"Yes."

"Very well. I'll see you at KXYZ tomorrow."

"Maybe you should consider staying somewhere other than home till this is straightened out."

"As I mentioned before, my house has the most elaborate security system money can buy. I choose to believe that *it* can perform as advertised."

I ignored the implicit insult but I was getting a little tired of her Evita routine. "Your choice," I groused.

"Oh, yes, Mr. Tanner. It's always my choice. Be early tomorrow, so you can have the studio secured before my arrival."

"Will do," I said, feeling the way I used to when my mother made me clean my room, which was that I wanted to make it messier.

Since I'd obviously been dismissed, I headed for the door. Before I could make my escape, Lark McLaren caught up to me. "I'm getting worried," she said.

"So am I," I admitted.

"There was something very real about that one."

"I agree."

"And very hateful."

"Yes."

"So what should we do?"

"Fly to Paris and wait it out in the bowels of the Ritz. But since that's not likely to happen, just try to be careful."

"I can only be as careful as Chandelier lets me. She's a brave woman, unfortunately. Foolhardy at times."

"One other thing."

"What?"

"This doesn't sound like a nutcase to me. It sounds like Ms. Wells is up to something the note writer wants her to stop. Get together with Chandelier and try to figure out what that is."

She nodded. "If she'll let me, we'll do it tonight. She has some telephone interviews, though, and a chat session on her Web site, then a photo shoot for a spread in *Bay Area Homestyles*. And Amber and Sally are coming to go over some last-minute changes in her tour. But I'll try to fit it in. Definitely."

I laughed at the evening's schedule Lark had described, which was more laden with effort and entanglements than my schedule for the rest of the month. "Just another evening at the Wells house?"

"Actually, this is a slow night. You can't imagine what it's like when she really gets rolling. When we're out on tour, I'm on the phone ten hours a day."

"When does she have any fun?"

"Never. She doesn't relax while she's touring, all she does on tour is hustle. She'll sign a book in the hotel john if they let her. I always have half a dozen copies in my backpack in case she meets a hot prospect en route to the loo."

"I'm beginning to sense why you don't want to be a writer anymore."

"I thought you might."

I waved good-bye and headed down the street toward the Lincoln. When he saw me coming, Jed Filson rolled down the window on the big car.

"One thing," I said.

"Shoot."

"If she goes anywhere but home tonight, or anywhere but to the TV studio in the morning, let me know as soon as possible."

"Right."

"She been hanging out in any strange places lately?"

Filson's stubble made room for a grin. "Hanging out in dives is her hobby. She prowls this city like a derelict, let me tell you. I been chasing bad guys around the bay for twenty years and she knows joints I never heard of, let alone been inside. Last week she spent a couple hours in some toilet out in the Potrero I wouldn't go in without a rifle platoon."

"You let her check out these places alone?"

"Only because she insists on it."

"What's she like when she comes out?"

"Like she's just had great sex." Filson shook his head. "The woman gets off on lowlife like I get off on the nags."

chapter *10*

I live in a four-unit apartment building on the south slope of Telegraph Hill. Broadway is below me to the south; North Beach below me to the west. It's my favorite part of the city and I've lived there almost twenty years, in apartment 3, top floor front; I've got a view and a parking place and I can walk home from the bar if I have to. During all that time, my neighbor down below has been a woman named Pearl Gibson. Pearl is eighty-four and she's a pistol.

Over the years I've learned a thing or two about Pearl even though we've never talked for more than five minutes at a stretch. She's been a widow since she was fifty. She had a son named Alvin, who died driving drunk up at Tahoe, and a daughter named Myra, who died in infancy from a viral infection that was never fully diagnosed. She doesn't seem to be wealthy but she has enough money to pay her rent and to order Chinese food delivered five nights a week from a joint on Grant Street that doesn't deliver to anyone else.

Pearl likes the Giants and 49ers, though not as much as she used to before everyone on the rosters was rich. She has a glass of wine at dinner, usually fumé blanc, and another an hour before bedtime, usually brandy—she thinks chardonnay is overrated, red wine keeps her awake, and hard liquor felled her father so she steers clear of spirits. She doesn't take a pill except aspirin for arthritis, feels physically fit as a fiddle, and hasn't seen a doctor since she broke her ankle eight years ago doing something she knew better than to be doing at her age, which was changing a lightbulb while standing on a rickety chair. She likes it when I bring her baked goods, especially cinnamon twists. I feel bad if I don't do it once a week.

And that's about it, the sum total of my knowledge of my neighbor Pearl Gibson, up to the point when I arrived home from Jimbo's at six-thirty that evening, still puzzling over the turn of events at the launch party. As I was climbing the stairway toward my place on the second floor, I heard a door grind open at my back.

"Mr. Tanner?"

I smiled before I turned around; talking with Pearl was always a trip. "Hi, Pearl. No pastry today, I'm afraid."

"That's all right. Suzie across the street brought me an angel food cake this morning. Old people like me are the only ones who still eat angel food cake, have you noticed that, Mr. Tanner? Why do you think that is?"

"Because angel food is too white and white isn't cool. And I really wish you'd call me Marsh."

"I've told you before—that would be forward of me and I wasn't brought up to be forward."

I grinned. "I've seen less forward women leaning against lampposts on Hayes Street. How are you feeling this evening?"

"I'm fine as always except for the arthritis. I trust you're the same?"

"I am, as a matter of fact."

Her look morphed into a combination of Joel Grey and Yoda. "Is that attractive young woman still coming to call on you of an evening?"

I blushed as if I'd been discovered in flagrante delicto. "Have you been spying on me, Pearl?"

She drew herself to full height, which was on the downside of sixty inches. "I most certainly have not. But there are certain sounds whose origins are unmistakable even to one of my age and impaired recollection. If you get my drift, Mr. Tanner."

Her drift was more like a tsunami. In the twinkle of her devilish eyes, my blush became a range fire. "I'm sorry we bothered you. I'll try to hold it down next time."

"Who said I was bothered? Quite the contrary, I assure you. I used to get rather noisy myself in the old days, or so I've been told.

Oh, my. Now you're discombobulated just when I need to ask you a favor."

I pretended I didn't resemble a walking tomato. Pearl always got me talking about things you shouldn't talk about with women her age. Which is probably why I liked her. "How can I help you, Pearl?"

She pointed back toward the front door. "The mailman left a bundle down by my box and it's far too heavy for me to lift. I wonder if you'd be kind enough to bring it up to me."

"Glad to be of service."

I trotted back down the stairs and looked toward the row of mailboxes that was set into the east wall. Below the four rectangular brass doors was indeed a hefty bundle, double-wrapped in twine. It looked to be mostly magazines, a dozen of them or more, along with some junk mail and catalogs and flyers and the like.

I grabbed the bundle at the knot and toted it down the hall. "Where do you want it?" I asked when I got to Pearl's door.

She backed into her apartment and pointed. When I looked to see where she wanted me to put it, I had to work to keep my mouth shut.

What I saw was the sort of fortress a child would build, a wall three feet high and even higher in spots, entirely surrounding her couch and occasional table but for a narrow opening that served as an entrance to the embattled sitting area. I thought of *WKRP in Cincinnati* and the invisible walls one of the characters had insisted were defining his office, but this wall wasn't invisible, it was just unusual, mostly because of its raw materials. Pearl's wall wasn't built of board or brick or Sheetrock, Pearl's wall was built of magazines.

Hundreds of them, glossy and thick and sturdy, piled neatly so the stacks wouldn't topple, a laminated fortification that hadn't been in evidence the last time I'd been in Pearl's place, which had been more than a year ago when I was recovering from a gunshot wound and Pearl had invited me down to give her the gory details while she made me some split pea soup.

After I placed the fresh bundle at the base of the wall, I wanted to say something pertinent but couldn't think what that would be. "That's a lot of reading material," I mumbled finally.

"Oh, I don't *read* them," Pearl scoffed as if I'd accused her of using them for napkins. She picked up a couple of copies off the nearest pile. "What would I want with *Road & Track*, for heaven's sake? Or *PC World*, whatever *that* is?"

"Computers."

"There. You see? I don't know anything about computers and I don't *want* to know anything about them. As far as I can tell, they make quality obsolete and quantity the measure of everything. If that's not enough, it takes longer in line at the supermarket than it ever did with cash registers."

Usually, a diatribe like that would have gotten me intellectually involved, in this instance by seconding Pearl's notion about the seditious onset of technology, but I was still staring at the wall of magazines the way I stare at the apes in the zoo, as if they have something to teach me. "If you don't read them, why do you have them?" I asked out of actual ignorance. "The subscriptions must have cost a fortune."

Pearl waved a hand with unconcern. "It's not that expensive, really, in light of the bigger picture. And besides, I don't have any choice."

"Why not?"

She squinted at me with sudden suspicion, as though I'd asked her age or her PIN. "All in due time, Mr. Tanner. All in due time. As soon as I'm back from Vancouver, I'll have news that will satisfy both you *and* Mr. Larson, that Nosy Parker."

"Who's Mr. Larson?"

"The *mailman*, silly. Surely you know Mr. Larson."

"We've met," I said, though I wasn't sure if we had or not.

Pearl looked at the clock that was ticking away at the far wall and threatening to disgorge a cuckoo. "I'm afraid I must ask you to take your leave, Mr. Tanner. I have to start packing. The plane leaves quite early in the morning, and the little blue bus will be here even earlier."

"What's in Vancouver?" I asked absently, still wondering about the periodicals.

"In due time, Mr. Tanner," Pearl repeated mysteriously. "In due time."

I shrugged and started backing toward the door. "Have a nice trip."

"Oh, I shall. It's cut-and-dried this time. Last time they tricked me, but this time I read the rules six times. Now if you'll excuse me, we'll have a nice chat when I get back. If you see Suzie, tell her the angel food was scrumptious."

As far as I knew, I had never seen Suzie in my life.

I bid Pearl a quick good-bye and lumbered up to my apartment, which was sufficiently drab to make me consider a change of decor every time I came home, especially in light of the inevitable comparisons between Jill Coppelia's place and mine. Mine always came in a poor second even when I was doing the measuring.

I fixed myself a drink, glanced through *Newsweek* and *Harper's*, and speculated idly if I had enough unread magazines around to build a fort myself. Then I heated a can of Healthy Choice soup after adding salt and Parmesan to make it a little less healthy, ate a banana while I waited for the soup to cool, and finished off my dinner with five or six Oreos. Or maybe nine or ten. By the time I'd finished my second drink I was ready to make the call.

The phone rang a long time, which was a hint I should have taken, especially when the answering machine didn't click on. Which most likely meant Jill was working and I shouldn't have been trying to horn in.

I had decided to hang up when she answered with a bleat of irritation, "Coppelia."

"You're home now, counselor. It's allowable to be polite."

"I don't feel polite."

"Don't sound it, either."

"How'd it go with your celebrity?"

"Great. I'm really good at this bodyguard business."

"That sounds sarcastic."

"She got a death threat while I was standing ten feet away."

"No."

"Yes."

"How could that happen?"

"I'll let you know when I find out."

The evasion stoked her anger. "Fine. Great. So what do you want with me?"

"That's a bit gruff, isn't it?"

"I *feel* gruff, I told you. Gruff, gruff."

"Well, Fido, the reason I'm calling is to get your comment on the story in the *Examiner* this evening that says the local grand jury's look into cop corruption is foundering badly. Or maybe that's *floundering*, I'm never sure there's a difference."

"My comment is, a flounder's a fish and a founder isn't."

"Then what's a founder?"

"Like Leland Stanford. He founded Stanford University. Or Steve Jobs. He founded Apple."

"Or Bill Clinton."

"What did he founder?"

"He found her in the Oval Office."

"A punster. God spare us."

"I apologize."

"Some things are unforgivable," she said, not entirely in jest.

"The conversation seems to have taken a wrong turn," I said when I couldn't think of anything else to say.

Jill sighed like wind through the willows. "So has my life. Professionally, at least."

Her despair swept through the line and made me shiver. "That bad?"

"At least."

"So I guess it's not a good time to ask how you enjoyed the after-hours activity last night."

She giggled and diluted her mood. "Very much. Except it didn't last long enough."

I reddened for the second time in an hour. "I could try Viagra, I guess, but I didn't think it was so bad. I also think when we get more accustomed to each other's—"

"I didn't mean *that* way, stupid. I meant the good feeling ended by the time I got to the office this morning."

"Oh."

She laughed. "Premature ejaculation is the least of my problems, believe me."

"Do you think that's an issue, honestly, because—?"

"Relax, Marsh. I'm joking."

I chose to believe her so I could choose to drop the subject. "The grand jury's not going well? Seriously?"

"Grand jury proceedings are secret."

"I know."

"If I divulged them, I could be prosecuted."

"I know."

"So, seriously? I'm toast."

"Why?"

"At this point there's no proof of anything more notorious than minor bribes and low-weight drug deals. If I don't have more by the end of next week, I'll have to wrap it up without seeking a true bill." She paused to ask a question that didn't need voicing.

"I told you before you got started that this was your baby and I wouldn't get involved with it," I said.

"I know what you told me, Marsh."

"I don't even know if I've got anything for you. Now that Charley's dead, my sources in the department are few and far between."

She fired for effect. "I think Charley told you lots more about the Triad than you've told me."

"He didn't. Not really. Though I guess it depends on what you mean by 'told.'"

"Jesus. You *are* like Clinton."

"He's a premature ejaculator?"

"You know what I mean."

I paused to let her cool down. "Maybe I should come over."

"Sorry, but I have two witness examinations to prepare tonight."

"I could bring a treat. Ice cream. Those brownies you like. We could take a little break."

"You know what happens when we take a break."

"Not always, it doesn't."

"Always."

"Really?"

"Yes, really."

"Good for me."

Her voice dropped to a level of despondency that was unique in our relationship. "I'm in big trouble on this, Marsh. I'm going to end up looking like an ambitious idiot who couldn't deliver the goods. I'm probably going to lose my job because of it."

I sighed. "Maybe I can help."

"How?"

"Give you a name."

"What name?"

"Not yet. I have to think about it first."

"Well, think fast, goddammit. If you have anything, I need it tomorrow night."

chapter 11

C handelier's ex-husband lived in surprisingly tasteful decorum on the western edge of the city in a mock-Tudor house with a nice view of the Pacific as it assaulted Ocean Beach with a succession of blunt instruments in the form of twelve-foot breakers. The house was new and incongruous in an area of more eclectic homes that had been warped by the rain, bleached by the sun, and rusted by the salt in the breeze off the sea. Many of them looked more like barnacles than dwelling places, but not the one I was visiting. How Mickey Strunt came to possess such handsome digs remained to be seen.

I knocked on his door at precisely ten o'clock. From the time it took him to answer, I guessed that in Mickey Strunt's world it was still the middle of the night.

After unlatching at least three locks, Mickey stood in the doorway like a toad just jolted out of hibernation. He was short and overweight, with vast patches of body hair on his chest and back and a bulge in his belly that looked like a Christmas prosthesis. As he stood scratching his balls and squinting his eyes, he looked as confused and vulnerable as a toddler. An instant later he retrieved his chosen persona and became as bellicose and belligerent as an adult.

"What the hell do you want?" he demanded with ersatz anger, his rotund arms crossed over a tank top that was numbered 23, his stubby legs sticking out of baggy red satin shorts that were also of the House of Jordan. The sleepwear was fitting, I decided—the only way Mickey Strunt would get to the NBA was in his dreams.

"Are you Mr. Strunt?" I asked unnecessarily.

He drummed his fingers impatiently, as though he were so busy the slightest interruption might delay his discovery of the origins of dark matter. "That depends. You a cop?"

"Not at all."

"Collection agent?"

I shook my head and stuck out my hand. "My name's Tanner, Mr. Strunt. I'm vice president for product development and concept content for one of this country's leading media corporations," I burlesqued heartily, playing the role I'd concocted on the way over, one that was calculated to find out if Mickey was threatening his ex-wife and, more important, to get him to stop if he was.

"Yeah?" Mickey shook my hand reluctantly, with all the spunk of a punk. "What's that have to do with me?"

"Simply this. My employer is considering a major commercial involvement with your ex-wife, and believe me, the operative word is *major.*"

Instantly roused by the scent of money, he struggled to remain impassive. "So?"

"Before we finalize any agreement, we need to know what kind of person she is. And what kind of relationships she maintains."

"Why?"

"We need to know whether she's worthy of a sizable investment, quite frankly."

Mickey shook his head in reluctant admiration. "Damn. The bitch made it to the movies without me." A moment later he drew in his wonder and redonned his mask. "Am I right or not?"

"I'm afraid I'm not in a position to comment on the specifics of our proposal at this time. It's a cutthroat world out there, as I'm sure you know, especially in the entertainment industry. We've found from experience that absolute secrecy in these matters is the only way to maintain a competitive edge."

His brain awash in fantasy, he didn't hear a word I said. "What's the deal? Miniseries? Feature film? Biopic? Multimedia release?"

I kept my nonexistent cards close to my nonexistent vest. "Let's just say everything and anything is on the table."

He literally began to drool. "She getting a producer credit?"

I shrugged casually, to suggest I answered such questions daily. "That's not my decision, but I wouldn't be surprised."

"How much are we talking? On the front end, I mean?"

I stayed silent and shook my head.

As if he'd mainlined a steroid, Mickey swelled toward the size of the Cliff House. "I'm gonna tell you what, Mr. Vice President of whatever, you *best* get it through your *head* that you're not going to *screw* her. Not if I have anything to say about it, and you better believe I *will.*"

I frowned in all innocence. "I'm sure I don't know what you mean, Mr. Strunt."

He sneered at my naïveté. "Here's the way it goes down or Chandelier doesn't play ball. First, gross profit participation is a must, plus a percentage of syndication rights and creator billing in any series spin-off. Second, sequel and prequel rights will double the pickup price. Third, dramatic rights to the main character are not exclusive. Fourth, electronic rights remain in reserve, with terms to be—"

The Hollywood jargon sounded as alien in his mouth as the particulars of particle physics. "You seem to know a lot about the entertainment business, Mr. Strunt," I interrupted.

"Ought to. I been in it for almost twenty years."

"Really? In what capacity?"

He started to answer, then slapped himself on the forehead in unconscious tribute to the Three Stooges. The blow seemed to dislodge his ingrown personality and replace it with a more civilized version. "I got the manners of a mule. Come inside, Mr. Tanner. Let me get you a drink or something. How about a beer?"

"Coffee would be nice."

"Instant okay?"

"Actually, I—"

"Got steaming-hot water right out of the tap. I can have a cup of Folgers in front of you in twenty seconds."

Mickey Strunt backed inside his house and made sure I followed him as he penetrated its core. I'd dangled the biggest bait you can use on a homo sapien in the nineties—participation in a movie scheme of any size, shape, or sleaze—and Mickey Strunt had bitten. I was getting to be such a good actor, I should have been making movies myself.

Predictably, the refinement of the structure was confined to the exterior—the living room was an idiot's idea of chic. The art had been bought in a mall, the furniture came out of IKEA, the wallpaper was whorehouse red flecked with metallic accents in the shape of potato chips, and the carpet pretended to be Spanish tile. There were empty beer bottles everywhere, a half-eaten pizza still in the box, and enough crumpled bags of Frito Lay and Kettle chips to gorge a Dumpster. But the junk-food wrappers were only accessories to the predominant paper product, which was skin magazines. A dozen or more littered the living room, hard-core editions known only to the cognoscenti and featuring behaviors and bodies that were decidedly abnormal if not anatomically impossible. The only point in Mickey's favor was that none of them featured kids.

Mickey scraped his idea of fine art off the gold velvet couch and motioned for me to sit down. "So you need some backstory from me, is that it? To put Chandelier in a context?"

"That's it exactly, Mr. Strunt."

"Call me Mickey. So I guess the rumors finally got down to L.A."

"What rumors are those?"

He puffed like pudding. "That I made Chandelier what she is today."

"Really."

"Hell, I don't like to brag, but I wrote her first three books myself."

"Really."

"Damned straight. Well, maybe not word for word exactly, but I told her what to put down. Hell, the main character's modeled after me."

I looked as puzzled as I felt. "The main character's a woman."

"Yeah, well, you know what I mean. The macho stuff—gunplay and martial arts and that shit—it all come from me. Hell, Chandelier didn't know a cap pistol from an assault weapon before I come along."

"When *did* you come along, Mr. Strunt?"

"Mickey. Back in '83."

"How did you and Ms. Wells meet?"

"I laid her carpet."

"You what?"

"Laid her carpet," he repeated proudly. "I laid rug in the east bay for eight years. Kramer Koverings, you probably seen the ads—guy laying green shag over a golf green at Tilden Park, that was me. I still get residuals."

"Really."

Mickey paused for breath. Something about the look on my face made him want to define the relationship with his ex-wife more precisely. "Yeah, yeah, I know what you think. You can't figure what a woman like Chandelier seen in a guy like me, but listen up. She wasn't who she turned out to be back then. Not by a long shot."

"How so?"

"She was fat, for one thing. Two-forty easy. And working for pennies at Kmart. On her feet all day stuffing size-twelve women into size-eight dresses. Compared to the duds she saw around there, I came on like the fucking king of fucking Egypt."

"She's undergone quite a change, then."

"Damn right she has, and I'm the one who got her going. When she got that first piddly-assed contract, I said, 'Babe'—that's what I always call her, Babe—I said, 'Babe, there's a pot full of money out there just waiting for someone to grab it, and that someone might as well be you.' Then I told her how to go about it."

"How was that?"

As lively as an inspirational orator, Mickey held up his fingers in turn. "She had to be glamorous but not ritzy; smart but not intellectual; funny but not silly; feminist but not butch; and hip but not political."

"Sounds like sage advice."

"Damned straight it was. So she goes to a fat farm and drops fifty pounds. And to a surgeon who cuts back her boobs, which I wasn't entirely in favor of, by the way. And to one fag to learn how to fix up her house and another to learn how to wear clothes. Two years and six books later, she gets a half-million advance from Madison House and ain't looked back since. And that's pennies to what she gets now."

"So you made her a star. Sort of like Pygmalion."

"More like Sonny Bono if you ask me—Pig whoever didn't have nothing to do with it. Without me, Chandelier Wells is still Betty Moulton under the flashing blue light. Yeah. That's right. I come up with the name, too."

"Seems to me you don't get nearly enough credit, Mr. Strunt."

"Mickey. Yeah, well, I can't eat credit, know what I'm saying?"

I nodded as he rubbed his fingers together in the universal tic of the hustler. "Which brings me to one of the reasons I'm here," I said.

I had his full attention. "Yeah? What's that?"

"We were wondering what kind of financial arrangement you have with Ms. Wells. Is it a formal one? Reduced to a writing of some kind?"

He shook his head. "Handshake deal, is all."

"Is your stipend regularized?"

"Say what?"

"Do you get a fixed amount of money from her per month?"

His look grew wary and defensive. "Fixed? No. I wouldn't say it's fixed."

"Then how is your compensation calculated, if I may ask?"

He had finally found something he needed to keep secret. "What the fuck business is it of yours, anyway?"

I got as prissy as I get. "I don't mean to pry, of course, but if we're to go forward with Ms. Wells in a major way, I need to know what kind of financial obligations she has already undertaken. Arrangements that might adversely impact any effort she would be able to make in our behalf."

My persistence made him angry. "Shit. I ask her for money and she gives it to me. When she feels like it. If I beg her hard enough. Is that what you want? Shit. I need a drink."

Mickey lumbered out to the kitchen and returned a moment later with a can of Colt 45. He held it up. "Got another if you want."

"No, thanks." Mickey plopped down on the couch with the grace of a cannonball. "I was wondering what's the most money Chandelier has ever given you at one time, Mr. Strunt."

He started to resist, then relented in service to the greater good, which was his future solvency. "What the hell. She gave me twenty grand once. To help me buy this place. Last month she gave me fifty."

"Thousand?"

"Singles. Fifty lousy bucks. She earns that in a minute. I should sue the bitch is what I should do. Got plenty of lawyers ready to take it on, too."

"How long have you and Chandelier been divorced, Mr. Strunt?"

"Mickey. We split twelve years ago June first."

"Did you get a substantial property settlement?"

His blush told me I'd touched a sore point. "I got zip, practically. She claimed she didn't have nothing, but she and her dyke lawyer hid most of her money offshore, I know that for an actual fact. But the idiot working for me couldn't prove it."

"Do you get alimony?"

"Alimony? Shit. *Guys* don't get alimony, you schmuck. Sorry," he added when he realized he'd insulted me. "The divorce thing still gets me hot."

I waved the apology away. "Understandable. One final point. If Ms. Wells signs with us, would you expect a participation of some kind, Mr. Strunt?"

"Mickey. Damn right I would." He drained his beer while he thought it over. "You can do that?"

"We could arrange some sort of consulting contract, I imagine."

Suddenly listless, Mickey lifted the can in a mock salute, unable to make himself believe he would ever be on easy street. "Well, here's to you, Mr. Vice President of whatever. Go to it, pal. Get me what I deserve."

I stood up. "I'll do my best," I said in all sincerity, and we shook hands once again. "By the way, when's the last time you saw your ex-wife?"

"Last month, like I told you."

"Is that your only contact? When you approach her for money?"

"Yeah," he grumbled. "Why else?"

"What about the child? Aren't you Violet's father?"

"Hell, no."

"Then who is?"

"Beats me, mister. And you know what? Chandelier don't know who he is, either."

---

chapter *12*

The television studio occupied the entirety of a nondescript stucco building five blocks south of Market and two blocks west of the Hall of Justice, beneath a web of freeway underpinnings that looked like an outtake from *Blade Runner*. Given the aggressive insularity of show business, I anticipated a lot of trouble getting to where I needed to get, but someone, probably Lark McLaren, had paved the way for me.

A cheery receptionist handed me off to a perky girl guide who took me through a labyrinth of offices to the door to Studio B. After making sure the red light was safely off, she ushered me inside and introduced me to a producer named Carmen, a hyperactive bundle of nervous anxiety clutching a clipboard to her chest and a pen in her teeth and who clearly saw me as another in a long line of potential glitches that could ruin her day.

The event Carmen was producing was called *Magda Makes Sense*, a noon-hour talk-show broadcast over the largest independent TV station in the Bay Area, featuring an Oprah wanna-be named Magda Danielson. Magda was a former Raiders cheerleader and current society grande dame who was married to an investment banker who had gotten rich giving seed money to Sun and Cisco in exchange for a portfolio full of common stock. Magda was smart and uninhibited and the show was popular and at times controversial, although I had to admit that my supporting evidence was only hearsay—I'd never seen Magda or her show before and neither had anyone I knew. It's amazing how much trivia you accumulate just by being alive.

"They told me you were coming but they didn't tell me why," Carmen was saying around the pen, manically and uneasily, her eyes flitting about the studio to be sure no catastrophe was in the offing so close to airtime.

"I just need to take a look around," I said as I took a look around.

"For what?"

I returned my gaze to Carmen. "Ms. Wells is a bestselling author."

She stuck her pen behind her ear and chewed her gum three times. "That's why she's here, isn't it?"

I nodded. "Bestselling authors have fans."

"Duh?"

"Most of Chandelier's fans are sweet and kind and generous."

"Goody for them. But what does that have to do with Magda?"

I spelled it out. "But some of them *aren't* sweet and kind, some of them like to make pests of themselves. And those are the ones I'm looking for."

Carmen frowned. "You mean stalkers and such?"

"Something like that."

She ran some scenarios through her mind. "That shouldn't be a problem, I guess. As long as you're not stumbling around the studio when we're live."

"You haven't seen any pests yourself this morning by any chance?" I asked as Carmen started to turn away.

Her lip wrinkled. "Only the ones who work here."

"No one out of place? Work being done that wasn't ordered? Phones being repaired that no one knew were broken?"

She shook her head. "Nothing like that is going on. I'd know if there was."

"Then I'll just poke around for a while."

A thought made her brow furrow with suspicion. "You won't be needing to talk to Magda, will you? She doesn't like it when her prep period is interrupted."

"Does Magda carry a weapon?"

"No. Of course not. Why?"

"Then I don't see why I would need to see her."

She started to go into it, then passed. "Good. Great. Fantastic. Well."

She started to walk away but I put out a hand to stop her. "It might help if I knew the schedule you'll be following."

Carmen looked at her watch, which was her only adornment. "Ms. Wells is due in ten and she's always prompt. She'll go straight to makeup, then Magda will speak with her in the greenroom at five till the hour. Airtime is noon sharp. Chandelier will come on at six after and stay till we wrap at twelve-thirty."

"Where's makeup and the greenroom?"

She pointed toward a blue door. "Through that, then look for the signs."

"Thanks. I'll let you get back to work."

Carmen dashed off to forestall some calamity that was visible only to her, and I began to tour the studio.

It was a hive of electronics, of course, a forest of cameras, lights, TV monitors, and computer screens that were linked by a tangle of cords and cables that made me envision vipers. The set itself was à la Oprah as well, with a couch and an easy chair separated by a coffee table with fresh-cut flowers spilling out of a blue ceramic vase. The backdrop was a phony window draped with a phony curtain that masked a phony view onto a real blowup of the Golden Gate Bridge as seen from the yacht club. The mundane decor in the middle of the high-tech accoutrements gave the enterprise a schizophrenic aspect, which maybe explains why TV does such bad things to our brains.

Studio B itself was essentially an open bay filled with communications gear, so it took no time at all to confirm that the only people in sight seemed essential to the production. I got fishy looks from time to time, as though I was suspected of being a mole in hire to union or to management, but otherwise they paid me no mind. Five minutes later, my only conclusion was that if I ever worked in TV, I'd want to be the lighting guy.

The studio was one thing but the rest of the building was another.

Half a dozen doors opened off the studio, and they led to a warren of rooms that served for everything from equipment storage to the dressing room for the star of the show. I opened all the doors that were unlocked, which numbered maybe a dozen. Most opened on to slipshod offices, desks topped with phones and laptop computers and walls hung with TV monitors and marking boards—producer-pods, I supposed, the offices of all those people listed in the closing credits. One large room held two entire sets—one for the newscast and another for a cooking show, mini-rooms on wheels that went to and fro to conform to the mandates of *TV Guide.*

Whenever I ran into anyone who asked if they could help me, I told them I was looking for a strange-looking guy from advertising. The theory was that my lie would elicit a response if anyone even marginally lethal had been seen in the vicinity. Of course that assumed Chandelier's nemesis would fit the description of odd in some sense of the term, which may have been a stretch given the variety of people who apparently had reason to do her harm. When I had no luck with sightings of strange men, I switched genders, but no one had seen the spacey woman from wardrobe, either.

The next door I knocked on had a sign that read MAGDA taped to it at a slightly crooked angle. Below that was a sign that said PRIVATE, with a handwritten notation that read "Magda Means *You*, Stupid." Stupid knocked anyway, and a muffled voice immediately cursed me. Since show business wasn't my life, I opened the door nonetheless.

Two women were in the room, which was mostly full of racks of clothes and piles of makeup receptacles. A young black woman wielding a powder puff the size of a muskmelon was dabbing it on various promontories on the other woman's physiognomy. The other woman had a black net over her black hair and a white towel draped over her shoulders. The only other garment I could see above the part of her that was hidden by the dressing table was a filmy black brassiere that seemed inadequate to its purposes, which was probably by design.

The woman in the bra looked up, but the other woman kept dabbing industriously, as though she were putting out a fire. "Who the hell are you?" the woman in the towel and bra demanded, in a pre-emptive tone that identified her as the Magda Danielson who made sense.

"Maintenance," I said.

"No one called for any maintenance. Can't you read? Get the hell out."

I shrugged. "Someone said a fuse went out and something smelled like burning rubber. But if you got no problem, I got no problem."

"Fine."

I looked back toward the corridor. "Seen my assistant around?"

"No," the woman who had to be Magda spat. "I have a show going on in ten minutes and guess what?"

"What?"

"It's not about you and it's not about fuses. So why don't you disappear."

I blew her a kiss and disappeared.

The next room I entered was painted green from floor to ceiling and carpeted in the same shade, one that suggested money. Sitting on matching green chairs and a green tweed couch were Chandelier and her tenders—Lark, Sally, Amber, and two other women I didn't recognize who apparently were there to fetch and carry. Chandelier's face was eerie with makeup—overly orange, overly smooth, and overly rigid, like waxed fruit. The rest of the women sat like pointers with a whiff of wild bird, which is to say they were alert to Chandelier's slightest whim.

When she heard the door open, Chandelier turned my way. "Well?"

"No problems as far as I can tell."

"You're sure?"

"I don't have a bomb-sniffing dog, but I'm as sure as a mere mortal can be."

"I guess that will have to do."

"Do you want me to stay for the show?"

"Of course."

"And afterward we're still at Steinway Books?"

She nodded. "I'll have Jed stop for a latte on the way over, so that will give you time to check it out before we arrive."

"Fine."

She turned toward Lark McLaren. "You're sure Magda has the questions I want her to ask?"

"I gave them to the producer ten minutes ago."

"And you got the pages faxed to the book clubs this morning?"

"On schedule, Ms. Wells."

Chandelier nodded absently, as if she didn't really care about the nuts and bolts of the business but couldn't keep from obsessing on them because she'd been doing it for years. "How about placement?" she went on. "Are our people out making sure the chains gave us the windows and end caps Madison House paid for?"

"They're checking even as we speak."

"Amazon, too?"

"Right."

"I damned well better be front and center in 'What We're Reading' this time around."

"You will be."

Without thinking, Chandelier shoved her fingers through her hair, got them covered with hair spray, and scowled. "Get Dianne back in here. Christ, she put enough hold on here to frost a cake. And you'd better make sure Magda's going to play ball with the questions. She gets testy when she thinks I'm suggesting that she doesn't do her homework. But I don't want any improvising, especially not this morning. When she improvises, she gets bitchy."

"Fine."

Lark plucked her cell phone out of her purse, and the diversion gave me a chance to duck out. I returned to the studio and found a director's chair tucked behind a make-believe bookcase and sat down to enjoy the show.

A couple of minutes later Magda Danielson came on the set, followed by her ubiquitous makeup person. This time Magda was wearing a blouse, a plunging black number above a snug-fitting pair of silver slacks—apparently once a Raiderette, always a Raiderette. Carmen rushed to her side and did whatever producers do in tones that were low enough to be dubbed a whisper. A cue-card man took his place behind the middle camera, and the light man turned some dials on his board that caused the candlepower in the room to quadruple. A ponytailed young man wearing a headset and kneepads approached from behind the blue door, crouched beneath the middle camera, and began to count down from ten. For the first time I appreciated the significance of the show going out live. My pulse began to race even though I was just an unlooker.

Just like that, Magda was talking, thanking her viewers for joining her, teasing them with Chandelier's imminent arrival, and chatting of the events of the day, which included a joke about Al Gore and another about Mrs. Clinton. After she segued into a commercial, Chandelier joined her onstage.

The makeup and lighting people made minor adjustments, the soundman clipped a mike to Chandelier's collar, the countdown started again, and Magda was introducing Chandelier as the most important voice in women's fiction since Margaret Mitchell. Chandelier accepted the compliment as her due, then gave Magda a return tribute that encompassed both Oprah and Diane Sawyer. As the mutual admiration society moved into second gear, and Chandelier began describing the plot of *Shalloon*, my mind began to travel elsewhere.

When it came back, Magda was asking Chandelier to tell her viewers how she got her start as a writer. Chandelier had obviously answered the question a thousand times and was ready when she got her cue.

"I started writing because I married a bum," she announced bluntly.

Magda's smile turned delicious. "The infamous Mickey, is that right?"

"That's right, Magda."

"Tell us more."

Chandelier settled in for a cruise. "I was twenty-nine, living in Hayward, working a dead-end job, and living in a depressing apartment I couldn't afford with a roommate I couldn't abide. I was new in town and had no friends, and a date was just something that grew on a tree. Then this guy came along to put in new carpet. We had a few chats and he asked me out. And I said yes. And he said nice things about me. And showed up on Sunday with a pizza and a cowboy movie and cleaned my car and unclogged my sink, so I thought what the hell. Maybe he drinks a little too much and he's crude and insensitive sometimes, and a bit of a racist and not actually that smart. But I'm not lonely anymore, so I'll marry him the first time he asks, and there'll be plenty of time to shape him up later. Which taught me my biggest life lesson."

"Which was?"

"Men don't shape up."

Magda whooped and slapped her knee. "Tell it like it is, girlfriend."

Most of the staff milling around the studio were women, and most of them started clapping. I tried to blend with the bookcase.

Chandelier was just getting warmed up. "After we were married, of course he got worse. He quit his job and spent the day watching TV; he drank twice as much as before, only now it was Heineken, not Bud; he demanded to be waited on hand and foot; and he complained if dinner wasn't ready on time or the mashed potatoes had lumps. Meanwhile, I took a second job to make ends meet, and a writing course on weekends at the community college as a way to get out of the house. Then he began to fool around."

Magda shook her head in elaborate commiseration. "They all do it, don't they? It's never whether, it's only when."

"That's certainly true in my experience, Magda, and the other thing about it is, they don't seem to enjoy it until they *tell* you about it, am I right? Which Mickey would do in glorious Technicolor during fits of drunken apology, just before he went out and did it again."

"What did you do about it?"

"I took it for six years."

"And then?"

"I threw him out."

Cheers from the staff; claps from Magda.

"Tossed his stuff in the yard, changed the locks, had the sheriff put enough of a scare in him to convince Mickey I was serious, and bought a gun in case he didn't take no for an answer. And that solved problem one. But not the other problem, which was money."

"What did you do about that?"

"A few years before all this, I'd written a book. My first one—*Pendant*—it's in its twenty-third softcover printing, by the way. Anyway, in order to keep my mind off Mickey and his antics, I wrote this book. The women in my writing group loved it but the men thought it was fluff. So I did another draft, right?—deferring to men, not women, the way we were brought up to do. The women loved the new draft even more, but the men still thought it was bilge. But this time I wised up and went with the women. I went to a writers' convention up in Seattle and met an editor who promised to take a look at my book, so I mailed it to her the minute I got back home. Two months later I got a letter with a three-book contract enclosed. And I've been writing ever since. And once I hit big with my fifth book, I got rid of my biggest problem."

"And what happened to dear Mickey?"

Chandelier laughed. "He's still around, unfortunately. Like that yeast infection you never quite get rid of." Magda and the distaff crew convulsed on cue, then they went on to discuss Chandelier's upcoming tour.

Which left me with two versions of Chandelier's past, one from Mickey Strunt and one from the horse's mouth. I didn't completely credit either one, particularly, but clearly the money Chandelier had given Mickey over the years wasn't necessarily because of his contributions to her books, it could just as well have been to keep him from suing her for slander while he remained a staple of her act.

As the interview was winding down, Lark McLaren sidled over to me. "That's really what hooks them, you know," she whispered.

"Who?"

"The fans. It's not the books they love so much. It's the bio."

chapter *13*

After she and Magda had hugged and kissed and exchanged competitive compliments, Chandelier's magical mystery tour loaded into limos and moved on to Steinway Books in Berkeley.

The store was on the north side of the city, not far from Chez Panisse and the lesser lights of a neighborhood that had become known as the Gourmet Ghetto. As befitted its commercial peers, Steinway Books was a fairly high-toned place, catering to faculty and students at the university and to the yuppies who lived in Berkeley for the political ambience but made their money across the bay in ways violative of most of the mores of their hometown. On the surface it was surprising that Chandelier Wells would be featured in Steinway's reading series, which usually catered to *The New York Review of Books* set. On the other hand, the books intellectuals actually read are often quite different from the books they enthuse about in public.

I got there in plenty of time to check out the store for thugs and bombs. The front room featured the new books, in shelves along the walls and on tables in the center, meaning the sight lines were fairly clear and unobstructed. The back of the store housed used hardcovers and paperbacks in a crowded maze that made it an easier place to hide out. The front was crowded with browsers, but in the back there were only a few obsessive collectors seeking overlooked bargains and a couple of undergrads in search of a cheap read. I checked the back room out pretty thoroughly, including the stock room and rest rooms and broom closet, and found nothing untoward except for a transient using the rest room as a public bath. The smell alone was enough to convince me he was what he purported to be.

The front of the store was an easier task, and the result was the same—nothing suspicious, nothing extraordinary. While I worked, I noticed a copy of Chandelier's first book in a glass case along with several other first editions—the one next to hers was *Look Homeward, Angel.* I picked up *Pendant* and looked inside. The book was signed by Chandelier. The price, written lightly in pencil in the upper-right corner of the flyleaf, was $2,100. After blinking to be sure I'd read the number correctly, I put the book back in a hurry, before I did damage I couldn't pay for.

By the time Chandelier and her entourage swept into the store, I was talking to the assistant manager. Her name was Kelly and she was eager to the point of ecstasy at what was about to occur.

"Lots of people in the store read Chandelier," she said with a grin, "but I'm the only one who admits it." When I asked if the owner had any aesthetic objections to Chandelier's official appearance, Kelly told me that Chandelier made such a fuss if she wasn't included in the series it was easier all around just to book her as a sideshow. But if there was any certainty in life, it was that Kelly didn't use that term to Chandelier's face.

Kelly hurried over to make Chandelier welcome, and I joined the crowd of some forty people sitting shoulder to shoulder in matching folding chairs set out in ranks of eight before a podium complete with microphone and water glass, waiting for Chandelier to start speaking. My fellow aesthetes were mostly middle-aged, mostly female, and either eager for the opportunity or slightly embarrassed at being where they were. A few of the latter even bolted for the door after squirming uneasily for a few moments, for fear of being discovered where they couldn't pretend that their presence had everything to do with Toni Morrison and nothing to do with Chandelier Wells.

As Chandelier waited to be introduced, I caught her eye and nodded to indicate that everything seemed okay. She didn't look as though she believed me. I wasn't sure I believed it myself. Berkeley wasn't called Berserkeley for nothing.

Kelly was effusive in her praise and Chandelier seemed equally appreciative of the opportunity to appear in one of the finest independent bookstores in the country. After both parties were adequately stroked, Chandelier began to read from *Shalloon*, specifically a scene where the heroine, Maggie Katz, meets the CEO of the cosmetics company suspected of corporate wrongdoing and parries a pass he makes at her. The prose was florid, the conflicting emotions explicitly staked out, the heroine's reactions gutsy but gentle, and her degree of revulsion at the pass somewhat less than absolute. By the time Chandelier was on the fourth paragraph, I was thinking more about an assistant DA named Jill Coppelia than a news reporter named Maggie Katz.

What I was wondering was whether I should give Jill the name of someone who could tell her and her grand jury something about police corruption in the city, and particularly about the gang of dirty cops called the Triad. Wally Briscoe was the guy I was thinking of. He was a cop and had been a good friend of my friend Charley Sleet. Even when Charley decided to start taking down the Triad on his own, he hadn't homed in on Wally even though Wally had been active in the Triad himself for some years before drifting to the edges of the organization. Wally wasn't my friend, particularly, but his relationship with Charley, plus my general inclination to steer clear of cops and DAs at least during business hours, made me reluctant to roll over on him. On the other hand, the woman I loved needed help, which was a pretty strong shove in the other direction.

I hadn't come to any conclusion about Wally Briscoe when Chandelier stopped reading, bowed to the quick burst of applause, sipped from the glass of water, and said she'd be happy to answer questions. Hands shot in the air like bids for Kennedy memorabilia.

Most of the questions were pat and predictable, I suppose—where do you get your ideas, are your stories based on real life or do you make them up, do you use a computer, do you have an agent, does your editor change your work very much, have there been any movies made from your books, if a movie *was* made, who would you want to play Maggie? But a few of the questions caused Chandelier to squirm just a little and fumble for answers that, when they came, seemed more thoughtful than rote—do you consider your books to be literature or merely entertainment (the latter), what's the difference between the two (entertainment caters to an audience; literature is self-centered), how do you think your work benefits society if at all (that's not for me to say, although some people do seem to be comforted or encouraged by Maggie's pluck and persistence), do you try to send a message to your readers and if so, what is that message (basically, that life is difficult but salvageable), are you a feminist (of course), are you antimale (not at all), are you in a relationship right now (I keep those parts of my life private), did becoming a famous writer do what you thought it would do for you in terms of happiness (almost but not quite).

Chandelier tiptoed through the rhetorical minefield with surprising deftness, then a young woman sitting three seats down from me stood up. She wore the Berkeley winter uniform of Birkenstocks, wool socks, baggy corduroys, rag sweater, and a knit scarf long enough to rope a steer. "My name is Lucy Dunston Bardwell," she began gravely, in the manner of a patriotic oration.

"Hello, Lucy," Chandelier replied easily as she glanced at the clock on the back wall, obviously wondering how soon she could head back for the city.

"Do you remember me, Ms. Wells?"

Chandelier squinted for better focus. "No. I don't believe so. Should I?"

"Six years ago, I was a student in a writing course you were teaching in the extension program at San Francisco Bay University."

Chandelier smiled broadly. "I remember those days very well. I had some good writers in those classes. Including you, I'm sure."

"I was working very hard on a novel back then. It was called *Childish Ways.*"

Chandelier's smile seemed to solidify just a bit, in the way clay becomes ceramic. "I don't remember it; I'm sorry. I read a lot of student work in those days. They sort of blended into one big book, I'm afraid."

Lucy Bardwell's stentorian voice didn't soften or subside. *"Childish Ways* is about a woman who discovers that her child is being abused at the day care center she chose to place her in."

Chandelier fidgeted uneasily. "What is your question? If you've finished the book, I suggest you send it to one of the agents I've listed in my article in the October issue of *The Writer* magazine."

"Two years after I took your class," the woman persisted gravely, "you wrote a book called *Infamy of Infants.*"

Chandelier nodded as if pleased to be able to agree with the woman. "Yes. That's one of mine. It's on a similar subject, as a matter of fact. I hope it was helpful to you."

Lucy Bardwell thrust out her jaw and crossed her arms. "I think it's the other way around, Ms. Wells."

Chandelier smiled condescendingly. "I'm afraid I don't understand."

"Infamy of Infants was also about abuse in a day care center."

Chandelier turned the color of Hawaiian Punch. "What is your point, young lady? I hope you're not seriously suggesting that I stole your *idea*. Among other things, ideas are not copyrightable. Only the *expression* of an idea has copyright protection. So even if I *did* borrow your idea, which of course I did not, you don't own *that* subject or any *other* subject." Chandelier looked across the room as if for a friendly face. "Can we move on now, please?"

Lucy Bardwell stayed standing. "I'd like to read a paragraph from my book if I could."

Chandelier leaned across the podium. "This is *my* reading, if I'm not mistaken," she proclaimed with lethal sarcasm. "I believe *most* of these good people are here to see *me*."

"I'd like you to let me read, please," Lucy Bardwell persisted, her expression as fixed as a museum guard's. "It won't take long to make my point."

"Is this a *published* book by any chance, Ms. Bardwell?" Chandelier asked meanly.

"No. But I mailed a copy to myself after I finished it so I could prove from the postmark when it was written, in case anyone ever—"

"Mailing a copy to yourself proves nothing, as any reputable intellectual-property lawyer can tell you. So we don't know *where* this little paragraph came from, do we, audience?"

The audience was immobile.

"This paragraph is one of many that was contained in the portions of the manuscript of *Childish Ways* that I submitted to you in class," the young woman plunged on. "And this among many other paragraphs turned up in *Infamy of Infants* in almost the exact same words."

Chandelier's tone turned arch and dismissive. "Have you consulted an attorney about this, Ms. Bardwell?"

"Yes, I have."

"Since you haven't sued me, I assume he told you that you didn't have a case."

"Quite the contrary. He said I had a solid case for infringement, but he also said I didn't have enough of a damage claim to make suing you worthwhile. In other words, he said you definitely hurt me, Ms. Wells, but not *badly* enough." Lucy Bardwell offered a rueful smile to the room. "If that lawyer had ever tried to get a book published in this day and age, he'd have a better idea of how badly I've been hurt," she added almost as an afterthought, accompanied by a drip of tears.

Chandelier seemed to double in size and triple in density. "Let me tell you something, young lady. With every bestselling book, every hit movie, and every hit song that comes along, some vultures like you comes out of the woods and claims they had the idea first. They make a big stink and the media hop aboard and repeat the charge and the reputation of the writer gets tarnished indelibly. But you know what, Ms. Bardwell? The vultures always lose. Sure, they may gouge a nuisance settlement out of the artist once in a while, but if the case goes to trial, the vulture *always loses.* The problem is, the media never cover *that* part of the story, do they? They've moved on to some *other* spurious allegation in an effort to get more readers or higher ratings, leaving the artist whose reputation they've raped trying futilely to regain her good name."

Lucy Bardwell stood her ground. "I'm not asking for money, Ms. Wells."

"What *are* you asking for?"

"An apology. And some help."

"I have no reason to—"

"I'm not claiming you stole my idea, I'm claiming you stole my words. Since I can prove that's the case, I want to know what you're going to do to see that my work gets published just as yours has been. Especially since *you* obviously thought it was publishable."

Before Chandelier could answer the question, there was a commotion from the other side of the room. Lark McLaren and Amber Adams were standing on either side of a third woman, who was wearing a floor-length black coat and a black hat in the shape of a floppy beret looking like something out of a silent movie featuring Gloria Swanson. The woman was clearly attempting to join the fray, and Lark and Amber were clearly trying to restrain her.

I stood up and put my hand on my weapon and walked toward the trio of women. When I got there, I recognized the woman in the beret as Viveca Dane.

"She did the same thing to me!" Viveca called out suddenly, even as Lark and Amber clutched at her arms. "Chandelier stole my character, my plot, my milieu, and my persona. She took everything I had, even my readership. Thank you for speaking up, young lady. Because someone has to *stop* her."

I closed to where I could prevent Viveca from using any weapon more potent than vitriol. For her part, Chandelier was cursing under her breath and gathering her things, preparing to vacate the premises.

"But you haven't signed books," Kelly the assistant manager squealed as Chandelier threw on her cape and grabbed for her briefcase, then fumbled with something below the podium and emerged with a small cassette tape that she shoved in her purse.

"You should screen your audiences more carefully, my dear," Chandelier said snidely as she strode across the room. "I don't come to these things to be insulted." She shouldered her way toward the door, then turned back. "I should have known something like this would happen in this town. If any of you still want signed books, they'll be available at Baubles, Bangles & Books over in the city. Where most of the populace is still sane."

With that final promotional plug, Chandelier was out the door, leaving a maelstrom of disappointment in her wake. I went outside, watched her stride to her majestic Lincoln, waited for her to get inside, gave a wave to Jed Filson, then returned to the store.

Viveca Dane and Lucy Bardwell were huddling near the podium, no doubt comparing causes of action against Chandelier. Kelly the assistant manager was trying to mollify customers who had already bought books by offering them a coupon good for a signed Sue Grafton as soon as the books came in. Lark and Amber and Sally were displaying various degrees of consternation, no doubt wondering whether the contretemps about plagiarism would put a crimp in their principal's soaring career.

And then the bomb went off, blowing in the front windows and showering us all with flying glass.

chapter 14

Lark McLaren was the first person out the door, and it was her incessant screaming as much as the shards of glass or the reverberations of the explosion that made me dash out after her.

When I spotted her, what I saw was a woman twirling frantically to and fro, not sure what to do or how to do it, sobbing and pointing and searching desperately for assistance as her voice splashed the day with terror. Beyond her was a sheet of orange flame lapping hungrily at the sky from within a cloud of roiling smoke that rose from the middle of the street. At the base of the flames was a crumpled lump of steel and glass that behind the aftereffects of the blast had become almost unrecognizable as the handsome old Lincoln.

By the time I reached her, Lark was standing so close to the wreckage she had to shield her face with her forearm to ward off the heat from the blaze. I stepped between her and the conflagration and turned her gently toward the sidewalk. Tears streamed down her cheeks, streaking them with makeup, and in the spotty light of the flames her eyes seemed ablaze themselves, matching meteorites burning toward the center of her skull.

"Help her," she burbled between convulsive sobs. "You have to *help* her."

Overwhelmed by likelihoods, Lark had become insensate by the time Amber and Sally rushed forward to help pull her away from the danger. When the three of them were safely on the curb, I turned back toward the car. Shielding myself as ineffectively as Lark had done, I moved as close to the blaze as I could, until my skin began to prickle and my eyes began to sting and my clothing became an analgesic compress that brought forth sweat and stink.

As flames pranced before me like amateur Rockettes and smoke swirled this way and that on random gusts of wind, I could see glimpses of my goal through brief chinks in the wall of flame. The bomb had been so powerful it had severed the front half of Chandelier's car from the back, in the vicinity of the front seat. The forward portion—engine and front compartment—was scorched and twisted beyond recognition as anything other than scrap. It was impossible that Jed Filson was any longer alive, unless he had been part of the plan and had triggered the explosion from a position of safety. I disliked that thought so much I waited till it vanished.

Incredibly, the rear portion of the car, especially the rear seat compartment, seemed structurally intact. If there was hope to be had, it was there, deep within the soup of smoke and fire.

As I inched closer to the wreckage, someone tugged at my coat. When I turned, Kelly, the assistant manager, thrust a fire extinguisher at me. "Maybe this will help."

"Maybe," I said dubiously, regarding what looked more like a toy than a deterrent to anything as terrible as the burning vehicle. I took the small red cylinder from her, pulled the pin, detached the small hose from its bracket, and turned back toward the car, feeling far more foolish than heroic.

"She's alive!" Lark McLaren screamed at my back. "See? That's her *hand*! She's *moving*! Somebody *help* her, for God's sake. Please!"

Canister in one hand and hose in the other, I took aim at the car and squeezed the trigger, producing a miniature cloud of dry white retardant that was so meager as to be whimsical. From behind my flimsy shield, I advanced toward the rear of the car.

The smells were of fuels and plastics and burning rubber. The noise was of approaching sirens and urgent warnings. I ignored as many of my senses as I could and moved ahead, energized by feelings of guilt and incompetence that warred with electric jolts of fear.

Heat greeted me, seduced me, then slapped at me. My scalp

seemed to be peeling away from my skull; my hands seemed to be boiling in oil; my face seemed to be bubbling and cracking like cheap paint. I kept going, the retardant thankfully blinding me to the fix I was getting myself into. If I had stopped to think, I would have run the other way.

When the heat seemed impenetrable and the extinguisher too hot to hold, I stopped spraying and looked. Five yards in front of me, the rear portion of the car was on its side, perhaps from a secondary explosion in the gas tank. What I was looking at was the top of the car, not the side, which meant the only way I could extract Chandelier would be to lean over the roof and pull her out through the window hole. As I was trying to summon the courage to do just that, I wrapped the extinguisher with my handkerchief to make it bearable to hold. It was then I saw what Lark had seen—a hand rising out of the gap in the steaming shell of sheet metal. Chandelier was reaching for help, which meant she was reaching for me.

I took three steps toward the car. Flame taunted me from all sides, impervious to the dregs from the extinguisher, seeming even to feast on them. Tossing the canister aside, I leaned forward to see if I could see Chandelier, extending my hand to where I thought I had last seen hers. My arm draped over the fire like beef on a spit; my face could have served as a griddle. The gases erupting from the wreckage seared enough of my inner and outer tissue that I was coughing and choking and crying simultaneously, rendering myself effectively blind.

Just then, like when the film breaks at the movies, everything went black. As I felt myself sag to the ground, helpless to do otherwise, I was engulfed in a thundercloud that seemed to fall on me from all sides, as if the bomb had brought forth a volcano from the inner earth. My reflexes told me to curl in a ball for protection, which is what I was doing when two gloved hands grabbed me under my arms and began to drag me away from the blaze. I struggled inanely for a moment, reluctant to surrender, then let him do his duty, which was to handle me like a baby.

When I was back to the curb, he put me down. From flat on my back, I looked up at the masked man in red helmet and black respirator and tried to thank him. My voice croaked like a bullfrog.

The fireman nodded and reached behind him as though he had an itch he needed to scratch, then produced a more formidable nozzle than the one I had carried.

"There's a woman alive in the backseat," I shouted, loudly enough for him to hear me over the wail of several sirens.

His helmet nodded in understanding, then he advanced on the Lincoln once more, this time with chemical spray shooting out of the hose from a canister three times the size of mine. Quickly, he was joined by others. Together, they looked like *Star Wars* extras. I watched them approach the flames with a mix of envy and relief, then lay back on the concrete to let it cool me.

Dumb with fatigue and rigid with pain, I rolled to a sitting position and watched the firemen do their work. Two of them were dousing the fire with chemicals, one was attacking with hose and water, and two more were reaching through the rear window to haul forth a form that was unrecognizable as Chandelier or as anyone else. When she saw the charred clothing and smoking hair, Sally Rinehart began to scream. Lark McLaren hurried to comfort her, and Amber Adams started to swear a blue streak. When an EMT got out of an ambulance and came over to ask if I was okay, I lied and said I was.

Minutes later, an ambulance roared off, carrying Chandelier Wells to the hospital. It was only then that I thought of Filson. When I looked toward the front half of the Lincoln, I saw a fireman staring down into the wreckage, then shaking his head. "This one's done," he said, loud enough for me to hear. A small part of me was relieved that Filson hadn't turned traitor to his boss.

As a pair of police cars squealed to a halt down the block, Lark McLaren squatted beside me and tapped me on the shoulder. She was flushed and smudged and breathless, but back in control and routinely efficient. "Are you all right, Mr. Tanner?"

"Close enough. How's Sally?"

"She's getting herself together."

"Good. Anyone else hurt?"

"No. Just . . ."

"Filson."

"Yes." Her voice was as soft as goose down.

"How's Chandelier?"

"I don't know. She looked awful but she was breathing. She even waved at me from the stretcher, I think. They've taken her to Alta Bates. I'll go there when they're finished with me here."

"I guess this means the tour is canceled."

"She never cancels. Only postpones."

"Well, I hope she's all right. When you talk to her, tell her I'm sorry her bodyguards screwed up."

"I'm sure nothing more could have been done."

"Something more can always be done. That's why I don't like the work."

Lark turned away, then looked back. "I'm sorry."

"For what?"

"I shouldn't have expected you to help. I wasn't thinking of the danger, I'm afraid. I was just thinking of Chandelier."

"Don't worry, that's not why I did it."

She started to go, then stopped again. "Jed was a little cavalier about the job, I think."

"I think I was, too."

"But in a way he saved her life."

"How so?"

"That funny old car? The Lincoln? He bought it from an African dictator when he first took the job. Mobutu, or one of those. Chandelier wanted a Mercedes, but Jed insisted on the Lincoln. It was built like a tank, he said—steel plates welded all around the rear seat. Cost a fortune to ship over here, but he said it would be worth it if anyone ever made a try for her."

I looked at the part of the wreckage that had remained intact. "I'd say he was right."

Just then a pair of Berkeley cops broke out of a pack by the bookstore and started walking our way. We stopped talking till they arrived.

The taller one looked at Lark. "You're the secretary?"

"Administrative assistant. Yes."

"Let's talk."

He motioned for her to follow him, which she did after patting me on the shoulder. "I'll see you at the hospital," I said at her back. She waved to show she'd heard me.

The second cop was short and stout and black, with a mustache and a bald head and a uniform two sizes too small. He winced when he sat on the curb beside me. "Disk," he said in explanation, then got out a notebook and consulted it. "You're Tanner."

"Right."

"You look like shit."

"Thanks."

"Tried to pull a Rambo, I hear."

"I'm not sure what I was trying to do."

"Need medical treatment?"

"Not yet."

"Good." He looked at his notebook again. "You're a PI."

"Right."

His eyes left the notebook and scrolled over my face. "You're the guy who shot Sleet a year or so back."

"You knew Charley?"

"Some."

"He was my best friend."

"Which makes it odd that you drilled him."

"*Odd* isn't the word for it."

He started to say something else, but gestured toward the Lincoln instead. "What happened out here?"

"Blew up."

"Bomb?"

"Probably."

"See it happen?"

"Nope."

"Know who did it?"

"Nope."

"What's your relationship to the victim?"

"I'm working for her."

"Full-time?"

"No."

"Doing what?"

When I tried to smile, my face wouldn't let me. "Bodyguard."

He chuckled mordantly. "Nice job."

"Could have been worse."

"Not for you." He pointed toward the front seat. "The dead guy your partner?"

I shook my head. "Full-time chauffeur. Met him yesterday for the first time."

"Where?"

"Jimbo's."

"Why there?"

"On the job. Publication party."

He nodded as if he understood. "Former feeb, I hear."

"So do I."

"Any chance this was terrorists?"

"Not much."

"Personal grudge?"

"Maybe."

"Sex thing?"

"Maybe."

"What else?"

"Disgruntled groupie."

"The Wells woman some kind of star?"

"Writer. Big seller."

"Yeah?"

"Yeah."

"Me, I only read Moseley. Got anything at all we can use?"

"Not yet."

"What's that mean?"

"I don't know."

His voice hardened and his hand gripped my arm till it hurt. "She's our job now, Tanner. Your job is to forget about it."

I looked at my swollen hands, then at the black hunk of scrap still smoking in the street. "That's going to take a while," I said.

chapter 15

By the time the cops were through with me it was pitch-dark. Traffic was still being rerouted around the crime scene like fireflies circling a haystack. A scruffy band of onlookers was still debating the causes of the blast—the fatwa against Salman Rushdie made the list (Steinway had *The Satanic Verses* on sale), followed by animal rights activists (Chandelier sometimes wore fur), and the Hayward branch of the Aryan Nation (three books back, Chandelier had come out against white supremacy). If I'd had any ideas on the subject, I would have kept them to myself, but as it happened, I didn't. All I knew for sure was that I'd been hired to do a job and hadn't done it.

Although I wanted to go to the hospital, I was pretty unpresentable, even for Berkeley. So I fought the battle of the bridge at commute time, got home in just over an hour, then took off my clothes and examined my burns in the mirror. When I saw what was going on with my hands, which had assumed the color and texture of watermelon without the water, I considered going to the hospital for treatment. Instead, I opted for two glasses of grapefruit juice, under the two-pronged theory that the worst part of burns is dehydration and grapefruit juice tastes bad enough to cure anything. After I showered as much of my body as I could stand to get wet and changed clothes with more pain than I'd experienced since I'd been shot, I decided to defer the hospital till later and got back in my car and drove west.

Millicent Colbert and her husband, Stuart, lived in an elegant stone structure on Santa Ana Way near the crest of St. Francis Wood, up the hill from Stern Grove about a mile east of the ocean.

The Colberts are the parents of Eleanor, a five-year-old girl who was carried to term by a surrogate mother and presented to the Colberts pursuant to their contractual arrangement with the surrogate. What the Colberts don't know, and neither does anyone else but the surrogate, is that the odds are better than even that I'm the father of the child. I didn't plan it that way, and in fact I took steps to prevent it, but for reasons of her own, the surrogate was so hostile to the prospect of giving birth to Stuart Colbert's offspring that she replaced the embryo implanted at the fertility clinic with one produced by the two of us, without my knowledge or consent. Her perfidy infuriated me when I learned of it, but it turned out to be the best thing that ever happened to me. Life can be funny like that. When it isn't being horrible.

Because I'd had something to do with salvaging the arrangement when the surrogate became balky at providing a child to the Colberts, Millicent considers me Eleanor's godfather even though I declined the honor when she offered it formally. Although publicly my status is only de facto, Millicent keeps me posted on Eleanor's progress and lets me visit whenever I want, which I make sure happens no more than once a month so I won't become either suspicious or a pest. Millicent is an excellent mother and Stuart's an adequate dad, but every time I leave their house, I wish I could take Eleanor with me.

I pulled to a stop next to the curb. People were coming home from work. The homes they entered were all huge, the cars they drove were all expensive, the lights in the windows that welcomed them were all bright and congenial. All kinds of wonderful things were going on inside those homes, no doubt, and some dastardly things as well. But when you've got the kind of money these people have, you get to keep both behaviors private unless someone shows up with a subpoena.

I rang the bell and waited. A moment later, Millicent opened the door. "Marsh," she enthused. "How wonderful." Her smile bloomed, then withered. "But I'm afraid Eleanor isn't here. Stuart just took her to a computer fair at her school."

"Computers at age five?"

Millicent laughed at the Luddite. "She's a real geek, Marsh; she's been on-line for almost a year. She e-mails children in France and Bulgaria."

"I guess I'd know more about that if I were on-line myself."

"You should be, you know. Then you could e-mail Eleanor every day."

"I don't have that much to say."

"It doesn't seem to stop anyone else."

She clutched my arm with her usual exuberance. I tried not to flinch as she ran roughshod over my burns. "Don't worry about Eleanor," I said. "This time I'm here to see you."

Millicent's blush was dramatic, so much so that she turned away so I couldn't see her reaction. I think she was afraid I was going to make a pass at her and what stirred her was that she wasn't sure how she was going to respond. Given our past, which featured lots of friendship and a little flirtation over and above our common bond with Eleanor, I was tempted to meet expectations. But the pain radiating off the scalded flesh beneath my sleeves helped me keep my leanings under control, as did a quick flash on the image of Jill Coppelia.

"Come in, Marsh; come in," Millicent managed finally, her usual graciousness momentarily shouldered aside by the uneasy ethic of the moment.

"I'll only be a minute," I said as she led me into her sumptuous home.

Stuart Colbert ran a women's clothing store, so he was up-to-date on fads and fashion and had the money to keep pace with each. As a consequence, the living room had been redecorated thrice in the five years I'd known them. At present, the drapes and carpet and wall coverings were baroque and overabundant, a riot of paisley weaves and floral prints complemented by the dozen bouquets of cut flowers strewn about the room in antique cuspidors and wooden buckets. The couch and chairs were formed of dainty frames and shiny fabrics, the tables were built of dark hardwoods no doubt appropriated from some colonial conquest. The fireplace was a work of art all to itself, a symphony of wrought iron and painted porcelain. I'm sure the room was a triumph for some celebrity decorator, but I would have gone crazy in the place myself.

Thankfully, we traversed the living room and entered the library, which was far more my style: leather and plaid, oak and brick. We sat side by side on the husky couch and crossed our legs simultaneously. "Do you want coffee, Marsh? Or a beer?" Millicent asked uneasily. It might have been the first time in our acquaintance that we weren't being chaperoned by a child playing somewhere in view.

"No, thanks."

"You look . . . distracted."

"I am, a little. And that's why I'm here."

She reached out a hand and touched my wrist, which happened to be where I was burned worst. This time I couldn't suppress the flinch.

Millicent frowned and lifted her fingers, then examined my wrist more closely. "What's wrong, Marsh? Are you hurt?"

"I got broiled just a little."

"Let me see."

Because I'm not nearly as tough as I act, I let Millicent play nurse. When she peeled back my sleeve she recoiled from what she'd exposed. "Good gracious. Don't tell me you were trying to make French fries again."

I shook my head. "I've moved beyond my Martha Stewart phase."

"Then what on earth happened?"

"I got too close to a car."

"But how did that . . . ?"

"The car was on fire at the time."

Her eyes widened. "It wasn't yours, was it?"

I shook my head.

"Then why were you so . . . ?"

"Because my client was inside it."

"What client?"

"Chandelier Wells."

Millicent's hands were a pantomime of prayer. "Oh, my God. Did something happen to Chandelier?"

"Her car blew up. Probably from a bomb. I was supposed to stop it and I didn't. Since you were the one who recommended me, I wanted to tell you before it hit the news."

Millicent hugged herself as though we were meeting in Nome. "A bomb? Really?"

"Afraid so."

"Good Lord. She's all right, isn't she?"

"I don't know. I doubt if anyone else does, yet. She had to have been badly burned, but I don't know the details. They took her to Alta Bates over in Berkeley. I'm going there after I leave here."

"Maybe I should go with you."

"I'm sure there's nothing you can do for her at this point. My guess is she'll be in intensive care for quite a while and in the burn ward for quite a while after that."

"How awful." Millicent thought it over, then stood up. "Well, there's *one* thing I can do, at least," she said firmly, then strode off toward the door. "I'll be back in a minute."

She left me to gaze around the library, at books I had read and others I should have, at souvenirs of her trips throughout the world with Stuart, at a rolltop desk I'd coveted from the moment I saw it, at attractive art and tasteful furnishings. At times like these, I get depressed about the things I don't have in my life, until I remember what such things cost in terms of pride and dignity and freedom. Then I cheer up till the next time.

When Millicent returned, she wore an air of self-satisfaction that puzzled me. "What?" I asked her.

"I called the hospital. They said Chandelier is critical but not grave."

"Good."

"And then I called my neighbor."

"Why?"

"You'll see."

I looked at my watch. "I should be going."

"Not yet. Please."

I didn't know what was up so I expressed my worst fear. "Is something wrong with Eleanor?"

Millicent smiled. "Eleanor's fine. Terrific, as usual. She's going to start dance lessons next month."

"Is that wise? I've known some ballerinas. Dancing's pretty hard on the body."

"Don't worry, silly. It's not really dancing. It's movement therapy."

"What does she need therapy for?"

Millicent wrinkled her lips in resistance to my question. "You sound like my mother. It's just so she'll do more with her body than she gets to do at school."

I was too tired to go into it. "You're the boss, but I don't see why a five-year-old kid needs some sort of therapy just to—"

The doorbell cut off my cry of impotence and insecurity and Millicent hurried to answer it. When she returned, she was followed by a distinguished-looking gray-haired gentleman wearing a shiny burgundy running suit and carrying a black bag. "Marsh, this is Kyle Bronson, my neighbor. *Doctor* Kyle Bronson."

I stood up and shook his hand. As we muttered the usual bunk, I figured out what Millicent was up to. "I don't need a—"

"You most certainly do," Millicent dissented firmly. "Roll up your sleeve or I'll do it for you."

I did as directed and the doc looked me over. The burns were mostly minor, with some second-degree on my hands and wrists and first-degree on my forehead and cheeks. He wanted me to go to the hospital for a more thorough exam, but when I told him I didn't have time, he put some ointment on the worst parts and bandaged them up. The ointment made me feel so good that I offered to pay him. He told me not to be silly. After some chitchat with Millicent about a man down the block who had shingles, Dr. Bronson went back home.

"Thanks," I said when he'd gone.

"You need to take better care of yourself."

I grinned my wolfish grin. "It's more fun when you do it for me."

She colored again and I was sorry I'd pushed the envelope, but on the theory that it was the flush of pleasure, not insult, I took her hand and kissed it. "You're the best."

"Thank you."

"I mean it."

"And I appreciate it."

As the silence grew uncomfortable, I stood up. "Tell Eleanor hi."

"Of course."

"And Stuart."

"Surely."

"I'd better go."

"Do you have to so soon?"

"I think I'd better."

She nodded as though she understood what I meant, which was that we shouldn't tempt fate any longer than we had to.

"Well . . ." she said.

"Well . . ."

"Tell Chandelier I'm so sorry."

"I will if they let me see her. For both of us."

"Don't blame yourself, Marsh. Please."

"Have to. The only other guy I can blame is dead."

I gave Millicent a peck on the cheek and she gave me a dispassionate squeeze and I decided she might not be as enamored of me as I thought she was. I decided that was just as well. Then I headed back across the bay and got there in half the time of my previous trip.

It was a little before eight when I parked at the hospital, and a little after that by the time I found my way to intensive care. Lark McLaren was sitting in the visitors' room looking wan and lifeless, as though she'd survived an explosion herself.

When she saw me, she rushed to embrace me, but stopped when she saw the bandages. "Mr. Tanner. How are you? I was worried that maybe you were badly hurt as well."

"I'm fine," I exaggerated. "How's Chandelier?"

Lark tugged me to a chair and sat me down. "Pretty bad, I think. They haven't told me much, but there're third-degree burns on her hands and face and legs; second-degree almost everywhere else. She's still in shock. They say she won't be out of danger for days."

"Burns are tricky," I said. "But that doesn't mean she won't make it. Have you seen her?"

She shook her head. "They won't let me. But she thinks it was Mickey."

"How do you know?"

"She told one of the ambulance attendants she thought her husband had done it."

I shook my head. "I don't think so."

"Why not?"

"Mickey's better off with her alive and earning big bucks, which I told him she was about to do. He's not in her will, is he?"

She shook her head. "No way."

"Who is?"

"In the will?"

I nodded. "Inheritance makes a nice motive. It says so in all the mystery novels."

Lark frowned. "All I know is what she told me once, which was that I would get a small bequest—fifty thousand—and Amber and Sally would, too, and the rest of the staff would get something similar though not as large. And the bulk of her estate would be split between Violet and the library."

"The city library?"

"Yes."

"What's Chandelier's net worth?"

"I don't know, exactly; she has a zillion accountants keeping track. But I think it's between twenty and thirty million."

I laughed. "I think we can add the librarian to the list of suspects."

Lark grasped my hand, then released it when she felt my twinge. "I don't know what to do. I feel helpless just sitting here, but I'm afraid if I leave, something awful will happen."

"All you can do is wait. And you can do that just as well at home."

Her cell phone rang. She took it out of her purse, then turned it off. "The publisher keeps calling. So does the press. So do her fans."

"Tell them everything's on hold and you'll make a statement when there's something to say. Tell the doctors in here to get the best burn people in the business on the case. Tell Amber not to leave town till I talk to her. And then go home and get some sleep."

"I've already done all that," Lark said, "except for Amber." Then she shook her head miserably. "Who could *do* such a thing?" she asked rhetorically, not really expecting an answer.

"I don't know," I said truthfully, "but if you've got no objections, I'm going to try to find out."

Ever the faithful employee, Lark frowned uneasily. "I'm not sure I can authorize the expenditure until Chandelier can—"

"There won't be an expenditure of anything but time. It comes under the category of saving face."

"Won't the police be unhappy if you interfere in their case?"

"I won't be interfering; I'll be aiding and abetting."

chapter 16

When I got home, the telephone was ringing. "Were you there?" she asked breathlessly. "Are you all right? What happened? Is Chandelier Wells going to make it?"

I chuckled at the torrent of words formed in questions I couldn't answer. "I was there, I'm fine, Chandelier's critical but not grave, and I have no idea what happened except for some reason her car exploded."

Jill Coppelia paused to take it all in. "You're sure you're all right?"

"A little crisp in spots. But, yes."

"Crisp from what?"

"I forgot you're not supposed to play with fire."

"It was really a car bomb?"

"I think so."

"You weren't *in* the car, I hope."

"Nope."

"Where were you?"

"Inside Steinway Books."

"The news said something about a driver."

"Chandelier and her driver were in the car when it blew. The driver didn't make it."

"Did you know him?"

"Not well."

"But why on earth did it *happen?* Who had reason to kill Chandelier?"

"I don't know," I said.

"A nut, I'll bet. Some fool who was sure God wanted Chandelier up in heaven with Him. Or down in hell with the devil."

"Maybe. But all kinds of people have a bone to pick with famous writers, it turns out."

"What kind of bone?"

"Ten minutes before the bomb went off, a young woman stood up at the reading and accused Chandelier of stealing her work."

"How would that happen?"

"Chandelier used to teach. The woman used to be her student."

"But still."

"But still," I agreed.

She paused to let things simmer back toward our version of normal. "Since you're all right, do you want to come over for a nightcap?"

"I definitely do, but I probably shouldn't."

"Why not?" she asked, not entirely without frost.

I laughed at her new mood. "Do you think it's at all significant that you cast a bad light on every ambiguous statement I make?"

This time her tone was rectitudinous. "I don't know what you're talking about."

"You always think I'm up to something and I usually never am."

"That's nonsense."

"I hope so."

"So are you coming over?" she asked again, still borderline huffy.

"I got kind of cooked, actually. I should let the medicine do its work."

"You went to the hospital?"

"No. Millicent Colbert's neighbor is a doctor."

"Millicent."

"Yes."

"You were there."

"Yes."

"Tonight."

"Yes."

"After the bombing."

"Yes."

She paused. "You and Millicent make me nervous."

"I don't go to see Millicent, I go to see Eleanor."

"Not entirely."

"Yes, entirely."

"Liar."

"Jealous witch."

"Am not."

"Are, too."

"Am not."

"Are, too."

"God, I love these mature conversations," she groused.

"You're a little touchy this evening, Ms. Coppelia."

"What if I am?"

"I'd like to know why."

Here came huffy again. "Maybe it's because I'm in a pantload of trouble and you can help me get out of it but you haven't lifted a finger."

"With the grand jury, you mean."

"That's what I mean, all right, Sherlock."

I don't love it when she calls me Sherlock. "I hate to break it to you, but helping you with the grand jury isn't necessarily my highest priority."

Her response was pouty and hurt. "I'm afraid I see that all too clearly."

"But helping our relationship is."

"Ha."

"It's true, whether you believe it or not."

"Well, good. I'm glad that what we have, whatever that is, is important to you."

"It is. Definitely. So I'm going to give you a name."

"What kind of name?"

"A cop. A guy who knows something about the Triad. Not everything. But something."

"Who is he?"

"His name is Wally Briscoe. He's a detective. Last I knew he was working out of Northside."

"Does he know you?"

"Yes, which means his name can't have come from me."

"No problem. So what's this Wally Briscoe got to sell?"

"Wally was in the Triad for a while."

"How do you know?"

"Charley told me."

"Ha. I *knew* Charley told you more than you—"

"Leave it alone. Please."

She stifled her usual dissension. "In the Triad for how long?"

"I don't know. But you can probably get all he has—he should be easy to break down."

"Why?"

"Because Wally's that kind of guy. And because he'll want to do something for Charley, even postmortem."

She hesitated long enough for me to begin having regrets. "I guess a 'thank you' is in order," she said at last.

"Then so is a 'you're welcome.'"

Her voice assumed its normal timbre, which was somewhere between friendly and licentious. "I'll try to come up with a more suitable token of my appreciation."

"I'll look forward to it."

"Are you sure you're all right?"

"I'm fine."

"Are you going to look for whoever blew up that car?"

"Yes."

"Will you be careful?"

"Yes."

"I'd appreciate it. Well, I should get back to work."

"Wally's not a bad guy," I said before she could hang up. "Do me a favor and go easy on him. Come to think of it, immunity would be a good way to go."

"I may not have the time for easy or the authority to grant immunity. But I'll do what I can."

"Thanks."

When I hung up, I was feeling as bad as I'd felt since the night Charley Sleet had died from a bullet from my gun. Love can make you miserable, I guess, and make you do things you shouldn't be doing. It's why Hallmark cards and country music are thriving.

I was thinking about the best way to get some sleep in light of my burns and my bandages when I heard a car pull up outside the building. Normally I wouldn't pay attention, but the bomb had excited my nerves to the point of paranoia, so I shut off the lights and went to the window and looked out.

A taxi had pulled to the curb. The driver was lugging a suitcase out of the trunk and the passenger, a woman, was laboring to get out of the backseat without help. By the time both the suitcase and the woman were standing on the sidewalk, I had recognized the passenger as Pearl. When the cabbie drove off without helping her inside with her bag, I put on my shoes and went down.

When I got there, Pearl was regarding her suitcase with a mix of dread and confusion, as though uncertain whose it was or how it got there. She didn't hear me coming till I touched her on the shoulder. "Pearl?"

She started, then looked at me with eyes blurred by apprehension. "Who are you? What do you want? I have no money, if that's what—"

"I don't want your money, Pearl. I'm Marsh Tanner." I pointed. "Upstairs."

She blinked and tried to focus through glasses thick enough to make that more difficult rather than less. "Mr. Tanner," she said finally. "What are you doing up at this hour?"

"Thought you might want some help with that suitcase."

The old Pearl was finally there. "As a matter of fact, I would. The driver was a beast. He didn't even inquire if I required assistance."

"Well, I can assist you just fine." I grasped the handle of the canvas case. "Shall we go up?"

She nodded and I lifted the suitcase and followed her toward the front door. The case was as light as if it were empty. The tag on it read VCV. I asked Pearl if she had enjoyed her time in Vancouver.

"I most assuredly did *not*," she spat without breaking stride. "They didn't even know I was coming. And they laughed when I told them what I had come *for*."

"Who are these people? Family?"

She opened the door and held it for me. "My family weren't criminals, thank you very much. I'm talking about the people at Worldview Enterprises."

"Who are they?"

"They run the sweepstakes I won."

We climbed the stairs in silence and I set the suitcase down by her door and waited for her to unlock it. "The what?" I asked while I waited.

"The sweepstakes. The one that benefits the World of Peace Program and gives a million dollars to the winner. The form they sent me told me I won. That the money was in an account in my name in the largest bank in Vancouver. It had to be real, it was a legal document. But when I went up there to claim my prize, they denied it to my face. And the bank had never heard of me."

After Pearl unlocked the door, I followed her into the apartment. "What made you think you'd won?" I asked.

She ignored the question. "Would you put the bag on the bed, please?" she asked, and pointed toward a door that was exactly where the door to my own bedroom was, one flight up. I took the suitcase in, absorbed the frilly neatness of a room that reminded me of the dollhouse my sister had played with forty years before, and placed the bag on the white chenille spread that covered the narrow bed.

When I rejoined Pearl in the living room, she was holding something in her hand. "This is how I know," she said, and handed me a document of several pages stapled at the top and collected beneath a blue binder.

The print was in a legal-looking font; the heading was OFFICIAL

JUDGMENT, DOMINION OF CANADA, STATE OF BRITISH COLUMBIA. The design was identical to that of court documents filed by attorneys in litigation or probate. In the place where the title of the cause of action is usually listed, the subhead read, "In the Matter of Pearl Gibson." The title of the document was "Certificate of Award of Grand Prize."

It certainly looked definite enough, as definite as legal documents get, that is, but finally I found the catch. On the overleaf, beneath a portion of the blue backing that folded to cover half the front page, was a small notation, in print so small I could barely decipher it, adding the following caveat: "If yours is the winning number, notification of your prize award will be sent in the following format . . ."

I looked at Pearl. "You thought this meant you won."

"Of course I did. Isn't that what it says right there?" She pointed toward the words OFFICIAL JUDGMENT.

I nodded. "Did you happen to read this part?"

"What part?"

I flipped the blue cover and read her the sentence.

"Let's see that," she demanded.

I handed it over. She squinted for several seconds, then held it closer to the light, then handed it back. "I can't read that."

"That's the idea. It means you're not a winner."

"I'm familiar with the English language, Mr. Tanner," she said in a voice as tiny as she was.

I gestured toward the magazines piled around the couch. "Is that why you subscribed to all those? So you would have a better chance of winning some sweepstakes?"

"Of course. Why else would I care about those stupid magazines? There's one in there about surfing, for Lord's sake. Do I look like a surfer, Mr. Tanner?"

"I'm not sure. I've never seen you in your bathing suit."

I didn't get the laugh I sought. "Don't tease me, please. Not tonight."

I apologized. "These sweepstakes are scams, Pearl."

"Why do you say that?"

"Because it's true. They prey on people who believe what they read and they cost people their life savings, sometimes. Lots of them are run out of Canada. I guess they don't have much of a fraud statute up there. Down here, it's illegal to require you to buy something to qualify for a prize."

"But don't you think I'd have a much better chance of winning if I—"

"I doubt if some of them even award a prize, if you want to know what I think. Not a million dollars, at least. And even if they do, they can't make you pay money to qualify for it."

"They couldn't do that, could they? Not give out any prize at all?"

I shrugged. "Just 'cause it's sleazy doesn't mean it can't happen. In fact, sleaze seems to be becoming the norm."

Pearl sagged to her chair and closed her eyes. "So I'm a silly old fool. Is that what you're saying?"

I listened to her breaths grow rapid and more audible. "Come on, Pearl. Don't let it get you down. You're no more a fool than I am," I added, then remembered the events of the day and wished I'd given her a stronger endorsement.

"You're being kind."

"I'm being honest. If you want me to, I'll have somebody come haul all these magazines away tomorrow."

"That would be nice."

"So you won't be entering any more sweepstakes?"

She opened her eyes and forced a smile. "I've learned my lesson."

"One thing I don't understand."

"What's that?"

"Why was it important that you win a million dollars."

She regarded the question with gravity. "It wasn't the money."

"I didn't think so."

She looked toward the picture on the wall of the pyramids of Egypt, the one taken by Pearl during one of her trips abroad. "It was a way to get attention, I guess. To have people make a fuss over

me the way they did when I was young. To be something more significant than a lonely old woman in a tiny little apartment who no
one but the mailman knows is alive."

"I know you're alive, Pearl. And I'm happy about it."

"You're a sweet man, Mr. Tanner," she said, then blew me a kiss
and asked if I would please excuse her, she needed to get some rest.

chapter 17

P ain and shame are potent in combination, potent enough to have kept me awake all night, writhing wildly to find a position that wouldn't aggravate my singed skin, employing a series of platitudes and psychic somersaults to evade the guilt of failing to do my job effectively. Chandelier Wells had been cruelly injured, perhaps terminally so, as a result of my inept approach to her care, and that was going to be difficult to live with.

It's a prejudice that's gotten in my way before, my inclination to dismiss the problems of the rich and the celebrated as trivial by-products of raging egos or ungoverned avarice or the public's pedestrian tastes. But over the years I have realized the prejudice is as much a function of my own shortcomings as those of the objects of my inbred disdain, so I should have been able to have put it aside whatever the circumstance and done my job properly. Usually I can, in fact, but this time I didn't. So I made the only resolve I could make, which was to find Chandelier's cowardly assailant before I did anything else.

I gave up the ghost at 6 A.M., left the bed behind, plowed through a breakfast of Grape-Nuts and potato-bread toast, and paged through the *Chronicle* without registering much of the news except for coverage of the bomb. The articles didn't tell me anything I didn't already know, except that Chandelier owned several parcels of choice real estate around town and was assumed to have made as much in her business dealings as she had from her book deals. At eight sharp I picked up the phone. It was time to find out if my client was still alive and if I was still in her employ.

After lots of beeps and clicks, Lark McLaren came on the line.

"This is Lark McLaren, administrative assistant to Chandelier Wells. How may I help you?"

Within the rote requirements of her job, Lark's voice sounded bleak and defeated, barely able to state her piece. After an instant's sympathy for what she must have been going through, I steeled myself for the worst.

"Lark, hi. It's Marsh Tanner."

"Oh. Hi."

"How are you?"

She hesitated, as if the subject were as complex as the Genome Project. "Who knows?" she offered finally. "I certainly don't see how I could be in very good shape, do you, Mr. Tanner?" The words were airy and random, the speculations of a soothsayer.

It was rhetoric best left unanswered. "Where are you? At the hospital?"

"The hospital," she repeated, made dumb by dread and exhaustion. "Yes."

"Have you been there all night?"

"More or less. I snuck out to Starbucks at seven for a mocha grande. It was cold by the time I got back."

"Is anyone there with you?"

"Sally was here for a while. And Meredith came over from the bookstore. But they had to leave so I've been holding the fort since two. Luckily, the enemy hasn't launched another attack." She giggled at her nonsense, then cut herself off with a groan when she realized that in the world she now inhabited, it might not be nonsense after all.

"How's Chandelier?" I asked.

"Not good."

"She's alive, I hope."

"For now she is. If you can call it that."

"What do the doctors say?"

"They say what they always say—it's too soon to tell."

"Is she conscious?"

"On and off. Mostly off."

"Have you talked with her?"

"Briefly. I'm not sure we communicated. I'm not even sure it was her I was talking to. They said it was, but . . ."

"What did she say? Anything at all?"

When Lark spoke, the words were thick and unwieldy, made awkward by the sludge of grief. "You should see her, Mr. Tanner. She looks like a fish fillet or something, with some kind of clarified sauce and some garnish scattered here and there around the edges. It's disgusting at first, but then of course it's unbearable because you imagine how much it must hurt. She can barely breathe for the pain. Her lungs are burned, inside, from breathing hot gases, and her lips are black and swollen, and . . . everything is so *hideous*. They say she'll face years of plastic surgery, even in the best-case scenario."

Lark started crying, not bothering to remove the phone from her lips. "You need to get some sleep," was all I could think of to say.

"I can't leave her to face it all alone. I just can't."

"Get Meredith or someone to relieve you for a while. She can send someone over from the bookstore, if nothing else."

"Everyone else has other responsibilities. I'm the only one whose full-time job is Chandelier."

"Mine, too," I reminded her. "I'll be there in an hour. I can stay till you—"

"No," she interrupted sharply. "Chandelier wants you to keep working. It's the only thing I understood unambiguously."

"The Berkeley cops are pretty competent, Lark. The odds are good that they'll wrap this up a lot sooner than I will."

Lark sniffed and sneezed and blew her nose, creating havoc in the phone line. "Chandelier doesn't trust cops, Berkeley or otherwise."

"Why not?"

"I'm not sure. Something in her past, probably. She lived a rather wayward life in the early days."

I took a deep breath and defined my duty more clearly. "You're sure she wants me to stay on the job in spite of what happened?"

"That's what she said."

"Does she think the author of the death threats is the person who rigged the bomb?"

"I don't know. But it makes sense, doesn't it?"

"Maybe, but sometimes good sense is the last thing that's involved in these cases. Did she have any new ideas about where I should look?"

"Not really. All she asked about was the book. Apparently sales of *Shalloon* have skyrocketed. They're going back to press to print another hundred thousand."

"Tough way to be a bestseller."

"It's always been tough. For Chandelier, at least. People have no idea what she's sacrificed to get where she is."

Where she was was in intensive care, but I had the sense not to point it out.

"Tell me about Violet," I said instead.

The shift surprised her. "Violet? What about her?"

"She was adopted, right?"

"Yes."

"Even though Chandelier wasn't married at the time."

"Yes. It's possible, sometimes. If you know the right people."

"Was it private or through an agency?"

"An agency, I think. I wasn't working for her then."

"Anything funny about it?"

"How do you mean?"

"Birth parent showing up and making demands for the child or for money. Agency causing problems. Someone claiming Chandelier isn't a fit mother."

Lark bridled and lashed out. "No. *Nothing* like that. Chandelier's a *wonderful* mother. Why are you asking these questions?"

"Mickey Strunt acted funny when I mentioned Violet's name."

"Mickey hated the idea that Chandelier had a child."

"Why?"

"Because he knew Chandelier wouldn't give a damn about him after Violet came into her life. And because he knew Violet would be Chandelier's only heir."

"Did Mickey ever do anything to Violet directly? Mistreat her in any way?"

"No. Never. Chandelier wouldn't have stood for it."

"Maybe Chandelier didn't know."

"Chandelier knows everything," Lark said, firmly enough to make me believe it.

"I guess I'll get back to work. But we need to take care of some things first."

"What things?"

"We should augment the security at the hospital. Put a guard on Chandelier's room to make sure no one makes another try at her."

Lark's voice fluttered. "You think that's really possible?"

"I'm afraid I have to assume it."

"But I don't know anyone who could spend time over here without—"

"I do," I interrupted. "A woman named Ruthie Spring. She's an experienced investigator and a former sheriff's deputy. If she's available, she'd be perfect. If not, I'll get Burns or one of the other big agencies to help out."

"Then you'll take care of it?" she asked, not bothering to disguise her relief at escaping yet another task being added to her already crushing burden.

"I'll handle it," I confirmed. "But we should also get a guard on Violet."

"But why would . . ." She gasped with incredulity. "Of course. If the goal is to cause Chandelier pain, harming Violet would make the burns from the bomb seem like splinters. My God. This is like the old movies Chandelier likes so much. *Cape Fear* or something."

"Do you know anyone who might be able to watch over Violet for a while?"

Lark paused. "I can't think. My mind is asleep, even if the rest of me isn't."

"Ruthie Spring has a woman she works with on occasion. I'll find out if Ruthie can bring her on board. If not, I'll try somewhere else. One way or another, there'll be someone on Violet by the time she gets out of school. Laurel Hill. Right?"

"Right."

"Just so you understand, I'm going for around-the-clock coverage. It'll cost big bucks, but if anything happened to either of them we'd hate ourselves for not going all out."

"I agree. Of course. And you'll take care of it?" she asked again, unused to anyone offering to lighten her load rather than add to it.

"No problem. Now you go home and get some sleep."

"I hate to wimp out."

"Don't be silly. You're not going to do Chandelier or anyone else any good if you're out on your feet."

Lark stifled a yawn and sighed. "How are *you*, by the way? You look like you've been skiing at Squaw for a month."

"I'm fine," I lied.

"I don't see how you could be. If you need medical assistance, I'm sure Chandelier would foot the bill."

"No need. I'll make the security arrangements and get back on the job."

"That would be fine."

"Go home," I ordered.

"I can't."

"Yes, you can."

"I . . ."

"Go. Now."

"Maybe to a motel. So I can be back in a hurry if—"

"Fine. Whatever. Just sleep. Is this number always good for you?"

"Yes. I have call forwarding to my cell phone. One number fits all." She choked back another sob. "Be careful, Mr. Tanner. Please. They tell me the burn ward's already filled up."

Lark McLaren hung up. As I was about to call Ruthie Spring, Ruthie called me. "What the hell, Sugar Bear?" she began. "I got to sit on your lap to keep you out of trouble?"

"Guess so, Ruthie."

"Car bomb?"

"Yep."

"Not the weapon of choice in these parts."

"Nope."

"You haven't gone spook on me, have you?"

"Not that I know of."

"Good. Those towel heads play rough. You responsible for the integrity of the vehicle?"

"Not directly. Guy named Filson had that part."

"The spud in the car."

"Right."

"But you feel guilty anyway."

"Right."

"Like you should have done more to prevent it."

"Right."

"Like if you were good at your job, Filson would still be alive and the Wells woman would still be a bitch on wheels."

"Something like that."

Ruthie clucked like a tom turkey. "That's a hobby you should give up, you know that, Sugar Bear?"

"I know, but apparently it's even harder than quitting smoking."

Ruthie laughed, then turned serious. "So how can I help?"

"If you're free, I'd like you to go over to Alta Bates and stand guard over Chandelier."

"How bad is she?"

"Bad. Have you got some spare time?"

"For you I do."

"Thanks, Ruthie. And it's on the clock. She's authorized the expense."

"On, off, whatever. Just so it don't come out of your pocket."

"No chance."

"That's what you said the last time."

"This time it's straight."

"It better be. When should I be there?"

"As soon as you can. Chandelier's in intensive care. A woman named Lark McLaren is the contact—you saw her at the book party. She's probably home asleep right now, but when she gets back, she'll get you up to speed."

"Check."

"If you have any trouble, call me. Do you have someone who can relieve you at night?"

"No problem. Cops likely to get sand in their shorts from me hanging around?"

"I don't know why they would. I'm the one they're going to get excited about."

I asked Ruthie if she knew anyone who could stand watch over Violet Wells for a few days, and she told me she did and would take care of it right away. We made some record-keeping arrangements, promised to get together that evening to compare notes, and hung up hoping there weren't any more bombs in the cards.

chapter *18*

I was down at the office, swilling coffee, eating a bagel, and putting together a plan of action that might smoke out Chandelier's attacker, when there was a knock on the door to the outer office. The only person I was expecting was a Berkeley police detective coming to take a formal statement about the bombing. When the guy came in wearing a tweed sport coat, open-necked polo shirt, and well-worn cordovan oxfords, I assumed that's who he was.

"Mr. Tanner?" he said as I invited him into the inner sanctum.

"I'm him. You must be from the Berkeley PD."

He sat down in the client chair, crossed his legs, and folded his hands in lazy nonchalance, as though he held a second mortgage on the place and I was two months delinquent. His face was round and full, but more forbidding than fat. His jaw was firm and his eyes were hard-boiled eggs and his matched set of inverted wrinkles suggested he spent more time scowling than smiling.

"Assumptions can get you in trouble," he said after he'd made a mental inventory of the room and didn't see anything that made him sweat.

"What kind of trouble?" I asked, just being sociable until he gave me a reason not to be, which he was sure to do sooner or later.

"For one thing, they can make you see a friend as an enemy," he was explaining.

"And vice versa, I assume."

"True enough."

I smiled, still the affable dunce. "Which is it in this case?"

"I'm most definitely a friend."

"Of whom?"

"You. And Ms. Wells. But mostly of Jed Filson."

"The limo driver."

He nodded somberly. "The late lamented Jedediah. Yes. Name's Hugh Cadberry. Like the candy only spelled differently." He extended a hand and I extended my body and we shook across the litter that always seemed to find its way onto my desk.

"What can I do for you, Mr. Cadberry-like-the-candy?" I asked as I retook my seat.

He didn't find my levity amusing. Given its quality, I didn't hold it against him. "Ever hear of something called ARFA, Mr. Tanner?"

I shook my head. "What is it, some kind of dog food?"

His laugh was enough like a bark to suggest my quip had touched truth. "ARFA is the Association of Retired FBI Agents."

"A boys' club."

"If you will."

"Sounds like fun."

Cadberry didn't look like fun had ever been on the agenda. "We have our moments."

"You're a member, I take it."

"Regional vice president."

"Congratulations. But I'm not retired and I'm not an ex-agent."

Cadberry looked at the painting behind my desk, the one that's worth more than the building. If he wondered how I'd managed to acquire such a prize, he didn't ask and I didn't tell.

"Jed Filson was a member in good standing of ARFA," Cadberry said easily, as though he were reading a box score. "When one of ours goes down, we make it our business to know why. We don't make a lot of noise and we cooperate with the authorities as much as we can. But our bottom line is, there are no unsolved cases when it comes to dead agents and no one or nothing gets in our way until we close the file."

"No open cases whatsoever?"

Cadberry shook his head. "Not on the West Coast. Not in the ten years I've been heading up the Investigations Division."

"Good for you. I see a national office in your future. Treasurer, maybe."

He froze as if I'd belched. "This is not about me, Mr. Tanner."

"It is so far."

He started to object, then shrugged. "You were hired to protect Chandelier Wells."

I just sat there.

"You didn't do it."

"Neither did the ex-agent."

He nodded. "Clearly. May I assume you're still on the case?"

"You may."

"In an investigatory capacity?"

"Among others."

He nodded. "Good. That's why I said that we're friends. ARFA can be a help to you in this, Mr. Tanner."

"Too many friends can fuck up the gumbo sometimes, Mr. Cadberry."

"Hard to see how that could happen in this case, isn't it?"

I smiled my friendly smile. "That's funny. I can see it pretty clearly."

"Assumptions again." Cadberry sounded like a bored lecturer in a required course. "We're like no other organization in this country, Mr. Tanner. We can bring so many chips to the table you can't count them—forensics, DNA work, fingerprint bank, liaison with international police agencies. We have access to virtually any federal resource we choose to consult, and we've got a skills bank among our roster of retired agents that makes any other investigative agency pale by comparison, including the active Bureau."

I crossed my arms and leaned back in my chair. "That's impressive, but if forensics and DNA are the key to this case, I'm sure the Berkeley cops will root it out."

He shook his head. "Not necessarily, I'm afraid. Cops can be slow as Sunday. There's a backup of at least six months at the state crime lab and their DNA base isn't even onstream yet. We, on the other hand, are fast as lightning. Especially when we have a head start."

I smiled. "This must be where I come in."

"Affirmative. You tell me what you know and we'll get a level-one inquiry under way right away. Keeping you apprised, of course. And giving you help if you need it. And credit as well, incidentally, in case you're concerned about that."

"The only place I need credit is at Wells Fargo Bank."

Cadberry shrugged like the holder of a pat hand who'd just been raised. "We might be of help on that end, too. We've been known to pay for professional assistance on occasion."

"The feds always were partial to mercenaries."

He made a fist, then released it unharmed. "Professionals assisting professionals. That's all it amounts to."

"What it sounds to me like is you're cutting in line, Mr. Cadberry. And pushing and shoving as well. I'd think the FBI would know better."

He recrossed his stubby legs. The crease in his trousers was as sharp as the edge on fine bond. I hated to think he'd dressed up just to meet me. "I can assure you we're all grown-ups, Tanner," he announced rather grandly. "This isn't a game."

"I haven't seen a grown-up since Eisenhower died," I said, for some reason unwilling to match his gravity. "Here's my problem, Agent Cadberry. The last time I looked, murder wasn't a federal crime, not even the murder of retired FBI agents. I don't see much of a role for you in this."

He glared at me with the accumulated steel of his years in the business, which was enough to get my attention. "This isn't the time or the place for a pissing contest, Tanner. If this turns out to have international implications, you'll wish you'd brought us on board."

"I don't see how this could possibly be international."

"Car bombs aren't common domestically, you know. Except for the Mafia, which you don't have much of out here."

"Chandelier Wells is a terrorist target, is that what you're saying?"

"I'm saying if you tell me what you know, we can labor in this vineyard beside you."

"And the tit for my tat would be what?"

"We keep you apprised. And take on anything you can't do yourself. We're already looking into the provenance of the explosive device, for example."

"Have you pitched this to the Berkeley cops?"

"Not yet. Have you met with them yourself?"

"Only briefly at the scene. I'm sure they'll be dropping by."

He nodded. "We've found it's best to go into those discussions armed with as much data as we can assemble beforehand."

I thought it over while Cadberry gazed on my painting with a look of what could have been resentment. Or maybe he figured I'd stolen it.

Ultimately I decided to play ball, at least in a limited way, for reasons that had to do with immunizing Chandelier Wells from further danger as best I could. "I'm afraid I haven't been able to assemble much data or anything else for that matter," I said, and proceeded to prove it.

When I was finished summarizing my work so far, Cadberry frowned. "That's it?"

"Afraid so."

"You like anyone in particular at this point?"

"Nope."

"What's your next move?"

"The woman at the reading."

"Slim."

"Emaciated, even."

"And then?"

"The ex-boyfriend."

"Buckley."

I nodded.

"High-profile guy."

"The highest."

"Probably have a roomful of lawyers, if you even get in to see him."

"True."

"I could tag along if you want."

"I've been in a roomful of lawyers before. It's as much fun as being in the men's room at a Giants game, but I think I can handle it."

Cadberry shrugged and stood up. "Well, good luck to you, Tanner. We'll be in touch."

"Look forward to it."

"Here's where you can reach me."

The card he tossed on my desk had a name and a number, nothing else.

Cadberry walked toward the door, then stopped and looked back. "My wife just loves her damned books. As far as Betty's concerned, this is the biggest case I've ever had."

chapter 19

The people at Steinway Books helped me track her down, thanks to the mailing list for their quarterly newsletter. Even so, it was almost noon by the time I pulled to a stop in front of a nondescript gray stucco building on Page Street not far from the UC Extension building.

Lucy Dunston Bardwell lived on the top floor of four, her apartment reachable only via a malodorous stairway that looked to have been the site of a food fight. Tongues of wallpaper lapped off the walls, nonskid rubber mats flapped loose from the tread like shingles in a windstorm, the banister had been ripped out and disposed of in some manner that was probably profitable, and the bulbs had been removed from the lights in the stairwell for reasons other than mood. The smells that flavored the stagnant air didn't come from sources I cared to deduce. Although it was high noon outside, in the stairwell it might have been midnight.

Peering through the man-made dusk, I knocked on the door to apartment 10. And waited. And repeated the procedure three times. And called out, "Ms. Bardwell? If you're in there, I'd like to talk to you. It's about Chandelier Wells."

After another minute I was about to reuse the fetid stairway when the knob rattled and the door inched open. The eye that peered out at me was as wild and wary as a cheetah's. "I don't know you. Who are you?" The question implied I couldn't be anything good.

"My name is Tanner. I was at the reading at Steinway Books yesterday afternoon. I thought we could talk about what happened to Chandelier Wells after you finished speaking."

"Are you a policeman?"

"No."

"A lawyer?"

"No, also."

"Then why are you here?"

"I work for Ms. Wells. I'm trying to find out who hurt her."

"I have no idea who hurt her."

"You don't seem all that chagrined about what happened."

Her lips curled in an enigmatic grin. *"Chagrined.* I like that word. It suggests charm and good humor yet it means just the opposite. As you seem to know."

I smiled and shrugged. "I read books once in a while."

"Really? What kind of books?"

"Ones that keep me awake." I looked back the way I'd come. "It isn't all that, shall we say . . . salubrious out here, Ms. Bardwell. I wonder if I could come inside."

She shook her head with amusement. *"Salubrious,* is it? Now you're showing off."

I admitted it.

She licked her lips while she pondered. "I suppose the police will be here sooner or later."

"Indubitably."

"Then I would be wise to have a dress rehearsal, I suppose."

She closed the door, unhooked the chain, opened it wide enough for me to enter, then closed and locked it behind us. I felt like a bit player in an Eric Ambler novel, delivering the key to the code.

The apartment was a drab and dingy studio, with a trundle bed along one wall, a pine table painted with pea green enamel along another, an orange butterfly chair in the corner, and an upturned orange crate in the minimalist kitchen that featured a hot plate that looked one fried egg away from a short circuit. No TV or stereo was in sight, only a small clock radio on the floor next to the bed and half a dozen white votive candles that had to stand in for a fireplace.

The most prevalent form of diversion was books. There were

dozens of them, piled everywhere, including on the window ledges and space heater. The ones I could see were by people like Gardner and Forster and Burroway and purported to teach their readers how to write. Interestingly, none of the books had jackets or even bright colored boards—they had clearly been bought used, castoffs acquired at garage sales and thrift shops, a treasure trove of intelligence plucked from the jetsam of this purportedly literary city by someone with a thirst for knowledge and an empty purse. Since I'd been in such straits myself in my early days, my respect for their owner began to rise. But I don't think it's a good sign when even writers can't afford new books.

Lucy Dunston Bardwell pointed toward a straight-backed chair near the green table and invited me to sit. The table seemed to serve as both dinette and desk. As I eased down onto the frayed cane seat, I noticed a notebook lying open on the table, spiral and college-ruled, of the kind I used to use in class to take notes when I was awake enough to write. The pages of this one were full of tiny handwriting done with blue ballpoint, then edited once with red ink and a second time with green. As a result of the multiple revisions, the page was completely filled with manuscript, in all the margins and between all the lines. I don't know how it measured up as literature, but if her goal was to minimize her use of foolscap, Ms. Bardwell was already successful.

I got as comfortable as I could in the rickety chair and looked at Lucy Bardwell, who had taken a seat on a pillow on the bare floor, then crossed her legs and clasped her hands as though I were some kind of seer. She wore what looked to be a homemade outfit—baggy parachute pants and an oversize rag sweater and battered Birkenstocks over gray wool socks that were nearly a quarter inch thick. I could have reproduced the ensemble for less than ten bucks in any Goodwill outlet in the city.

"Is Ms. Wells okay?" Lucy Bardwell asked all of a sudden.

"Not really. She's badly burned. They're still not sure she'll make it."

"You mean she might die?"

I nodded.

She bowed her head and murmured what could have been a prayer. "I'm sorry."

"You didn't sound very sympathetic when you accosted her at the reading."

Her eyes filled with the bright light of virtue. "I didn't accost her, Mr. Tanner. What I said was entirely true. She stole my ideas and my words, and now that she's rich she should pay for it, somehow. But not like that. No one deserves that, except maybe the editors in New York who keep rejecting my work." She rolled her eyes to show she was joking.

I smiled. "So you didn't hire a hit man to take her out?"

Her look darkened. "No, but that's nothing to joke about, surely. Murder has never seemed very funny to me."

"Me, either," I admitted. "Is there anyone who might have been angry with Chandelier on your behalf?"

She frowned and gnawed her lip. "I don't know what you mean."

"Father or brother or boyfriend? Someone who might think Chandelier had gypped you out of a major career as a writer but with her out of the way you might get it on track?"

She blinked and looked toward the window, which looked out on to an air shaft and a solid brick wall. "My father is dead and my brother's in Sweden and the only lover I ever had committed suicide six years ago."

"I'm sorry."

"So am I. I'll never get over it." She pointed at the notebook I'd seen on the table. "One reason is, it's very hard to do this by yourself."

"Do what, exactly?"

"Write."

"Write what?"

"Novels and short stories."

"How long have you been doing that?"

"Eleven years. Going on twelve."

"That's a long time."

She nodded. "It's similar to solitary confinement, I imagine."

"How so?"

"As authoritarians seem to have known from time immemorial, sitting alone in a room for extended periods can make you crazy."

"Is that what you are, Ms. Bardwell?"

She seemed to treat the issue as a serious one. "Not yet, I hope. But I'll probably be the last to know, don't you think?"

"Well, you don't seem crazy to me."

She accepted the compliment graciously. "Thank you very much."

"Are you still taking writing classes?"

"I can't afford any more classes, but even if I could, I'm not sure they're what I need at this point."

"What do you need at this point? Money?"

She smiled with shy deprecation. "Last year I earned four thousand two hundred dollars waiting tables at the local Denny's and I actually managed to live on it." She gestured at the room. "My life is hardly splendid, as you can see. But what I need most isn't money, what I need most is optimism."

"About what?"

She shrugged as if the answer were obvious. "My future. My work. My life. I've written four novels and twenty-two short stories. None have been published, none have been taken on by an agent. Even I know that it seems silly to go on at this point, insane, really, but for some reason I'm afraid to stop."

"Why is that?"

She couldn't meet my eyes. "I guess because I'm afraid my work is all I have."

"Maybe writing's not what you do best," I said quickly, to head off a case of the doldrums. "Maybe you'd be happier doing something else."

She shook her head with the vehemence of a zealot. "Writing is my life. It's all I do, all I think about, all I dream about, all I want out of existence."

"But you are writing. You're just not getting published."

She shook her head in sympathy with my ignorance. "I'm not one of those who want to 'have written,' Mr. Tanner. I work my butt off. I write ten hours a day, six days a week. So I'm not in it for the glory, I'm in it for the joy of creation and the music of the language, and for what I learn about life as I write. But writing good prose is only half the Holy Grail."

"What's the other half?"

"Readers. I need to know people are being touched by what I do; that my work makes some sort of difference in their lives. Not by answering the great ethical questions or anything—I'm not a philosopher or even an intellectual. But I do want to give people joy. And peace. And escape from the hardships of their lives for a while, which is the gift my favorite books have always given me." She looked up at me and grinned shyly. "That's probably too much to hope for, isn't it?"

"No. Not at all," I said, mostly because I hoped it was true.

"The sad thing is, I'm a good writer. Not to brag or anything, but a wide variety of people have told me that over the years, including Chandelier Wells, if you can believe it. But it's not enough to be good, I've discovered. You need something extra. A hook. A gimmick. A kick in the teeth to some jaded editor who thinks she's seen it all before. And in my case, that something was *Childish Ways.* The topicality of the subject matter, the gritty humanity of the protagonist, interplay of terror and romance in the plotline—all the elements of commercial success were there. But Chandelier stole them and published them and kept my life from moving on. Do you wonder that I'm furious at her?"

"What I wonder is if you did anything but berate her at the reading."

"You don't think I had anything to do with that explosion, surely?"

"I don't know if you did or not."

She gazed around the room as though she hoped I would do the same and read its message accurately. "All I do is write, Mr. Tanner.

And go to church. And work at the restaurant. And sit with my mother on Sunday afternoon while she listens to the radio preachers. I have no money; I have no lover; I have no children; I have very few friends. Two, in fact, and one of them lives in Oregon. Truth to tell, I have no life at all beyond the lives I create in my books and my stories."

"I'm sure you're exaggerating."

"I'm really not, as it happens. The only things I have other than my work are my honor and my dignity and my effort to do no harm to the world. I recycle, I keep the heat below sixty-eight degrees, I take public transportation, I'm a Big Sister when I'm not too tired. The only things that keep me going are my belief that I'm a good person and my dream of becoming a writer. Intentionally injuring another, no matter how odious that person is or how much pain she's caused me, would destroy both of my lifelines, Mr. Tanner. I'm afraid you're barking up the wrong tree."

"Only in one sense," I said, then stood up and stuck out a hand. "I wish you well, Ms. Bardwell. I'm sure good things will happen if you persevere."

Her grin was brash and irrepressible. "I've been persevering for eleven years. I'm not about to stop just when I've gotten good at it."

chapter **20**

L ucy Bardwell's reclusive quest for literary achievement weighed
heavily on me as I drove toward downtown. I didn't know anything about her talent, but in her lonely devotion to art and
in the sacrifices she had made to pursue it, she was more of a writer
than most, at least in my judgment. Unfortunately for Lucy, my
judgment didn't count. Unfortunately for me, I didn't seem to have
the will or the passion to make such an effort myself, on behalf of
anything. Except maybe Jill Coppelia.

I was on my way to the offices of Thurston Buckley, the real
estate tycoon who had been smitten with Chandelier Wells and
whom Chandelier had allegedly dumped, but by accident I found
myself driving down Folsom Street past the offices of the *San
Francisco Riff.* In light of the paper's flagrant enmity toward Ms.
Wells, I decided to make a detour.

The *Riff* was a self-styled alternative newspaper, the latest in a
long string of such publications that sprouted with regularity in
the Bay Area and whose lineage went back to the *Berkeley Barb.*
The *Riff* was more prosperous than most of its ilk, and since it was
given away free at what seemed like ten thousand locations in the
city, it had a wide circulation and, on occasion, a surprising degree
of clout, especially with regard to social and multicultural issues.
Although not nearly as much as its arrogant editorials implied.

I read the *Riff* myself from time to time, mostly for the weirdly
inventive cartoons and the masochistic and irreverent sex column,
but I skimmed the book, movie, and restaurant reviews as well,
since they catered to inclinations and budgets more like my own
than those the *Chronicle's* pompous experts addressed. Their in-

house book critic was Allen Goodhew, who advertised himself as a former publishing executive, which might mean he had been a senior editor at Knopf or that he had a Xerox machine in his basement or Pagemaker on his computer.

I parked in the small gravel lot next door and entered the similarly modest brick building, a two-story former warehouse with the faded remains of a Burke's Cartage and Storage sign still clinging to the side, a thriving coffee roaster on the ground floor, and the offices of the *Riff* on level two. The office was sparse and cluttered, with rock posters on the walls, computers on the desks, rows of reference materials on the bookshelves, and coffee cups on every available surface, no doubt in tribute to the addictive powers of the aromas rising up from the roaster below. I got my daily dose of caffeine merely by inhaling.

When I finally found someone who would talk to me, it was in the person of a young woman named Wendy Lowenstein. She was dressed in a black floor-length skirt, a purple skintight leotard, and an oval band of pink lipstick that was double the width of her lips. Around her hips was a braided sash, apparently fashioned out of someone's neckties.

When I asked if Allen Goodhew was around, she wrinkled her nose and shook her head. "I doubt it. He usually makes it a point not to be."

"Do you know where I can find him?"

"We're not supposed to say. Especially about our precious Allen."

"Why not?"

She adjusted one of the many silver rings that wrapped her fingers like hose clamps. "Allen makes people mad. Especially writers. Or victims, as he calls them. A fantasy guy broke his nose one time after Allen called him a Terry Brooks without balls." She pointed left and shuddered. "The bloodstain is still in the carpet. Allen is very . . ."

"Acerbic."

"Yes."

"Callous."

"Yes."

"Vituperative."

She frowned. "What are you, some kind of wordsmith yourself? I suppose you want a piece of him, too."

I shook my head. "I'm what you might call a source. Goodhew called me a couple of days ago and left a message on my machine. I used to work for Chandelier Wells. Apparently I have some information he's interested in."

"Derogatory, I'll bet."

I smiled. "Massively."

"Allen hates her, for some reason."

"So I hear. Why do you think that is?"

"Knowing Allen, she probably split an infinitive."

"Surely it's more than that. In his last review, he called her a syntactical slut."

"He's called her worse than that, believe me, though not in print, fortunately for our libel insurer. But with Allen, all it takes is bad writing. Really. The guy's a fanatic about prose. He lit into my piece on genital accessories so rabidly I thought he was going to wring my neck."

"He's going to wring *my* neck if I don't get this information to him."

"Well, the only thing I can tell you is that he hangs out in the bar down the street."

"There are lots of bars down this street."

"McGuinn's."

I nodded. "Thanks." I turned to go, then looked back. "What does he look like?"

"Short. Skinny. Pizza face. Ponytail." She smiled at a private thought. "He doesn't bathe all that often, so if you don't see him right away, you can probably smell him."

"You sound like you know Mr. Goodhew pretty well."

She wrinkled her nose and nodded. "Yeah. Typical, I guess."

"Typical how?"

"I knew him lots better than he knew me."

I set off down the street in search of a bar that trafficked in literary criticism. In the fifties, that would have included half the gin joints in town. Now, McGuinn's might be it.

It was a typical south-of-Market Irish pub. The decor was obsolete and untended, the customers insular and aloof, the bartender huge and intimidating and in this case scarred above both brows from the bare-knuckle brawls of his youth. I started to ask about Allen Goodhew, then realized I didn't have to.

He was sitting in a booth in the back, wearing a wrinkled tuxedo jacket over a faded gray sweatshirt and hunched over a notebook in which he was scribbling as fast as he could with a black enamel fountain pen. Although it wasn't much after noon, he was nursing a pint of dark beer. He looked more like a punk rocker than a scribe, and he was twenty years younger than anyone else in the place.

Without being asked, I slid onto the bench across from him. "Let's talk about Chandelier Wells," I said when he didn't bother to look up, firing my best shot first.

The pen he was using looked sleek and expensive. The journal he wrote in was the size of a menu and bound in black leather. The ink he applied to its milky white page stopped flowing in midsentence.

The eyes that peered up at me were bleary and bloodshot and vague. "Who the hell are you?"

"A fan."

"I don't have any fans. Thank God."

"Not you. Chandelier Wells."

He snapped the cap on his pen and leaned back. His smile was lazy and pejorative and exposed a row of teeth that were stained the color of weak tea. "You don't *look* like a moron."

"Looks can be deceiving. For example, you don't look capable of murder. Or even planning it. But that doesn't mean you aren't."

"What the hell are you talking about? Who am I supposed to have murdered?"

"Not murdered. Only attempted."

He shrugged with elaborate unconcern. "Who's the lucky survivor?"

"Chandelier Wells."

His smile recombined to become a gloat. "Let me guess. The weapons were my trenchant textual analysis, my scathingly scrupulous aesthetics, and my crushingly apposite wit."

"The first time, yes. The last time, you used more potent ammunition."

"Like what?"

"A car bomb."

He shook his head with disgust, as if I had suggested we dance to the monotonous jig being piped through the loudspeakers. "What are you, friend, some pathetic pop novelist trying out a puerile plot device to see if I bite? Or are you merely a minion of the local gendarmerie?"

As if he was used to bringing the world to a halt with his quips, he uncapped his pen and began to write in the journal again. Without a word of warning, I shoved his hand away from the page and closed his journal. "Chandelier Wells was badly injured over in Berkeley yesterday. As I'm sure you know."

He replaced the cap on his pen with the precision of Eastern ritual. "How would I possibly know that?"

"The papers. The nightly news."

"I don't read papers and I don't own a TV."

"How noble of you. How do you fill your spare time?"

"I read decent prose when I find it, which is so seldom as to be terrifying, and I record my observations of the passing scene over my morning stout."

"A postmodern Samuel Pepys."

Goodhew bowed with false modesty. "That remains to be seen." He reopened his journal and sipped at his beer, rereading his prose and pondering his place in the pantheon.

"You're notorious for your enmity toward Ms. Wells," I went on. "Have you ever met her?"

He shook his head. "I've read her pallid prose. Believe me, it's as close as I want to come. Admittedly, that's close enough to render anyone of taste and discernment homicidal."

"You take her seriously enough to be a suspected assailant."

"Suspected by whom?"

"Me."

"And you are?"

"A private detective."

"Another Chandler wanna-be." Goodhew rolled his eyes toward the roof. "Spare me, O Lord."

"Maybe I'll spare us both. Prove to me you didn't do it. Then I can get out of here."

His thick brows lifted and his pink eyes bulged. "A car bomb? Please. I'm not a Neanderthal. I possess far more effective means to accomplish my goals."

"Your reviews?"

He nodded.

"I hate to break your bubble, but Chandelier's crying all the way to the bank."

He seemed genuinely indifferent to the implication of impotence. "For now, perhaps. But reason and refinement will prevail. They must, or the world is no longer fit to occupy."

I smiled. "When you find evidence to support your faith in reason and refinement, let me know."

He shrugged and grinned and adjusted the clamp on his ponytail, suddenly a bashful boy. "Why do you think I don't watch TV?"

I gave him time to finish his beer. "I still don't get why you're so hostile toward Ms. Wells," I said as he wiped his lips on his sleeve. "She's hardly the only popular novelist who isn't William Faulkner."

"The Chandelier, as I call her, embodies all that's wrong with the modern woman. She's arrogant, assertive, humorless, graceless, and oblivious to her artistic irrelevance. The worst of it is, Chandelier Wells actually believes she can write."

"So do a couple of million readers, apparently."

His sneer was world-class. "Idiots also, of course. We have bred a generation of subliterate dunces. In their day, Shakespeare and

Mozart were popular artists. In the aesthetic of the baby boomers, the successors are Chandelier Wells and Yanni."

"You're a bitter man, Mr. Goodhew."

"There's so much to be bitter about," he exulted pleasantly, then looked at his watch. "You should hear me when I've had a couple more pints and have a subject more worthy of my energies than the Chandelier."

"Where were you yesterday at three?"

"How should I know?"

"Were you drunk?"

"Probably."

"Here?"

"Of course not. I have more appropriate places to spend my afternoons than toilets like this."

"Who were you with?"

"Only my muse."

"Girlfriend? Boyfriend?"

"Both on occasion. Neither at the moment. Which is more of my life story than you're entitled to." He put his pen in his pocket. "One of us needs to move on."

Since I'd had more than enough, I stood up. "The bomb thing looked pretty professional, Mr. Goodhew. But if it wasn't, if it was some childish stab at fomenting cultural revolution, you'll take a fall. You're not nearly as smart as you think you are."

"Which still makes me the smartest man in the room."

"Only after I leave," I said, and left him to war with the world with his pen.

chapter *21*

Thurston Buckley ran his extensive real estate empire out of the top floor of his own building on the corner of First and Market, one of several titanic structures he had developed and leased to a variety of well-heeled tenants. Like most San Francisco architecture, the Buckley buildings were lackluster in design and unimaginative in execution, but exceedingly productive of profit—Buckley always made the list of the city's wealthiest residents, as did his second ex-wife, who had made off with enough of Thurston's money in their bitter divorce to become a player in the social whirl herself. As was her new husband, the lawyer who had represented her in divorce court.

I'd never met Thurston Buckley, but what I'd heard of him I didn't like—he was typical of much of the new class of wealth in the state, wholly lacking in subtlety and restraint, wholly convinced of his own acumen whatever the subject at hand, wholly oblivious to his lack of any significant attributes other than arrogance and assets. I wasn't looking forward to meeting him, let alone probing his love life.

The odds of getting in to see Buckley seemed slim, even though I'd called for an appointment. When a secretary as smoothly solicitous as a tour guide ushered me into the boss's office first thing, I figured she thought I was a cop. When I looked into the massive room, what I saw was Thurston Buckley perched like a bull rider on a high-backed leather throne behind a rough-hewn wooden desk that was as large as a garage door, as thick as a railroad tie, and raised a foot off the floor by a brushed-chrome base that passed for solid silver.

When he saw me admiring the desk, Buckley beamed with pride. "Single slab of cedar. Over a thousand years old, from up near Sierra City. Drives the tree huggers crazy when they come around to hit me up for donations." He stood up and extended a hand. "Thurston Buckley."

Predictably, he made the handshake a contest. I managed to hold my own, which discomfited him. "Marsh Tanner."

"Take a load off, Tanner." He gestured toward a two-toned leather chair, the color of pus and the color of mud.

After I sat down I looked him over. He was dressed like an urban cowboy, complete with snaps and boots and jeans and a silver buckle the size of a CD. His beard was more white than black, and his hair was long enough to be braided but wasn't. He fancied himself a tough customer and was so full of himself he was bursting— potbelly, thick lips, huge hands, big head, broad smile. Even his teeth seemed outsize—a row of domino tiles sparkling within a pulpy purse. The term *larger-than-life* was coined for men like Buckley. So was the term *raving asshole*.

Buckley was looking me over, too, of course, and what he saw didn't dent him much. "My girl thought you were a cop when you called," he said with what seemed like amusement.

"What a shame."

"If you claimed you were, it would be a felony."

"If I claimed I was, you're right."

"But you probably didn't."

"Probably not."

"Just played the role and let her jump to conclusions."

"Show business is my life. Stanislavsky."

His smile morphed toward a snarl. "I don't like smart-asses."

I nodded in mock sympathy. "Self-loathing is an insidious thing."

Flushed and furious, Buckley remained in his chair only with effort. "You've got three minutes."

"First of all, where were you yesterday at three o'clock?"

He surprised me by answering the question. "Right here."

"Doing what?"

"Same as always—making money."

"Witnesses?"

"Probably forty or so if I bothered to check, which I'm not going to do."

"Anyone in the room with you?"

"My girl, from time to time. And my assistant, from time to time."

"Your girl is the one who brought me down here?"

"Right."

"And your assistant is who?"

"Julien Towne. Sharp kid. Prep school back East; lawyer; MBA. I pay him more than he's worth just to listen to him talk."

"Where is he now?"

"Phoenix."

"Doing what?"

"Same as usual—making money."

"When will he be back?"

"When he's made the deal I sent him down there to make."

"How long will that take?"

"A day. A year. Whatever. If the deal's done right, time doesn't matter." Buckley looked at me as though he expected a contradiction and was ready to rebut it.

I was happy to disappoint him. I never ask a question about the business world because I never get an answer that makes sense. "Have the Berkeley cops been in to see you yet?"

"If they had, you wouldn't be here."

"Funny you didn't ask why they might show up."

He swiveled in his chair and looked out the window, at a view that extended across the bay and over the Berkeley Hills to the bulge of Mt. Diablo rising like a blister out of the warmth of the San Ramon Valley. "I heard what happened to Chandelier over there. It figures they'd want to see me eventually. Hell, everyone in town knows we had a thing for a while."

"I hear the thing got sour for you at the end."

When he swiveled back to face me, his complexion had started to mottle. "Bullshit. It didn't work out. We mutually agreed to break it off. The woman I'm seeing now is fantastic. Twenty-four; tits as hard as bowling balls. I'm sure Chandelier has someone new in her life as well." He shrugged an overly casual disclaimer. "Life goes on. It was fun while it lasted. They always are."

"Mutual is not precisely the way I heard your breakup described," I said amiably.

"No?"

"What I heard was, she dumped you and you got ugly about it."

His flesh seemed hot enough to throw off steam. "My question to you is this, Mr. Peeper—how would anyone but me and Chandelier know what the fuck kind of breakup we had?"

Because he was so proud of it, I decided to ignore his rhetoric. "I heard you were incensed when she told you it was over. I heard you threatened to make her life miserable."

"Bullshit. All bullshit."

"Since she's about as miserable as you can get right now, it makes me wonder if you followed through. I mean, you're clearly a can-do guy, Mr. Buckley. I figure you don't make idle threats."

He glowered down at me from his throne as though he'd majored in monarchy in college. "You got that right for a change. But like I said, I didn't threaten the bitch. I just found another filly."

"What happened? You have problems in the sack? Or maybe you don't like women who make more money than you do."

"The day she makes more money than I do will be the day they serve shit to the sultan." He stood up and stepped off his cloud of chromium and loomed over me like an overaged bouncer. "Get the fuck out of here. Now."

I stayed put. "You build lots of buildings, Mr. Buckley. You must have plenty of guys on the payroll who know their way around explosives. Like the ones that blew the hell out of Chandelier's Lincoln and killed her chauffeur."

"Stop trying to dump that on me."

"But you're such a nice receptacle."

He grabbed my arm at the biceps and squeezed. "No one talks to me that way, goddammit. I'm going to kick your ass all the way to the elevator if you don't get moving."

I yanked his hand off my arm and stood up. "I also figure you're such a blowhard, there's someone around here who heard you hatch the plot. When they realize somebody died and Chandelier got badly hurt, sooner or later they'll crack."

He made a fist with his meaty hand and squeezed with the power of pneumatics. I expected to see drops of blood. "I can break you in half with one hand."

I smiled. "Only if the hand held an ax. Have a nice day."

"Fuck you."

When we were through playing rooster and I was back in my office, I called Lark McLaren's cell phone number, hoping that if she'd gone home to sleep she'd had the fortitude to turn off the phone.

She answered after the first ring.

"Hi. This is Marsh Tanner."

"Oh. Good. I was afraid you were another reporter."

"It's swarming season, I take it."

"Like flies on . . . well, like flies. Have you learned anything helpful?"

"I learned Thurston Buckley is a jerk."

She laughed feebly. "I could have told you that. So could Chandelier."

"And I don't think Lucy Dunston Bardwell had anything to do with it."

"Who's she? I forget."

"The woman at Steinway Books who accused Chandelier of stealing her work."

"Oh. Her. She seemed so . . . sincere. And so pathetic. What is she, some kind of nut?"

"Actually, she's a very committed writer, almost to the point of monasticism. And not at all pathetic."

"Well, Chandelier wouldn't do a thing like that. Never."

"No?"

"No. People send her ideas all the time. Out of the blue. More than she could possibly use. She has no need to steal one."

"I'll take your word for it," I said, while I wondered if she was protesting too much, then wondered if it mattered. "I think Allen Goodhew is off the list as well."

"You're sure? He's such a monster. At least in print."

"Off print, too. But he's a talker, not a doer. Plus, if Chandelier didn't exist, he'd have to invent her. Beating up on bestsellers makes him feel like a man."

"So you don't have a suspect yet?"

"I can't cross Buckley off the list, but I don't have anything that says he did it, either."

"He was very upset with Chandelier."

"And now he's very upset with me. But that's not anything you can take to a grand jury. Have the retired FBI boys been in touch with you yet by any chance?"

"I . . ."

"They talked to me so I'm sure they talked to you. And told you not to mention it."

"You're right. They just left."

"They tell you anything you didn't know?"

"No."

"Not even about Filson?"

"They asked lots of questions but they didn't offer much in return."

"That's been federal policy for the last hundred years. You tell them anything you haven't told me?"

"Of course not."

"Good." I took several seconds to gather my thoughts. When a few had been gathered, I asked, "Does Chandelier pay her sources?"

"I don't think so."

"Never?"

She considered it. "I suppose she might if it was . . ."

"Juicy enough?"

"Yes."

"Is there any way you can find out for sure?"

"I'd have to talk to her accountant, probably."

"Put that on your to-do list, okay?"

"But why?"

"I'm not sure. But what I think we need to do at this point is find out if Chandelier was doing any research for her new book."

"I don't know if she was or not."

"Can't you dig up her notes?"

"If there are any, they're all in her computer and I don't have the password."

"Do you know much about computers?"

"Some. Not a lot."

"Play around with hers and see if you can crack the code. Or get her to tell you, either one."

"She never talks about what she's working on. Ever. She thinks it's bad luck."

"Then you need to become a hacker. Or hire one."

She hesitated. "Mr. Tanner?"

"What?"

"I've been thinking, you know? About who might have done this."

"Good."

"There's this guy. Most of Chandelier's fans are women, but this one guy—he may be gay, I don't know—but he shows up at lots of readings dressed like one of Chandelier's characters. And quotes lines from her books. And brings her candy and cheap jewelry."

"Sounds creepy."

"It is creepy. But I didn't see him at Jimbo's, and that's even creepier. I was thinking he might be mad at her for some reason."

"Why?"

"I don't know. There's been some tiff about her fan club newsletter, I know. I think he was involved with that, somehow."

"What's this guy's name?"

"Randolph Scott."

"For real?"

"Probably not."

"Where does he live?"

"Somewhere in the Castro. He brings Chandelier this wonderful pastry from a Mexican bakery called Charro's."

"I'll check him out," I said reluctantly. "But it doesn't sound like fun."

"And I'll play around with the computer. That doesn't sound like fun, either."

chapter 22

I went for an early dinner at MacArthur Park. When I got back to the office, the phone was ringing—Ruthie Spring was reporting in.

"So what's going on?" I said after she'd asked if I had time to chat.

"Nothing out of the ordinary," she answered. "Chandelier's still in intensive care; the docs are doing their thing, the entourage is hovering, and the flowers are piling up like tumbleweeds in a Texas sou'wester. This woman is more than a writer, Marsh; she's some kind of love goddess or earth mother or something. Her fans are flooding the place with everything from Holy Bibles to echinacea, to say nothing of the flock that's gathered in the lobby sniffing and sobbing and carrying on like the Baby Jesus just stubbed His toe. I haven't seen anything like it since Elvis tumbled off the toilet."

"Have you checked the lobby out?"

"The assembled multitude? Sure."

"Any kooks?"

"They're all kooks. Why the hell else would they be here?"

"Any of them look capable of building a car bomb?"

"Most of them don't look capable of boiling water, if you ask me. But I can't say any of them look evil."

"How's Chandelier?"

"The good news is she's going to live. The bad news is, she's not going to want to for a while. Lots of pain; lots of grafts coming up; lots of scarring; and lots of scary pictures looking back from the bathroom mirror."

"But she's out of danger?"

"So they say."

"Can she talk?"

"Barely. The McLaren woman was in there for quite a while, but she didn't get much done, is what she said. When she came out, she was crying."

"Is Lark still around?"

"Home sleeping. Said she'd be back by six. Nice girl," she added cryptically.

"Yeah."

"If you weren't so dazzled by the assistant DA, I'd do a little matchmaking."

"I'm twenty years too old for Lark McLaren, Ruthie."

"Men are never too old, Marsh. And women are never too rich."

I laughed even though she'd said it a hundred times. "Anything else I should know?"

"Not really. Some of the Wells crew could use some manners," she added as an afterthought.

"Such as?"

"The Adams woman is a pain in the ass."

"She's an agent. She's supposed to be a pain in the ass."

"The McLaren girl said something interesting about her."

"What?"

"That Chandelier had gotten so big in the business, she was the Adams woman's only client."

"So?"

"So Chandelier is thinking about making a change."

I perked up. "She's getting a new agent?"

"Thinking about it. That's what Lark told me."

"Why?"

"Something about the last contract. Not enough front money; not enough promotional commitment; not enough share of some kind of royalty; and not enough something I didn't understand."

"Given what ten percent of Chandelier's take must amount to, that makes a nice motive."

"My thinking, exactly."

"Vengeance, too, I imagine."

"Vengeance isn't unknown in show business, from what I read in *People* magazine," Ruthie observed dryly.

"Chandelier isn't really in show business, is she?"

"Shit, Marsh. You got any doubt about it, come take a look at the lobby."

I decided she had a point. "Anything else?"

"Not that won't keep."

"Okay, Ruthie. Hang in there. We covered around the clock?"

"Snug as a condom on a kumquat."

"I'll be in and out. Call the cell phone if you need me."

"When I need you, I use a candle, Sugar Bear."

I hung up the phone before things got any more risqué. Ruthie had a way of implying that if she had her way, we'd be screwing three times a day. I couldn't quite convince myself it was entirely a joke.

Ten seconds later, the phone rang. "Hey," Jill Coppelia said.

"Hi."

"Where've you been?"

"Sleuthing. You?"

"Working. We brought Wally Briscoe in."

"And?"

"He opened up just like you said."

"And?"

"He didn't know everything but he knew something. Especially about one of the killings."

"How'd you get him to talk?"

"We gave him immunity, just like you wanted. He won't face prosecution unless he lied to us. And we'll give him protection and relocation assistance, till things die down, at least."

"Thanks."

"It was more for the city than for you."

"I know, but thanks anyway."

Jill paused. "He asked if you were the one who gave him up."

"And you said?"

"I said I couldn't comment."

"I'm sure that reassured him."

"Don't be that way, Marsh. We've got some hard evidence now. And places to look for more of it."

"Good," I said, without meaning it.

"So I do want to thank you."

"No problem."

"Yes, it was. I know you didn't want to give Wally up. I know it's not your style."

"Style's not all it's cracked up to be."

"Or maybe style is all there is."

"God, I hope not," I said.

"Well, I know you did it for me, or for us, and I want you to know I appreciate it."

My hands began to sweat and my brow felt feverish and it didn't have anything to do with Wally Briscoe. I tried to keep things official. "I'm glad you've got something for the grand jury."

"By tomorrow we'll have more. Two-thirds of the investigators in the office are assigned to my case."

"This might make you famous, you know."

She thought about it. "So famous I'll have to resign, I imagine."

"Why?"

"If I bring down as many dirty cops as I think I will, no one in the department will work with me again. In fact, they'll probably try to sabotage every case I bring."

"It won't be that bad, surely."

"It has been in other places."

"What would you do if you resigned? Defense work?"

"I don't know, but I hope not. Nowadays all I think of when I think criminal defense are those pathetic lawyers crawling all over TV talking about O.J. and Monica and JonBenet."

"If not defense work, then what?"

She paused for so long I thought she'd hung up. "That might depend on you," she said softly.

Which put me in the grip of quasi-influenza. "In what way?"

"Whether you wanted to be with me. Whether you wanted to stay in the city or go somewhere else. Whether you wanted to keep being a detective or throw caution to the wind and try something new."

"Wow," I managed.

She laughed. "To put it mildly."

"So where would we go if we went?"

"Someplace warmer. And friendlier. And less crowded."

"What would we do when we got there?"

"Something fun."

"For a living, I mean."

"Something fun," she repeated.

"When would this odyssey take place?"

"After the grand jury returns a true bill, at the earliest."

"And the latest?"

She hesitated. "Never, I suppose."

"Never doesn't sound good."

"No, it doesn't."

I took a breath and held it, then exhaled in a low whistle that mimicked the teakettle I had become. "This has been quite a phone call."

"We've had several of late, as I recall."

"But none quite so portentous."

She laughed. "You're scared to death, aren't you?"

"Not quite," I said, but it must have been a lie because I was sweating like a hog in the stockyards.

When Jill spoke again, her voice might have been a child's. "Can you come over tonight, Marsh? So we can talk some more about this?"

"Probably. What time?"

"Nineish?"

"Fineish."

"It's cold today. I'll make chili."

"Great," I said, even though I'd just had some.

"And corn bread."

"Perfect."

She sighed with contentment, as though she had reached some sort of verdant plateau. "Are you making any progress on the Wells case?" she asked after her rapture began to evaporate.

"No."

"None?"

"None. Have you ever run into an organization called ARFA, by the way?"

"The retired FBI guys."

"That's the one. How do you know about them?"

"They've assisted us in some prosecutions over the years. Mostly drug stuff with multinational implications—they've got a hell of a Rolodex, let me tell you."

"So they're legit?"

"As far as I know. Why? Oh. Chandelier's driver was a former agent."

"Right."

"Well, they're good. If I were you, I'd let them help in any way they can."

"Just like I helped you." When I heard the rasp in my voice, I knew I was in trouble.

"Hey, now, buster. Wait just a damned *minute*. I'm not a tyrant. No one got coerced in this thing. You didn't do anything you didn't do of your own free—"

"You're right," I interrupted. "I'm sorry. I'm still a little worried about Wally."

"Well, don't be. Wally will be fine. And so will we. The only thing you have to do is let us."

"And the only thing we have to fear is fear itself."

"Jesus," she said.

Jill hung up and the phone rang again. "Mr. *Tanner*. I've finally tracked you down."

"I didn't know you were hunting me."

"No. Of course you didn't. I left a message with poor Lark McLaren, but she's so distraught she can't be expected to—"

"Who is this?" I demanded, irritated at the implicit belittlement of Lark McLaren.

"My name is Gert Blackwood," she said in a chirpy voice. "I handle all of Chandelier's publicity."

"You work for Madison House?"

"Chandelier employs me directly. We've worked together ever since I put her fifth book on seventeen bestseller lists."

"I didn't know there *were* seventeen bestseller lists."

"Well, there are. And more besides that. My favorite's the one in Modesto. You wouldn't believe how long Chandelier stays on that one."

"What can I do for you, Ms. Blackwood?"

Her voice became artificially grave, in the manner of a politician on the Fourth of July. "This is a delicate time, Mr. Tanner."

"Especially for Chandelier."

"Indeed. My point is, the wrong kind of publicity could be fatal to her career. Unfounded rumor would be particularly dangerous, especially since we don't know the identity of the actual perpetrator of the crime. We don't, do we?" she added, throwing me a rope of redemption.

"Not as far as I know," I admitted.

"That was my understanding. Which makes it all the more crucial that comment on the case be coordinated by this office."

"I have no idea what that means."

"It means any comment to the news or entertainment media, or to law enforcement authorities, should come from me and no one else."

"I should keep my trap shut, in other words."

"If you put it that way, yes. In the best interests of Ms. Wells, of course."

"I don't make a habit of talking to the media, entertainment or otherwise."

"Good. Very good."

"But whether or not I talk to the cops will be entirely up to me."

Her voice turned from a wren's to a crow's. "But don't you see how that could—"

"Chandelier isn't the only one who has a career to protect, Ms. Blackwood."

"I see."

"I'm glad."

"I'm sure Chandelier will be disappointed when she hears of your attitude, Mr. Tanner."

"My attitude is the very least of her problems, Gert."

The phone made a loud noise when I dropped it into its nest.

chapter 23

wo minutes later, someone pounded on the office door. When I opened it, two familiar faces were glaring at me from beneath the moon of white light in the hallway.

I didn't know their names, but they had paid me a visit a year or so ago, after I'd gotten home from the hospital where Charley Sleet's bullet had put me. They had been there to warn me to keep my mouth shut about whatever I thought I knew about the Triad. Since I hadn't followed orders, I expected more of the same.

"We meet again," I said as they occupied the outer office the way alligators occupy a swamp.

"Tanner," they said simultaneously, as though my name were some sort of password. One of them had a scar across the bridge of his nose as though someone had honed a knife on it. The other had a chipped tooth, as if he'd opened too many bottles of beer with it. The one with the tooth had been at the power house the night I was shot, begging Charley Sleet to spare his life. Since I'd shot Charley before he got around to adding the tooth to his list, I figured the guy owed me a favor, but I was pretty sure he didn't see it that way himself.

I invited them in. I sat behind the desk; the scar took the client chair and the tooth perched like a moving man on the arm of my decrepit couch. I had a smile on my face; they looked sober and businesslike. I thought I knew why they were there, but they proved me wrong.

"I'm Detective Prester," the scarred one said. "This is Detective Storrs."

"Pleased to have names to put with the faces," I said, mostly because cops always expect due deference. "I take it you're here to chat about the Triad some more."

They looked at each other with a passing imitation of perplexity. "We're not on the Chinatown detail, Mr. Tanner," Prester said. "We're here at the request of the Berkeley PD to talk about what happened to a woman named Chandelier Wells. We understand you were on the scene at the time of the incident."

Their demeanor couldn't have been more professional; their approach couldn't have been more cordial; their mission couldn't have been more appropriate. Which meant either they'd had some electroshock since I'd seen them last or they were setting me up for a fall I couldn't foresee at the moment.

"I didn't see the explosion, if that's what you're asking," I said carefully.

"No? Where were you when it happened?"

"Inside Steinway Books. Where Ms. Wells had just given a reading from her new novel. *Shalloon*, it's called. Maybe you've read it."

I might as well have been whistling the Mass in B Minor. "And you were there in what capacity?" the scarred one pressed on.

"Professional."

"And what profession would that be?"

"Personal security."

"Bodyguard, in other words."

I shrugged. "I've been called worse."

"No shit," the tooth mumbled.

"Maybe you can tell us how that job came about," the scarred one was saying, still amiable and still therefore incongruous.

I considered my response. Private detectives don't have privileges to assert on behalf of their clients. At best we can sneak under the tent of an attorney's work product from time to time, but that probably didn't apply in this case, even though Chandelier's attorney had been the one to bring me on board. Eventually they could compel me to talk or go to jail, but that didn't mean I had to blab everything I knew to the first cop who came calling. Of course in the age of Ken Starr and Bob Barr, asserting your civil rights is tantamount to treason, so I began to wonder if I had a spare tooth-brush to take with me in case the cordiality was a pose and they decided to haul me off to the slammer.

I took the middle ground, partly to get rid of them as soon as I could and partly to assert my independence from Gert Blackwood, the publicity woman who had insisted that I make like a hand pup-pet and speak about Chandelier only through her.

When I had finished my recital, the two detectives looked at each other and then at me. "That's it?" Storrs asked.

"That's it."

"You don't know who or why?"

"No idea. But I'm working on it."

The scarred one shook his head. "It's a police matter now, Mr. Tanner. The Berkeley department would like you to step aside."

"I only step aside for kids and old ladies."

"That's not very smart, if you don't mind my saying so," Prester said affably. Far too affably.

"I don't mind, Detective. I've been called stupid lots of times. Almost always by people stupider than I am."

Storrs stood up and made himself a menace. But Prester backed and filled, so Storrs did, too, much to the regret of my poor little couch, which cried out in anguish when Storrs dislocated its arm. "Okay, Tanner. Let's keep this civil. What was the relationship between you and the driver? Filson?"

"None."

"You weren't working for him?"

"No."

"Or he for you?"

"No."

"You're not part of some federal criminal investigation?"

"I'm a cheap-suit PI. Why would the feds even know I exist?"

"The feds use all kinds of people as informants. Even nobodies like you."

I shrugged. "Who the hell would I inform on?"

Prester smiled. "You tell me."

"You're fishing in the wrong bucket, Detective."

Prester didn't seem to take it personally. "How about the woman?"

"Chandelier Wells?"

"Yeah."

"What about her?"

"You claim you were her bodyguard."

"You claimed that—I didn't."

"Is that all you were?"

"If I was that, that was all."

"Jesus," Storrs muttered. "You sound like the captain. And he sounds like a fucking shyster."

"You weren't digging up dirt for the Wells woman?" Prester persisted.

"Why would she need dirt? Is she taking up horticulture?"

Prester kept a lid on it, but only with effort. "Don't be so fucking cute. The kind of dirt I'm talking about she could put in one of her books."

"You mean was I doing research for her?"

"That's what I'm asking."

"Getting background information she could incorporate in a new novel?"

"Yeah."

"Like solving a case the cops couldn't handle? Or uncovering one the cops weren't pursuing?"

Finally, Prester got mad. "Something like that, asshole. Yeah."

"No."

"No what?"

"No, I wasn't doing anything like that. I was guarding her body. Period."

"You could use some lessons," Storrs grumbled heavily, then lapsed back into the role of adjunct.

"The car wasn't my responsibility," I said, as petty as a kid squealing on his brother, then quickly wished I hadn't.

"That's a hit tune with all the fuckups," Storrs said, still taking potshots when he could.

"You know Wally Briscoe, am I right?" Prester asked in all innocence, apparently out of the blue.

"Casually. Yeah."

"He was tight with your buddy Sleet."

"That's right. What about it?"

"Wally sang to the grand jury this morning."

"Yeah?"

"Yeah."

"Sang about what?"

"Some shit he calls the Triad."

"Which you know nothing about."

Prester nodded twice. "Which we know nothing about."

"What's that have to do with me?"

"Just thought you might be interested. They subpoena you yet?"

"The grand jury? No."

"Wonder why not."

"Maybe it's because I've got nothing to tell them."

"Or maybe it's because you told them what you know already."

"Why would I do that?"

Storrs flashed a grin so lubricious it dripped. "So you could keep putting the wood to that lady DA."

I stood up and balled my fists and placed them on the desk, knuckles down. "If you leave right this minute, you won't get punched in the mouth."

Storrs popped to his feet and strutted like an underdog at the weigh-in. "Please. I'm begging you. Take your best shot."

"Last time you begged, it was for Charley Sleet to spare your life. Lucky for you, I stopped him."

"You saying I owe you, shithead?"

"I'm saying get out."

They wanted to go to duke city, the way cops always do when you challenge their primacy, but they eventually thought better of it as I figured they would. Whoever was issuing the new marching orders had told them to tread softly and carry a limp stick, at least when it came to Chandelier Wells.

Without further ado, they shouldered their way out my door like beef cattle set free from a pen. Their fury was occupying so many of their senses they barely noticed the man coming down the hall in the opposite direction. But he noticed them. All of them there was to notice.

He was tall and thin and preppy-looking and he wasn't any more inclined than I had been to defer to the minions of the local law. As a result, there was a brief collision. The SF cops muttered expletives, then glared at the visitor as though he had a dozen wants and warrants, then continued on their way without a word of greeting or apology. I guess law enforcement reflects the society it polices. These days, I don't encounter common courtesy more than once a month.

As Prester and Storrs clomped down the stairs to the street, the tall man stopped at my doorway. "You Tanner?"

"That's me."

He put out a hand. "Lieutenant Hal Bridger. Berkeley PD. Like to talk to you about what went down in our fair city yesterday."

I pointed toward the stairway. "I thought you were having the local boys take care of things on this side of the bay."

He shook his head in puzzlement. "We tend to do our own work when we can. And most of us have learned how to drive over the bridge."

"You don't know those guys are city detectives? Prester and Storrs?"

"Never heard of them."

"You didn't ask the department to send someone down to talk to me?"

Bridger smiled. "The guy who's going to do the talking to you is me."

I led him into the inner office and poured him a cup of black coffee. He didn't waste time getting down to business and I covered my part in the bombing in five minutes. When I'd finished, he stood up and paced the room.

"She's a celebrity," he said, thinking out loud. "I can understand a fan or a stalker or even a competitor like the Dane woman taking some sort of potshot at her. But this was a professional job—Semtex explosive, digital triggering device, multiple charges expertly placed. The only thing that saved her life was that ugly old Lincoln. Those Africans know how to weld steel."

"So you don't think it was an amateur."

"No way."

"How about an independent contractor?"

"A contract?" He shook his head. "Possible, but I doubt it. A jilted lover usually wants to see the damage face-to-face."

"Not always."

He nodded. "Nothing's always in this business. The other thing is, how did they get past Filson? He was an experienced agent."

"I think Filson thought like I did—some nutcase with a bone to pick who was all bark and no bite. Neither of us was sufficiently serious about the job."

I was hoping for a rebuttal, but I didn't get it. "Let's say it was a pro," Bridger went on. "Some sort of terrorist thing. How would the Wells woman get involved in something like that?"

"Book research, maybe," I offered. "She liked to write pretty close to the bone. Maybe she stumbled on to some sort of plot."

"That's quite a reach. I mean, why would a stone-cold terrorist give her the time of day?"

"Fame or fortune."

"Maybe," he said dubiously.

"Revenge?"

"Better."

"Misdirection?"

"Best."

"Filson told me she loved hanging out in low-life places. Maybe she came across something by accident."

"If so, it's going to be hard to trace. Filson didn't keep a log." Bridger paused and grinned. "Of course we seem to have help."

"The senior citizens."

Bridger nodded. "I assume they've been in touch."

"Yep."

"Guy named Cadberry."

"Yep."

"Seems capable."

"Yep."

"But he's a fed."

"So he is."

"Which means we'll never know what he's up to."

"Probably not. But it did occur to me after I talked to him that we might be barking up the wrong tree in this."

"How so?" Bridger asked.

"What if Chandelier wasn't the target? What if Filson was? And what if his pals on the pension patrol know it?"

"Then that would be a brand-new ball game, wouldn't it?" Bridger asked himself. Then he pointed to the painting on the wall. "That real?"

"Yep."

"I'll be a son of a bitch," he said, and stood looking at it for the next five minutes.

chapter 24

Jill Coppelia lived at the dead end of a dead-end street in the Cow Hollow section of the city, a reclusive pond of privilege east of the Presidio and south of the Marina. The house was a granite and slate mini-château, with a small yard in front and a larger garden in back with enough vegetation to give an illusion of space and privacy even though the neighbor's house was less than fifty feet away. Its interior trappings were understated but luxurious, courtesy of the trust income Jill received every month by way of her late father's fortune. She didn't talk about her money, ever, or flaunt her wealth or demand my fealty to it, but Jill was quite a rich woman. It was one of three things that bothered me about her. The second was that she made her living sending people to jail. The third was that she thought I should cut back on the Oreos.

I parked at the curb and rang her bell at nine-ten. She let me in, let me sit, let me sip a cold beer, let me admire her new lounging outfit, and let me kick my shoes off and get comfortable on her blue-and-white silk couch, all without uttering a word more than the minimum. The couch was Italian, the beer was Czech, the outfit was a French version of black stretch pants below a billowy white top with a nicely scooped neck. Like the outfit, the atmosphere in the room was entirely warm and accommodating in terms of style, but tentative in interpersonal terms, as if we were about to debate religious differences or our positions on impeachment.

Even so, without intending to, I found myself grinning because Jill was such a lovely sight. "So how are things at the Hall of Justice?" I began since she seemed to be leaving it up to me to launch the ship.

She curled her feet under her and leaned back on the couch. "Better."

"Than what?"

"Than yesterday."

"That's good."

"It's actually going to happen, I think. I'm going to make a real dent in the venality in the police department, Marsh. I'm going to root out lots of bad apples."

"The barrel could certainly use it."

She waited till she had my attention. "And then I'm going to quit."

"The job?"

"Yes."

"For sure?"

"Absolutely."

"Well, congratulations."

"Thank you."

"Sounds like you got someone besides Wally to talk to the grand jury."

She nodded. "These things are like avalanches. Once they get rolling, everyone wants out of the way."

"So they won't get buried in indictments."

"Right. The trick is to convince as many as you can that the avalanche has already started."

"Which you managed to do."

"With the help of Wally Briscoe. Right. And the way to get out of the way of the crush is to cut a deal."

"With you."

She nodded. "We got eight more statements this afternoon. Good ones. From good cops, mostly, who saw things they didn't feel comfortable seeing and decided to do what they should have done a long time ago. We've got eight indictments for sure, but there'll probably be more than two dozen by the time we're finished."

"That'll make some waves around town. You could probably be the new mayor."

Since politics was the last thing on earth she wanted to be part of, Jill ignored my idiocy. "It's a guy named Hardy, it turns out."

"Who is?"

"The head honcho. Vincent Hardy. Top dog of the Triad. Ever hear of him?"

"Nope."

"Sergeant out of the Potrero. Twenty years on the job. Third-generation cop; second-generation crook."

"Too bad."

"Our hope is that when he goes down, the Triad will go down with him."

"And you'll ride off into the setting sun with a hearty 'Hi-o, Silver.'"

She adjusted her position and took a sip of her wine. "The question is, will my faithful Indian companion be by my side?"

"Meaning me."

"Very perceptive of you, Tonto."

I smiled at the memory of a bad Lone-Ranger-and-Tonto joke having to do with Tonto disguised as a pool table, then drained my beer and asked for another, not because I wanted her to fetch it, but because I wanted time to think. After Jill left the room, I stood up and strolled around, admiring the California-school art and colorful blown glass, trying to decide what to say in response to her question, trying not to see this as the most important moment of my life.

When she returned, I sat back down and did a dance I've done before, though not yet with Jill. "I'm not sure this is the time to get into this, actually."

"By this you mean . . . ?"

"The future."

"Ah. You mean Gore versus Bush; the Giants versus the Dodgers; the Internet versus traditional retailing . . ."

"*Our* future," I amended.

"Ah, squared."

"Things are pretty tense right now. For both of us. You've got the grand jury and I'm in the middle of the Wells case. Which I've screwed up totally so far. On top of that, I gave up Wally Briscoe. I'm not in a good mood about that, either. So maybe we should . . ."

"Wait."

"Yeah."

"And discuss this later."

"Yeah."

"When things have calmed down."

"Right."

"So we can analyze it objectively. Without being swayed by emotion and stress."

"Yeah."

"Bullshit."

"What?"

"*Bullshit*, Marsh. Jesus Christ. I thought you'd been paying better attention."

"To what?"

"To *life*, goddammit. Things *never* calm down, haven't you noticed? Emotions are *always* involved. Or should be. I mean, if you don't have any *emotion* about me, if I don't stir up any *feelings* in you, if you're perfectly *neutral* about whether we spend the rest of our *lives* together, then we don't need to have this discussion *ever*."

"I didn't mean that, Jill."

"Didn't mean what?"

"What you implied. I wasn't talking about us being calm, I was talking about the other stuff easing up a bit."

She shook her head with transparent disgust. "Typical man."

"How?"

She used her hands like Bernstein. "You think there's us over here and the rest of it over there. And you can make changes in one thing without having any effect on the other. Well, what women know from day one is that if you care about someone, which means if you're really in *love*, then it's *all* us. Every bit of it. The intimacy, the professional problems, the cooking dinner, the commute to work, the cleaning the toilet, the politics at the office—all of it is *us*. There's no you and me anymore."

"And that's the way you feel about me?"

"I think so."

"You're not sure?"

"I think I'm sure."

"You think so."

"Hey. I've never done this before, you know. It's not like I can look back to my third marriage and say I feel exactly like I felt back then."

"Okay. Bottom line is, you think you're sure you want to be with me."

"Right."

I smiled. "That's good. Because I think so, too."

"Really?"

"Yes."

"You're sure?"

My laugh sounded as hollow as my head. "I'm not sure certainty is an option at my age."

"Come on, Marsh."

"Okay, Jill. Yes. I'm certain. More certain than I've ever been about anyone in my life." I shook my head in wonder. "First Wally; now this. You're quite a woman, Ms. Coppelia."

"I'll take that as a compliment, but you should know that I expect you to get better at it."

I blushed and said, "I'll try."

"Since we're sort of on the subject, I also want you to know that I'm going to want to get married someday. I'm warning you now. If this thing we have keeps going forward, I'm going to want it the old-fashioned way."

"Fine by me."

"And I'm going to want to discuss kids."

"Our kids."

"Of course."

"I think I'm a little old for—"

"So am I. But the point is, we're not *too* old. Not yet. So we need to discuss it."

"Okay."

"Not now, though."

"Okay."

"Later."

"Okay."

"After you propose to me."

"Oh."

"After you get down on one knee and pop the question."

"Ah."

"And give me a ring."

"Ah, squared."

She laughed. "You look slightly terrified."

I blushed. "I am."

"Why? Because you don't want this to happen?"

I shook my head. "Because I do."

She leaned over to kiss me. When she had finished, I stretched out on the couch and pulled her down on top of me. She put a hand behind my head and pressed her lips on mine and we kissed long and hard, breathing with the sounds of surf, tasting each other the way we tasted ice cream and chocolate.

I slid my hand down her spine and made us increasingly contiguous. After a moment, she raised up far enough to tug her shirt above her breasts, then wriggled forward so I could feast on them without risking injury. I was more than happy to oblige, just as Jill was happy to oblige me. We spent the next ten minutes doing what the other liked, though more avidly and extensively than ever before.

As I was trying to remove some more of her clothing, the telephone rang. After silently cursing the fates, I paused to let Jill decide what she wanted to do. Seconding my emotion, she grunted sourly and shook her head, then started to undo my belt.

After the fourth ring, the answering machine clicked on. "Jill? Mark Belcastro. They found Briscoe twenty minutes ago, sitting in his car out at Ocean Beach. There were two slugs in the back of his head and his tongue was sliced off at the root. Guess the lab boys will tell us whether he was tortured before or after he was shot. Not that it matters, I guess. I kind of liked the guy, you know? I mean, he wasn't a killer, he just wasn't strong enough to say no to the ones who were. Anyway, I thought I'd let you know before you turned on the late news. Hope I didn't ruin your evening."

Although she struggled to get up, I kept Jill where she was and spoke into her ear in a voice I didn't recognize as mine. "I thought he was in witness protection."

"He was. Sort of. We do the best we can, but we don't have the resources the feds do. I'm sorry, Marsh. I thought we had it covered."

"Where's your gun?"

"Why?"

"Just tell me."

"In the closet. Top shelf."

I sat us both up. "Where are you going?" she asked.

"To get the gun."

"But why?"

"I'm spending the night. I want some firepower at my disposal in case they decide not to stop with Wally."

chapter 25

I lay awake all night, first in Jill's bed, then on her couch, then in her easy chair, thinking of Wally Briscoe and my role in his violent death. Try as I might, I couldn't evade the indictment that I had served as Wally's executioner.

A year ago, I'd killed Charley Sleet directly, with my own weapon. But Charley had initiated the drama, Charley had forced my hand, Charley had wanted it to be me who ended his life. Not some crooked cop, not a rapacious disease, but me. His best friend.

But Wally wasn't a friend, Wally Briscoe wasn't even a line in my address book. Wally hadn't asked for what had happened and Wally hadn't deserved it. He was just a weak and frightened man, like millions of similar men, trapped in a world he couldn't govern, a world he couldn't hide from, a world that preyed upon his weakness and used it for its own ends. What I had to live with from this day onward was that a part of that venal and vengeful world was me.

Not for the first time, I had objectified someone because it served my purposes to do so. Because of what was happening in my personal life, I had made Wally a token of my affection, a gift-wrapped charm I had given to the woman I was seeing, a sacrifice on the altar of what I thought was love. My actions, by any measure I knew and observed, were inexcusable. As far as I could remember, it was the worst thing I'd ever done to another human being. I had no idea how to atone for it, though I spent the long dark hours of night trying to find a way.

As subtly as a rumor, dawn finally made an appearance, months after Jill had gone to bed, days after she had fallen asleep, hours after I'd moved to the chair from the couch. To wrestle my mind off my transgressions, I got up, got dressed, got fed, and called Alta Bates Hospital, taking the phone to the kitchen so as not to wake Jill.

Lark McLaren answered in a voice that echoed my dreary mood. I asked her how it was going, knowing it couldn't be going well. "Okay, I suppose," she murmured wearily. "I'll be better when I get some food in me."

"Chandelier still improving?"

"That's what they say. I don't see much sign of it myself. I can hardly bear to look at her. And she can hardly bear to move."

"Doctor knows best."

"Not always, in my experience," she countered grimly.

"Mine, either."

"Have you learned anything?"

"I'm afraid I'm not making much progress. How did it go with the computer?"

She took a breath and blew into the receiver as though it needed cooling. "I got into the system okay, but I can't find any files on a new book—nothing shows up on any of the directories. The old book does, and the research notes she made for it, but not a new one. If she's done anything yet she must be using a secret file with some sort of coded access."

"Would the new book have a title?"

"I'm sure it does—the title's the most important part, at least for Chandelier. Titles set the mood, is what she tells people—it's like naming a baby. The title's the first thing she writes down and she doesn't let anyone change it no matter how goofy it sounds. I mean, *Ship Shape*? The sales reps hated it. They told her Barnes and Noble would put it on the travel shelf and her fans would never find it. But Chandelier wouldn't budge."

"No indication of subject matter either?"

"Not that I could find. It could be anything. She wrote a book set in the hardware business once, because her father had worked for TrueValue."

"Well, keep trying."

"I will."

"Does she only have one computer?"

"No, she has a laptop and a desktop."

"Did you check both?"

Lark sniffed. "The laptop burned up in the fire."

"So all her research might have gone up in smoke?"

"Maybe. But she usually downloaded into the desktop every night when she got home. She put her current thoughts on the laptop—ideas for new books, for promotion, for jacket covers, for scenes and characters she might want to use later on. But she knew better than to keep them there because she had a laptop stolen from her car when she was at a reading in Los Angeles one time. She always put the daily input on the big machine and backed it up on a Zip drive."

"Which you checked."

"Which I checked. Several times."

"I guess we need a geek."

Lark McLaren laughed, which lifted my mood as well. "Anything but that."

"Sorry, but if it's okay, I'm going to send someone to the house to play around with the machine."

"Okay. I'll tell the staff to be on the lookout for a pocket protector."

"In the meantime, take care of yourself."

"You, too, Mr. Tanner."

"Marsh."

"Marsh."

"Well, I'm off to see the rabid fan."

"Randolph Scott."

"That's him."

"You'll be amazed."

"It doesn't take much."

"Well, good luck."

"Thanks."

I started to hang up but Lark wasn't finished. "Mr. Tanner?"

"Yes?"

"I wanted to tell you, I just love Ruthie Spring."

"Me, too."

"Meeting her is the only good thing about this whole mess."

"I'm glad there's something. Speaking of capable women, where can I find Amber Adams?"

"She's staying at the St. Francis. I'm not sure what her schedule is today. I think she goes back to New York tomorrow, though."

"If you talk to her, tell her I'll meet her at five in the hotel bar for a drink. The one that specializes in beer."

"I'll tell her, but I can't guarantee she'll show up. Amber doesn't pay much attention to anyone but Chandelier."

Half an hour later, when Jill came out of the bedroom dressed for work, I handed her the gun. "Take this with you."

"Why?"

"You know why."

She looked at the rumpled couch and the crumpled chair. "You've been thinking."

"Right."

"All night. You're afraid they'll come after me."

"Something like that."

"I'm not the only prosecutor on this case, you know. There's Cassidy. And Schmidt. And sometimes even Sisco. Getting rid of me wouldn't accomplish anything."

"Crooked cops don't tend to be rational. If you're ready, I'll take you to work."

She shook her head. "I'll drive myself. But thanks for the offer."

"I'd rather take you."

"I know you would. But while I'm still on the public payroll, my safety is not your concern."

"Like hell it isn't."

"Officially, I mean."

"Then maybe it's time to get unofficial."

She laughed. "You're cracking, Tanner. Walls are crumbling; rust is blowing away. I'll have you eating out of my hand in no time."

Given the doomfilled thoughts of my night, it was hard to see it as a blessing.

After Jill left for work, I drove out to Henry Street, which was in the Castro District not far from the Davies Medical Center. The house was a confection of white stucco and red tile, with a yard of green icing, two sprinkles of Japanese maples, and a trim of white-washed rocks so uniformly round they could have come from a pastry gun. In spring, the flowers in the beds would be awesome. In summer, the days would be foggy and cold till well after noon.

I knocked on the door and waited. The man who finally opened it was still in his red silk housecoat and black silk slippers. And white silk ascot, blue silk pajamas, and red silk sleeping cap complete with pointed top and ball of white fur. He was round and jolly, with bright blue eyes and short brown hair and puffy pale flesh that seemed ageless and untouched except, perhaps, by a magic face cream he'd ordered from the TV.

He remained as cheerful as Santa as I took a brisk inventory. "Mr. Scott?"

"Yes?"

"My name's Tanner."

I put out a hand and he took it in both of his. "Charmed." He invited me in even before I asked him to. If he was a car bomber, I was a taxidermist.

The man who called himself Randolph Scott led me into a small living room decorated in powder blues and lemon yellows, with woven rag rugs tossed over the linoleum floor, dainty knit shawls tossed over the backs of the furniture, and so many art deco fixtures on the walls and in the ceiling it gave the place the aura of a high-class brothel. Here and there a variety of cut-glass vases held enough outsize silk flowers to stock a florist. It was a sunny home for a sunny person. I figured I'd be in and out in three minutes.

"You aren't a Witness, by any chance, are you?" Randolph asked as I sat on the couch at his invitation.

"Jehovah's Witness?"

He nodded, then took the chair across from me and crossed his legs and cocked his wrist and looked at me with eager expectation. "I have the most delightful discussions when they stop by. God is such a provocative concept, don't you think?"

"I don't know about God, but His missionaries certainly are."

He squinted for an instant, indicating his vanity didn't admit to eyeglasses, then regained his smile. "You don't look like a professional proselytizer, Mr. Tanner."

"Only to abolish the DH, I'm afraid."

He frowned. "I'm sorry, I don't know the reference. Is it some sort of sacrament?"

"Only in baseball. The designated hitter. I was trying to make a joke."

He was unfazed by my nonsense. "What can I do for you, Mr. Tanner? And, yes, I'm legally Randolph Scott of San Francisco, changed from Joey Cox of Stockton when I turned twenty-one."

"Nice to meet you, Mr. Scott. I'm here to talk about you and Chandelier Wells."

Impossibly, his mood became even brighter. "How nice. There's nothing I'd like better." Then, as if he were auditioning for a role as a manic-depressive, Randolph Scott began to cry. "Of course it's unbearable what happened to her. I'm quite undone by it all. If I hadn't been ill, I would have been there myself. Perhaps I could have prevented . . . no. That's silly. I don't suppose you're bringing good news," he added hopefully.

"I'm afraid not totally, but the doctors say she's improving. I understand you're one of her most loyal fans."

"The *most* loyal," he corrected firmly, with the first sign of psychopathy I'd seen.

"That kind of thing is difficult to measure, isn't it? Loyalty. Devotion. Dedication."

"Not if you have devoted your life to *this,*" he said proudly, and stood with a purposeful lunge. "Please follow me," he ordered somberly, and led me down the hall to what I nervously assumed was a bedroom but instead was an elaborate shrine to the divinity of Chandelier Wells.

In the center of the room were three rows of shelves that reached from floor to ceiling and were crammed full of volumes and mundane memorabilia. According to Randolph, the shelves contained all the books Chandelier had ever written, in all editions, in all the languages in which they had been published, plus various objets d'art that related to themes in her stories.

Randolph took my amazement for admiration. "They're signed, too. Every one. I go through the line six times on occasion. Since 1995, she's signed them 'to my #1 fan.' Isn't that special?"

"Very."

When he beckoned, I followed him to the rear of the room. Behind the shelves was a small sitting area complete with chair and table and lamp and rug. Photos of Chandelier covered all of the available wall space, ranging from small snapshots that Randolph had undoubtedly taken himself to glossy publicity photos of Chandelier in a variety of professional poses in the studied formality of Karsh. Audiobooks of Chandelier's work were piled high by the stereo, bound galleys lay scattered around the chair like discarded playing cards, and posters of blown-up book jackets were propped against the wall like the overflow in an art gallery. Most dramatic of all, a life-size cardboard cutout of Chandelier Wells, smiling broadly and extending her hand in greeting while clutching a copy of *Shalloon* to her chest, was welcoming a pagan into the fold.

"This is quite a memorial," I said with titanic understatement.

"They're all Chandelier's things, you know," Randolph announced proudly as he gazed at his cozy lair. "Even the chair is one she threw out back in '94."

"How did you manage to get hold of it?"

"I go by her house every day, the street in front and the back alley. You'd be surprised what I find tossed away for the trash. I've got a storage unit *full* of her things. I rotate them in and out of the house, to keep the memories fresh."

I was intrigued in spite of myself. "Do you go through her garbage?"

Somehow I'd insulted him. "I would *never* do that. It would be an intolerable invasion of privacy. I only take what they leave out in the open."

"But you go by her house every day."

"When she's in town I do. Unless I'm sick. And sometimes even then."

"Why do you do it?"

His look suggested I belabored the obvious. "To see her, of course."

"You see her every day?"

"Oh, no. I don't see her for months on end. She travels a lot. On vacation or on promotional junkets. I'd love to follow along, but I can't afford it."

"Does she know you do this?"

"Oh, yes. She knows I'm there. She knows if she needs me for anything, I'll be there at noon sharp every day."

I guess I didn't believe him. "You're at her house every day at noon?" I said dumbly.

"I get there by ten, usually. She never goes out before ten. Not since she made it big."

"When was that?"

The answer was automatic. "*False Hope.* Nineteen eighty-nine. Six hundred and ten thousand copies printed; four hundred and eighty-three thousand copies sold. In hardcover."

"What about paperback?"

His smile was as smug as if he'd written the book himself. "One million six. She's over three million now, of course."

"The paperbacks cost, what? Five bucks?"

"Back then, yes. They're six now."

"And she gets what?"

"Five percent."

"That's not much, is it?"

His jaw thrust out like a spatula toward quiche. "I'll say it's not. She's getting screwed, big time. I don't know why Amber doesn't make Madison House take the softcover rights to auction."

"Still, five percent of six dollars is thirty cents, times three million is nine hundred grand. That'll buy a lot of pens and pencils."

He shook his head." It's not the *money*," he said, repeating the axiom I'd first heard from Lark. "Everyone thinks it's about money, but it's not."

"Then what is it?"

"The status. The legacy. The comparison with other writers. Barbara Winston gets a full fifteen percent royalty on *her* hard/soft deal with HarperCollins and she's not *half* the writer Chandelier is. And she gets a bigger advance as well. Of course she doesn't earn out—Chandelier is the only writer of romantic suspense who actually *earns back* her advance. But you don't hear about that, do you? All you hear about is the precious *millions* that hacks like Barbara Winston receive from the idiots who publish her. Ms. Wells lets too many people take *advantage* of her, is the *problem*. Amber should put a stop to it, but for some reason she doesn't."

"You know Amber?"

"Not really. Just what I read in the trades. *Publishers Weekly*, mostly," he added when he saw my look.

"I'm surprised Chandelier's getting ripped off. I heard she was as hard as nails."

His voice softened as if he were talking about an infant. "Oh, she tries to be. And she seems that way sometimes. But deep down she's a pussycat. Would you believe she gives me a trinket whenever she sees me?" He pointed. "See that shelf? I call them my treasures. They're things Chandelier gave me herself. Her very own possessions that she said I can keep." In the umbra of his rapture, I examined the shelf myself.

If I hadn't known they were treasures, I would have assumed they were junk. There were lipsticks and compacts and brooches and bracelets. And key chains and coffee cups and writing pens and bookmarks. And on and on, arrayed on trays of black velvet like ancient artifacts, all junk Chandelier Wells clearly had no use for, all nostrums that made life worth living for the former Joey Cox.

"Would you like to see the outfits?" he asked quietly.

"What outfits?"

"The ones I wear to the signings. They're exact in every particular. I have at least one ensemble for every one of her books."

"I'll have to pass on the outfits," I said. "Let's talk about what happened to Chandelier two days ago."

"Do we have to?"

"Just for a minute."

His eyes filled with tears for a second time. He pulled a silk hankie from his sleeve to dab at them. "It's so tragic. I've been to the hospital three times. I bribed a nurse to give me updates every two hours." He paused. "They say she's going to be fine. She is, isn't she?"

"I think so, over time. Do you have any idea who might have done something like that to her?"

His expression turned stern and judgmental, reminiscent of my ninth-grade music teacher. "I have many ideas. But no proof."

"Give me some examples."

"Her ex-husband is a brute. And Viveca Dane is a jealous harridan. And Lisette Malcolm, well, don't get me started on Lisette."

"Who's she?"

"The former editor of the newsletter, among other things. Before I took over and made it intelligible."

"Lisette didn't take it well?"

"She was livid. She threatened to burn down my house. Lord knows what she tried to do to Chandelier."

"Chandelier fired her?"

"She had Lark McLaren do it. But of course Chandelier made the decision."

"Where's Lisette hang out?"

"In Hayward. She's a librarian. And a very spiteful person."

"I'll have a talk with her." Though only as a last resort.

"If you do, tell her I'm not going to print her silly little piece on food metaphors. I didn't find it to be at all worthy of publication in the *Chandelier Chronicles.*"

I told Randolph I'd try to remember to pass along the rejection. "Tell me this, Mr. Scott. When you're at Chandelier's and she goes out somewhere, what do you do?"

He blushed. "I follow her."

"Always?"

"Always."

"Why?"

"To be near her. To be ready if she needs me."

"Needs you for what?"

His shrug was heedless of burden. "Whatever."

I gave in to my urge. "Why is she so important to you?"

"Do you really want to know?"

"Yes. I do."

He looked momentarily stricken, then straightened with pride and purpose. "In today's vernacular, I have no life. But when I'm reading Chandelier's books, I have the most wonderful existence imaginable."

"How so?"

"For one thing, I'm Maggie Katz's best friend. Her confidant. Her soul mate. We go many places and see many things and she tells me her innermost thoughts every step of the way. And every time we go on an adventure, we make the world a better place." He lifted his gaze to the bookshelves. "On my own, I do nothing. But with Chandelier, I move mountains. And for that, I owe her my life."

"What if she stopped giving you presents? What if she asked you not to follow her around anymore?"

Randolph shrugged in Zen-like unconcern. "It wouldn't matter. Whatever she wants is what I want. That sounds pathetic, I know. But it's truly what I feel. Before Chandelier, I was nothing. I hated myself. I wanted to die because I felt so useless and so foreign. But now I have a purpose. And my purpose is Chandelier Wells."

I waited for his thoughts to return from the world of yearning and romance. It was a world I had once known well, though not for forty years. "Were you following her last week, Mr. Scott?"

"Yes, I was."

"Her driver told me she was making the rounds of some pretty rough places."

He shuddered, then nodded. "She went into neighborhoods that looked like war zones. I was horrified."

"Where were they?"

"Mostly South of Market. I know they claim it's coming back, but really."

"SOMA, you mean?"

"Farther south than that. The Potrero, mostly. Out past China Basin."

I perked up. "Where did she go in the Potrero?"

"Two places. One she was in for just a few minutes. The other she was in for more than two hours."

"What kind of place was it?"

"A bar. Saloon. Tavern. Whatever noun is most disreputable."

"Do you remember the name of this joint?"

"The Porthole, I think it was called. A horrid little place on Illinois Street. Out by the bay."

chapter 26

Illinois Street out by the bay was where I'd been shot, and where I'd shot Charley Sleet, and where the Triad had set up head-quarters in an abandoned power house not far from the Potrero police station. Suddenly Chandelier Wells and her apparent quest for a new milieu for a saga of romantic suspense had come uncomfortably close to Jill Coppelia's effort to clean up police corruption in the city. The same professionals who had killed Wally Briscoe could have set and triggered the bombs beneath Chandelier's car. The possibility sent me racing back to the office bathed in the sweaty stink of foolishness and frustration. I had the phone in my hand before I sat down at the desk.

Lark McLaren didn't ask many questions when I suggested that Violet Wells be kept home from school that day, and that if at all possible she and her nanny should be whisked off to some secluded hideaway for a while. What Lark had seen and done in the past forty-eight hours must have made anything at all seem possible, even conspiracies that victimized little children.

"I haven't had time to find a geek," I said when I'd finished making arrangements for Violet's safety. "You'll have to do it yourself."

"Do what, exactly?"

"Look for a file under the name or password of Hardy. Vincent Hardy. Also the name Triad. Also Wally or Briscoe. Also any synonym for cops or corruption."

"You sound like you've learned something."

"I don't know if I have or not. But if any of those files show up on Chandelier's computer, it will be the first real lead I've turned up."

"Okay. I'll run through the files again and let you know what I find out."

"Also, if any city cops come around the hospital and ask to see Chandelier, don't let them. Have the doctors keep them out, then have Ruthie Spring call the Berkeley police and tell them a witness to the bombing is in danger. If they won't come, call the FBI. Use the name Hugh Cadberry, he's a former agent. Also call the San Francisco DA's office. Ask to speak to Jill Coppelia. Tell her you need a protective order for Ms. Wells against an outfit called the Triad. She'll know what you're talking about."

Lark's voice was thin and incredulous. "You're scaring me, Mr. Tanner. Who is this Triad you keep mentioning?"

"I'll tell you later."

"But what's going on? What do the police have to do with it?"

"I think Chandelier's next book was about police corruption in the city. I think she came across some information that made her a danger to some crooked cops. She may have been attacked to keep her quiet."

"By *police?*"

"Maybe. Right now, the thing to do is make sure Violet and her mother stay safe."

Lark paused to absorb the implications. When she spoke, her voice was tiny and removed, reluctant to ask the question. "Mr. Tanner?"

"What?"

"If it's really the police, how do we stop them?"

"I wish I knew," I said, and hung up after I told her not to worry. I didn't expect her to follow my advice, since I didn't expect to follow it myself.

The more difficult call was to Millicent Colbert. A threshold question was whether the call should be made at all. As far as I knew, only Eleanor's surrogate mother knew I was her biological father. That was the way I'd decided to play it after I'd learned what had happened with the embryo, and that was the way I wanted to keep it for the good of all concerned except me. A cautionary call to

Millicent might frighten the Colberts for no good reason, which might in turn jeopardize the comforting genealogical myth that had been accepted as fact for the past five years.

On the other hand, I visit Eleanor a lot. And take her to the zoo and the planetarium and for walks in parks and on beaches. Anyone interested in learning what things I hold dear in this world would easily discover that Eleanor was on the top of that list, whatever the precise parameters of our relationship. The consequence of such information falling into the hands of people as ready to do violence as the Triad was unthinkable. Which is why I picked up the phone thirty seconds after I put it down.

The Colberts have a cook and a maid, and I spoke to the latter first, a young Latina named Victoria, who told me about Eleanor's latest exhibition of precocious behavior before she put me through to Eleanor's mother. When Millicent came on the line, there were giggling noises in the background, gleeful eruptions from the delightful little girl whom my brush with the Triad might have put in jeopardy.

When I told Millicent who it was, she bubbled the way she always did when we talked. "I was just *thinking* about you. Eleanor has been very emphatic that she wants to see Mr. Mush."

"Mr. Mush misses her, too," I said, feeling not nearly as stupid as I sounded.

"Why don't you come to dinner tomorrow night? Stuart is in New York at some spring showings."

When Stuart's out of town is when I get invited to dinner. Millicent knew I didn't like him much and vice versa. "I'd like to," I said truthfully, "but I can't."

She paused. "What's wrong, Marsh? You sound worried about something."

"I am."

"About what?"

"Eleanor. And you."

"Why are you worried about us, for heaven's sake? We're fine. We're—"

"Just listen to me for a minute," I snapped, more brusque than I'd ever been with her. "This has to do with my work. I'm involved in a case where some nasty things have been happening."

Her voice sobered. "The car bomb. I know. It's horrible. I'm going to the hospital later today to try to see Chandelier."

"There's more to it than Chandelier, I'm afraid. The nastiness I'm talking about includes murder."

"Murder? Of whom? Chandelier's driver, you mean?"

"Plus a policeman named Briscoe. His body was found out at Ocean Beach last night."

"But what does that have to do with Chandelier? Or with us?"

"I'm not sure. But for Eleanor's sake, I can't take any chances."

Her voice became shrill and insistent. "Are you all right, Marsh? You sound like you're in pain. You didn't get shot again, did you?"

"I'm fine," I insisted, despite my emotional state to the contrary. "And I'm glad you and Eleanor are, too. I want to be sure you stay that way."

"Why wouldn't we?"

"Some pretty bad people may be after me and some of them may be cops. They may want to get leverage on me so I won't tell the grand jury what I know about their off-duty activities."

"But what does that have to do with *Eleanor* or me?" she asked again, as if her cocoon of safety were impregnable and any penetration of it unthinkable.

"The bad guys may know how much I care for you both. If they try to stop me from doing what I'm doing, they might hurt one of you. Or threaten to. So I'll keep my mouth shut."

Her voice was electric with worry. "You're serious, aren't you, Marsh?"

"I'm afraid so."

"Eleanor's life may be in danger."

"Possibly."

"What do you think we should do?"

I broached the plan I'd hatched on the way back to the office. "Doesn't your sister live in Ohio somewhere?"

"Shaker Heights. Yes."

"Take Eleanor back there for a week. Be spontaneous. No big deal; just some sisterly bonding. But do it now."

"You mean today?"

"Yes."

"I don't know if I can—"

"*Today,* Millicent. I'll have a travel agent book a flight for late afternoon. As soon as you're ready to go, call me on my cell phone. I'll send an operative to pick you up and take you to the airport."

"Why don't I just take a cab? I—"

"The operative will make sure you're not being followed."

"Surely it's not—"

"I can't take that chance," I interrupted. "And neither can you."

"I can't . . . I've never . . . I still don't understand why we're *involved* in all this."

"I don't know that you are. I just know that if anything happened to Eleanor, I don't think I could stand it. Especially if it was my fault."

"I couldn't either."

"Then pack your bags for Cleveland."

She hesitated. "Marsh?"

"What?"

"If this sort of thing is happening now, it's possible it'll happen again, isn't it? I mean, given what you do? I guess what I'm asking is, will Eleanor ever really be safe as long as you make your living exposing killers and bombers and criminals?"

I tried to find an answer that would reassure us both, but I didn't come close.

As I was about to leave the office, the phone rang. "Tanner? This is Hugh Cadberry."

"The ex-agent."

"That's affirmative."

"What can I do for you, Hugh?"

"I wanted to give you a heads up that we've satisfied ourselves that the incident in Berkeley had nothing to do with Jed Filson."

"That will come as a surprise to his family, given the fact that the incident killed him."

"What I mean is, Mr. Filson was not the target of the explosive device."

"You're sure about that?"

"To a reasonable degree of certainty."

"That means you know who did it."

"Not necessarily."

"Oh, I think definitely necessarily."

"You're entitled to your opinion, of course."

I laughed. "You retired guys are so radical. Well, here's a heads up for you Hugh. They're going to fall."

"Who?"

"The dirty cops. And if any feebs have anything to do with them, they're going to fall, too."

"I don't think there's anything to worry about on that score, Mr. Tanner. A federal agent would hardly be stupid enough to be involved with an organization like the Triad."

"Who said anything about the Triad?"

"You did."

"No, I didn't. Which raises another point."

"What's that?"

"If the Bureau has someone under cover in there, they'd better get him out."

chapter 27

The bar in the St. Francis Hotel opened off Powell Street onto Union Square, which meant at any hour of the day or night it was filled with foot-weary tourists quenching their thirst with suds before heading back to Neiman's or Macy's or Nordstrom's, or riding off to Fisherman's Wharf via the ever-popular cable cars. I found a table in the corner, ordered a Grolsch from the matchlessly blasé waiter, and waited to see if Amber Adams would show up. I was virtually certain she had nothing to do with the attack on Chandelier Wells, but it was too early to head for the Porthole, so I might as well hear what she had to say.

I was on my second bottle before she showed. She was irritated before she sat down and even more so when she absorbed the kind of joint she was in. "I haven't drunk beer since I was a freshman at Skidmore," she muttered as she regarded the encyclopedic listing of brews on the wall behind the bar. Her mood was a match to her outfit, which was a clone of the one she'd worn every other time I'd seen her.

"I imagine they could come up with something more potent if you want it," I said, not caring much if they could or not.

"Let's try a Boodles martini. Very dry. Very large."

I passed her preference along to the waiter, who had doubts they could come up with the Boodles. Amber allowed as how Tanqueray would suffice. Then she crossed her arms and waited for me to justify the affront to her tippling. "Well? Why am I here?"

"To talk about Chandelier."

"I talk about Chandelier all day every day and it usually produces a profit. The question is, why should I talk to you?"

"Because someone committed a serious crime against her person, and a serious crime usually comes packaged with a serious motive."

"So?"

"I hear you have one."

She tried a blithe simper but didn't quite pull it off. "One what?"

"Motive."

Given the time to mold it, her expression became gloriously disdainful. "Now what on earth would make me want to do bodily harm to my dear friend and client?"

"I understand she was about to change agents."

Amber blinked, then blanched, then colored, then vamped to hide her surprise. "What idiot told you that?"

"I'm not at liberty to say."

"Well, I'm at liberty to say it's bullshit. I made Chandelier what she is today. She knows it and I know it and neither of us has a problem with the status quo."

"That's not the way I heard it."

She swelled with righteousness. "She told me her new book would be the biggest yet. Why would she tell me that if she was going to fire me?"

"I don't know. Maybe she wanted to sharpen the knife before she stuck it in your back."

I'd intended to provoke and I did. "I've put Chandelier's books in twenty-two languages in twenty-six countries," Amber bellowed. "I got her the biggest advance Madison House ever paid, to man, woman, or child. I got a sixty-forty split on foreign reprints and seventy-thirty on all book club money. She's had a movie of the week and there are two miniseries in preproduction. She was the first female suspense writer to have *merchandise*, for Christ's sake. There were Maggie Katz sweatshirts and book bags in 1991."

I smiled. "But what have you done for her lately?"

"What do you mean?"

"I hear she's upset about her royalty rate."

"I'm surprised you even know what a royalty is."

"I'm not sure I do, but I think it means money, and in my business, money makes motive."

Her look became autocratic. "Chandelier gets a straight fifteen percent for each hardcover sold, and that's from book one. That's a better deal than ninety-nine percent of the industry has."

"How about paperback?"

"Hard/soft with Madison House. We've got to keep them in business, after all."

"Why?"

"Because they do a good job. And they were there for us in the beginning."

"So you're loyal."

"Damned right I am. Which makes me a princess in this business, let me tell you."

"Is Madison House publicly held?"

She hesitated. "Not yet."

"But about to be?"

"So I hear."

"Do you own stock?"

"I . . ."

"I can find out if I dig hard enough."

She shrugged. "I have a few shares from the private placement. Why?"

I smiled. "Just seeing how much loyalty is going for these days."

She leaned forward so abruptly I thought she was going to spit in my face. "You don't know what you're talking about, Mr. Private Eyesore. Just before I came out here, I met with my tax accountant. Do you know how much I earned last year? Huh? Just from my little one-woman agency?"

"How much?"

"Five hundred and forty-two thousand dollars. Plus another fifty in investment income, not including my retirement accounts."

"Very impressive. Until you realize that's only ten percent of what Chandelier earns. Am I right?"

She swore. "I'll bet I gave more to charity last year than you've earned in the last decade."

"No takers."

"The point is, I'm set for life. Financially. Psychologically. Philosophically. Which means money doesn't matter anymore."

"Actually, everyone in this case keeps telling me it's not *about* money."

"Then what *is* it about?"

"Status. Esteem. Self-respect. All that touchy-feely stuff. Which, as far as I can tell, sounds a lot like the testosterone struts that men are always accused of."

Her lip curled dismissively. "Ha. That may be true for the rest of them, which I doubt, by the way. But for me it was *always* about money."

"Until now, you mean."

She blushed at being trapped in a contradiction. "Until now. Right."

"So losing your only client wouldn't bother you."

She clasped her hands and glared at me above two rows of white knuckles. "Do you know how many manuscripts I get in the mail every day? From writers who would cut off their left tit if I'd agree to represent them?"

"How many?"

"Twenty. On a slow day. And they're not all from Iowa housewives, either. Not that some of our biggest sellers didn't start out as housewives," she added, just in case a housewife was in earshot.

"So Chandelier is immaterial to you."

"I didn't say that."

"So it *would* bother you if she fired you."

"Of course it would. But not enough to blow her to smithereens. I'm not Sicilian, for God's sake."

I shrugged. "Okay."

"Okay what?"

"Okay, I believe you."

"As simple as that?"

"Yep."

"Why?"

"Because I think I know who did it."

"Who?"

"I'll let you knew when I can prove it. Hell, maybe I'll even write a book about it."

She chuckled. "You've probably got a few good stories in you at that. True crime can be huge, you know. You could be another Ann Rule."

"I'm afraid there's a bit of a problem."

"What's that?"

"The last story I told got a guy killed."

"Sounds like a seven-figure advance, plus another mil for the film rights."

chapter *28*

W hat'll it be?" the big man asked.
"Beer."
"Tap or bottle?"
"Bottle."
"Bud or Miller?"
"Miller."
"Coming up."

The bartender went down-bar to do his thing and I looked around the Porthole. It was near to 9 P.M. The bar was almost full. The decor was boat stuff and sports gear. The clientele was exclusively male, predominantly middle-aged, and excessively boisterous in a manner that suggested competition and compensation. If there was a customer in the place who wasn't an off-duty policeman, I couldn't pick him out of the crowd.

The Porthole was a cop bar, the watering hole for the Portrero station a block up Twentieth on Third Street. The only question left was whether it was also the designated drinking establishment of the cops who called themselves the Triad. I figured I could find that out in about five minutes.

I downed my beer quickly, then waited for the bartender to notice I was dry. When he drifted my way, I asked for another. When he brought it, I gave him a new fifty. He looked at it front and back and laughed. "Ugliest damned thing I ever saw."

"I couldn't agree with you more," I said truthfully.

"I seen shit paper classier than that."

"Looks like something some tin-pot dictator printed up in the hope someone would take him seriously."

"Hell, the MPC the fucking army put out in fucking Nam was

better looking than that piece of shit and the army fucks up everything."

I had an opening so I entered it. "You pull a tour yourself?"

His look took on a wary focus. "Two."

"What unit?"

"American."

"DMZ."

"Close enough. You?"

"Ninth Division."

"Delta."

I nodded. "My feet aren't dry yet. What MOS?"

"Eleven Bravo and proud of it. You?"

"Military police."

"Yeah?"

"Yeah."

"Long time ago now."

"Yeah."

"Thirty years."

"The nightmares aren't that old, though."

He shook his head. "The nightmares are always brand new."

The bartender rubbed the bar though it didn't need rubbing. I'd taken him to places he tried to stay away from and he was lost in a time it still hurt to remember.

"The all-time shitty war," I grumbled absently.

"Not if the civilians had turned us loose."

"You figure Charley would have quit eventually?"

"We bomb the dikes in Hanoi, he'd *chu hoi* in a New York minute."

I shrugged. "Maybe; maybe not. We dumped more tonnage on the North than we did on the Krauts in the big number two. I never saw much quit in the little bastards myself."

The bartender's smile turned sadistic. "Everyone's got quit in them. You just got to push the right button."

He went down-bar to do business, then drifted my way a few minutes later and tossed my change down in front of me. "You on the job in the city?" he asked.

I shook my head. "Private agency."

"Yeah? How does that work out?"

"I'm not getting rich. On the other hand, I don't have a shift captain or a time card. Or even a Fourth Amendment."

He laughed. "I hear you. Loud and clear."

"You own this place?"

He shook his head. "Bunch of cops got together and bought it a few years back."

"I'd peg everyone in here for blue."

"You'd be ninety percent right."

"You ever on the job yourself?"

He shook his head. "Brought part of an RPG round back to the world in my thigh—couldn't pass the physical. Been pouring booze for twenty-five years. Once I quit indulging myself, I got pretty good at it."

I nodded peaceably. It wasn't the time or the place to debate war or alcoholism, though some might argue that they had similar roots in the psyche.

I decided to pursue what I came for. "Know a detective named Prester? Scar on his nose about here?"

"Sure. I know Curtis."

"He come in on a regular basis?"

"All the Portrero bulls do. Why? You got business with him?"

"Maybe. How about a guy named Hardy?"

The bartender froze as if I'd said a prayer to Ho Chi Minh. "Who?"

"Hardy," I repeated. "Vincent Hardy. Patrol sergeant up the hill."

His face was as bland as meringue. "Don't think I know the man."

"Really? He's been out here a long time."

The bartender shrugged. "Maybe he had a problem with rum and got religion. What do you want with him?"

"A trade."

"Trade of what?"

"Information."

"For what?"

"Some equity in the enterprise."

His frown was puzzled but provoked. "Information about what?"

"Certain prosecutorial activities down in the Hall of Justice."

His puzzlement became confusion. "*What* kind of activities?"

"Prosecutorial. As in grand jury."

"And what would you want in return for this so-called information?"

"Equity. Like I said."

The response disgusted him. "Shit, I don't know what that means."

"Let's just say I want to join the club."

"What club would that be?"

"You know. The one that used to meet in the brick building down the street."

His expression claimed his ignorance was all-pervasive. "Don't know nothing about it."

"If you say so."

"I say so."

Since that tack had taken me nowhere, I motioned for him to bring me another beer. While he was gone, he stopped to talk in whispers to a guy at the end of the bar, a gruff and grizzled character I'd never seen before. The guy down the bar looked me over, then said something to the bartender, who nodded his understanding, then brought me my third beer.

"That club you mentioned," he said as he picked up two bucks from my change.

"What about it?"

"I think it's private."

"How private?"

"Blue only."

"Sounds like discrimination. Which would be a violation of my civil rights."

"Tell it to a lawyer, pal."

I was as persistent as a poodle. "Maybe it would be in their best interest to diversify."

"Why would they want to do that?"

"Maybe that's the only way to stay in business, given the people who want to shut them down. Plus, I think I could be helpful in furthering the ends of the organization."

"What ends would that be?"

"Making money."

The bartender squinted at me. "What's the name?"

"Tanner."

"And you're a PI."

"Right."

He gestured left. "Guy down the bar thinks you're the one who shot a cop named Sleet."

"The guy down the bar is right." I raised my glass and saluted him.

The bartender regarded me with calculation. "Sleet wasn't real popular down this way."

"No? Why was that?"

"Kept sticking his nose in other people's business."

"Well, he was a good cop."

"Says who?"

"Says me."

"He was also a rat fink."

"Yeah?"

"Yeah."

I leaned forward so he would catch every word. "The rat fink would have sent Detective Storrs to the squad room in the sky if I hadn't put a stop to it."

"So I hear. So what?"

"I figure that earns me a favor."

"Which would be?"

"A face-to-face with Vincent Hardy to discuss my membership application."

He thought about it. "What happens if the favor don't happen?"

"I discuss the club with someone else."

"Who?"

I shrugged. "The grand jury would be one possibility."

"So you know about that."

"I know enough about that to have an interesting chat with Mr. Hardy."

"Maybe you could chat with Prester instead."

I shook my head. "I tried that before. It wasn't productive."

He nodded his understanding, as though talks with Prester were always that way. "Where can I reach you?" he asked, so I told him.

chapter 29

The call came just before midnight, waking me up about two hours after I'd convinced Jill Coppelia to spend the night with her best friend in the office so she'd be hard to find in case the Triad wasn't through with its housecleaning.

"You Tanner?" a raspy voice asked.

"When I'm awake."

"You the guy that wants a meet with Hardy?"

"It's been a lifelong dream."

"I heard you were a smart mouth."

"And I heard you weren't."

"Fuck you. Be at the impound yard in an hour. Know how to get there?"

"I got my finger broken down there one night."

"Yeah? What happened? She cross her legs?"

"A cop named Mandarich thought it would teach me a lesson."

"Did it?"

"Not the one he thought it would."

The voice laughed. "Mandy. What a putz. Sleet took him out, was the way I heard it."

"Me, too."

"Execution style. While Mandy was down on his knees, begging Sleet not to shoot."

"That's the way it was."

"Couldn't happen to a nicer guy."

"My feelings exactly."

His chuckle was a chilling obituary. "Sleet was one of a kind."

"Yes, he was."

"Tough as a stump."

"Tougher."

"You're the guy took him out, am I right?"

"That's right."

His laugh sounded like advancing thunder. "You and Vince will have a nice conversation."

"I look forward to it. But I've got a problem. My car's on the fritz. I'll have to borrow something somewhere. I can't make it to the impound before two."

He paused long enough to consult a clock. "One-thirty or he's gone."

"It's a date," I said, and hung up. Despite the dangers involved, I regarded it as a good sign that the Triad felt enough under pressure to take prophylactic measures.

I dialed the friend's number and had her wake Jill. By the time she came on the line, there were two women mad at me before I'd spoken a word.

"Marsh? What's the matter? What time is it?"

"Midnight."

She coughed and sniffed and cleared her throat. "Is anything wrong?"

"I hope quite the opposite."

She hesitated long enough to make a reasonable assumption. "What's the matter? Is little Marshie lonesome?"

"Little Marshie is lonesome and Little Marshie is horny, but that's not why Little Marshie woke you up. I'm going to meet with Vince Hardy in an hour."

Her breath sizzled like steak. "Where?"

"The impound yard."

"Where's that?"

I told her.

"What's the meeting about?"

"First I'm going to sell you out; then I'm going to make him want to kill me."

My statement of mission jolted her fully awake. "Sell me out? What are you talking about? And why will he want to kill you?"

I ignored her questions and asked a few of my own. "Have you got any cops you can trust absolutely?"

"Some."

"How many?"

"Belcastro says he has a dozen or so for sure."

"Get on the horn. Tell him to round them up. And make sure none are from the Potrero station."

"At this hour? Why? And why not Potrero?"

I ignored her again. "How well do you get along with the Coast Guard?"

She paused. "Tell me you're not on a sinking ship."

"Only metaphorically."

After I told her what I had in mind, I got dressed and oiled my gun. I was pretty sure I wouldn't have to use it, but if I didn't have it with me, someone might wonder why not. At one-fifteen I got in the car and took Montgomery to Market, then Fourth across the bridge, then drove south down Third Street and took a left on Twentieth, knowing they were playing me for a patsy, hoping I wasn't being a fool, and that if I was, no one but me would have to pay the price.

The impound yard could serve as a diorama of the dark side of the moon or the slums of East Oakland or any other godforsaken place that needed illustration in miniature. Basically, it was a hive of seized or abandoned vehicles, most of them dented and rusted and rotting, beyond utility to anyone but a scavenger or a junk-yard dog. But since some of them were evidence and might have to be retrieved at some point, at least theoretically, little plastic triangles had been placed with the delicacy of a nosegay on top of each roof. Each triangle was stamped with a number that matched with a printout in some office at the Hall of Justice, so a given vehicle could be tracked down when and if the occasion arose in the form of a defendant's discovery motion or an ADA's last-minute trial preparation.

When I'd first run afoul of the Triad, this was where they'd taken me to persuade me to tell them the whereabouts of their nemesis, Charley Sleet. Since at the time I didn't know where

Charley was—he'd just broken out of jail and was on the run from the entire police force—it had been easy to maintain my integrity. But they'd broken my finger anyway, just to make sure I knew they were tough. I'd known it already, but some people are given to histrionics.

The Triad hadn't found Charley, Charley had found the Triad. And executed two of its leaders, though not, apparently, the very top dog, since he'd had the luck or the foresight not to be present that evening. Then Charley had shot me trying to make me shoot him. As I cruised past the vacant lot where the tragic farce had gone down, I paid silent homage to my departed friend.

As I hoped, they were waiting when I got there. In fact, I was pretty sure they'd had a tail on me since I'd left my apartment, and I was also pretty sure they had a lookout ready to sound a warning if I'd brought along some form of cavalry to back me up or bail me out. I parked beneath a streetlight that was pathetically inadequate to the gloom of the night, then got out of the car and waited for them.

The wind banged metal against metal somewhere in the shipyard at my back. The smells that aggravated my nostrils were of seaweed and dead fish. The cop in mufti who got out of a plain brown Lumina and lumbered toward me like an upright walrus didn't improve the atmosphere.

"Tanner?"

"Present and accounted for."

"You packing?"

"Of course."

"Where?"

"Back of the belt."

He frisked and disarmed me, then ejected the ammunition clip and put it and the pistol on top of the Buick. "Hardy wants to know why you're here."

"Hardy will have to ask me himself."

"It don't work that way, pal."

"It does now."

He shrugged. "You're the one wanted the meet," he grumbled,

and turned back toward his ride. I felt as if I were bargaining for a used car and being bluffed above my budget.

Two could play the game of chicken, of course, so I opened the door to the Buick and bid the doorman good-bye. "Wait," the cop said as I was about to get back in the car. "I'll go see if he'll see you."

I leaned against the fender and waited. The cop went down the road to a new blue Chrysler that was parked in the shadows of a hulking storage tank at the far end of the lot. A moment later he trudged back. "Vince'll meet." He pointed. "At the car."

I followed him back to the Chrysler. As we approached, a door opened and a man got out. He was large and muscular, filling his black turtleneck and canvas cargo pants with muscle and swagger. He wore a shoulder holster on his flank and a black SFPD baseball cap on his head. His eyes were lazy and lidded, but I doubted they missed much of interest. His mouth was toothy and genuinely amused, the way sharks sometimes look, as though he were in his element and I were an unwitting new snack.

Hardy put me in mind of someone, and suddenly I realized it was Charley. Except if what I'd heard about Vincent Hardy was true, he was the anti-Sleet, the antithesis of everything Charley believed, Darth Vader to Charley's Luke. It would be a pleasure to put him out of business. It might also be a bloody mess.

Hardy inspected me the way he would a new weapon. "You're Tanner."

"Right."

"Sleet's buddy."

"Yep."

"You think you got something I need."

"Yep."

He looked beyond me toward the hulk of the decrepit shipyard blotting out the sky at my back. "You didn't do anything stupid like bring backup, I hope."

"Nope."

"Why not?"

"Like you said. That would be stupid."

He considered the quip, then nodded. "Okay, make it quick. What the fuck do you want?"

"A piece of your action."

"What kind of piece?"

"Four thousand a month."

"That's a big piece."

"I've got a big prize."

He crossed his arms in easy anticipation, as if I'd offered to tell him a lawyer joke. "What prize is that?"

I made him wait for it. Somewhere, a siren mocked our lawlessness. Behind Hardy's hat, a top-heavy freighter steamed out of the bay with the grace and displacement of a hippo. The smells of leaking fuels mixed with the odor of decomposing marine life to make a stench as potent as kraut. The wind still whistled; the fog was still tangible and cautionary; the only humans in sight probably wanted me dead. I didn't hear anything alien or alarming, but I didn't know what that meant.

"I've got a girlfriend," I said when it was time to move things along.

"Great. So do I. Three of them, in fact."

"Mine is an assistant DA."

Hardy nodded with satisfaction, as though he'd beaten the information out of me. "So I hear."

"Then maybe you also heard she's running the grand jury looking into your little boys' club."

"I heard that, too. So what?"

"I can tell you what's going to happen in that grand jury before it happens."

His shrug was massive and self-explanatory. "Why would I care?"

"Because they're after the circus that's called the Triad and you're the ringmaster."

"Says who?"

"One of the witnesses before the grand jury."

"What witness?"

"Wally Briscoe."

His snort was brusque and autocratic. "Briscoe's not going to be a problem."

"Not anymore," I acknowledged. "But there are other witnesses where he came from. Do we have a deal or not?"

His sneer was damning and dismissive. "I still don't see what I get out of this."

"You get to know the evidence the DA's got against you. You get to know what times you need an alibi for, what forensics you need to explain, and what witnesses you need to discredit. And you get all that before you get your subpoena."

He started to walk away, then didn't. "Guaranteed?"

"Solid gold. But I need something in addition to the four thousand bucks."

"What's that?"

"Protection."

"From what?"

"From you."

"What kind of protection are you talking about?"

"I need a statement that you gave the order for Briscoe to be killed."

That his concurrence was immediate was the most frightening thing so far. "Okay. You got it."

"And I need the names of the triggers."

"Storrs and Prester."

"And I need to know that you or your people set the bomb that blew up Chandelier Wells."

"You got it," he said with a grin, as though we'd just perfected a juggling routine.

"And I need all of it in writing."

His smile turned sloppy and insecure. Without a word, he turned toward the Chrysler. "Kill him," he said to someone inside.

As two guys got out of the Chrysler and poked their handguns at me, Vincent Hardy turned back to me and smiled. "You want to know your mistake, Mr. Private Cop?"

"I'm always up for self-improvement."

"We *already* got a line to the grand jury."
"Not Jill Coppelia," I blurted, more as testimonial than question.
Hardy shook his head.
"Then who is it?" I asked.
But no one heard me.

chapter 30

The first shot cut Hardy off in midword. The second was a head shot that took out one of the guys with a gun trained on my chest. The third wasn't fired with a pistol, it was a volley of words made indelible by someone holding a bullhorn. "Freeze! Police! Drop your weapons and hit the dirt. You know the position. Assume it!"

After that came the floodlights, accentuating every evil detail of the impound yard, animate and inanimate, alive and dead. I stayed as still as I could and kept my hands in the air, hoping they'd know me as a good guy.

They had come over water, not land as the Triad had expected, the way Wolfe had come against Montcalm at Quebec. Lucky for me, the element of surprise had produced the same result—the grungy citadel that was the staging ground for the Triad's reign of terror fell quickly and decisively, with little in the way of resistance. The genesis of the assault—that someone in the police department would actually try to shut him and his criminal enterprise down—seemed more shocking to Vincent Hardy than the ambush itself.

Hardy wasn't a fool. Once his adjutant had been taken out, he didn't move a muscle except his lips, which stretched in a sardonic smile as his hands moved away from his sides in the universal gesture of surrender. The smile suggested what I already knew to be true—that this wasn't the end of the game, this was only halftime.

"I covered my ass, you pimp," Hardy hissed above the commotion that swirled around us. "I'll be back on the street before noon."

"Maybe," I acknowledged. "Or maybe you finally went too far. Maybe someone took the baton from Charley and decided it was time to purge the department of scum suckers like you."

His teeth gleamed like fangs. "There's nobody in this outfit with that kind of guts now that Sleet's in the ground."

I looked to my left, toward the platoon of cops who were rounding up a dozen or more of Hardy's henchmen. "I think the captain over there might disagree with you," I said as I watched Mark Belcastro fit a pair of plastic cuffs around the wrists of one of the men from the Chrysler.

"Belcastro eats shit," Hardy swore, then put his hands on top of his car and waited for someone to arrest him. If I believed the New Age mantra that all things happen for reasons, I'd believe that my finger had been broken in this very spot a year earlier to make this moment possible.

Impressed by their efficiency and élan, I watched Belcastro's troops round up the members of the Triad who were present for the festivities. The exercise culminated in the arrival of a paddy wagon to haul away the catch of the day. Such was the professionalism of the squad, none of the Triad put up an ounce of resistance, not even when Belcastro read them their rights.

Of the dozen men put in custody, none were Prester or Storrs. But if Belcastro had employed the eavesdropping equipment I'd suggested to Jill that he bring, Hardy's casual indictment of the two detectives would be admissible evidence and it would be only a matter of time before they were brought in. And if Jill was as good at her job as I thought she was, there would be so many cops rolling over on their confederates to cut themselves a deal, the Triad would be out of business before the end of the week.

I was halfway back to the Buick when Belcastro looked over at me from the paddy wagon and nodded, which I interpreted to mean he'd gotten what he needed to enable Jill to indict and convict. A moment later, as he was being herded toward a squad car and kept away from his mates, Vincent Hardy called out for the others to keep quiet till they talked with a lawyer, but his mandate seemed more plaintive than defiant. After that, one of the Triad men let out a loud curse as he was unceremoniously hustled into the paddy wagon by a cop who had taken the same oath to serve and protect the city as had his prisoner.

My gun was off the roof of the car and back in its holster when I felt a hand on my arm, then a kiss on my cheek. "Thank you for this," Jill said softly. "It will save us a lot of time."

I turned and gave her a hug. "And get you a lot of convictions."

"I hope so. You're all right, aren't you?"

"I'm fine. Though for a minute I was worried you were going to be late to the dance."

"Turned out the Coast Guard couldn't help. We had to use a fireboat."

"Nice job of improvising, counselor."

She grinned. "We got it all, too—video and audio both."

"That's great." I lowered my voice. "Did you hear the part about the mole in your unit?"

She nodded. "We think we know who it is. We had some suspicions ourselves, so we pretty much cut him out of the loop several weeks back."

"Good."

She couldn't suppress a wider smile. "God. I'm so wired I could fly. I'm starting to see why men like war so much."

"Maybe Spielberg will make a movie of it."

Something in my tone made her calm down. "I'm being silly, I know. If they'd started shooting, it would have been terrible. For one thing, you might be dead."

"Or hiding under a Honda, at least."

Her expression turned grave. "I hope this makes up for Wally Briscoe."

"It will," I lied. "In time." After absorbing the moment for another minute, I added, "There's one other thing that might help."

"What's that?"

"The FBI might have someone undercover inside the Triad."

"Really? What makes you think so?"

"The speed with which an ex-agent decided the car bomb that hurt Chandelier Wells wasn't targeting his pal Filson."

Jill's features furled prettily. "I don't know if that's a good development or not. The feebs foul things up as often as they help out."

"Just wanted you to know the score."

"Sure. Thanks." Jill looked once again at the benighted surroundings, this time with a proprietary air of obvious satisfaction. "I guess it's under control."

"Looks that way."

"I'd better get some sleep before the arraignments."

"Good idea."

"Will you call me tomorrow? I should be back in the office by eleven."

"Sure."

"I really do appreciate this, Marsh. The city will be lots better off with these guys behind bars."

"I know."

"Well . . ."

"Well . . ."

Like ballplayers after a big win, we were reluctant to leave the field, so we didn't. "Belcastro will want a complete statement from you, probably," Jill commented absently.

"Anytime."

"Their lawyers will be all over you, too. Trying to break down your testimony."

"I've dealt with lawyers before. If it gets to be a problem, I'll get one of my own."

"We could send someone down to advise you, I'm sure."

"I'll let you know."

"Well . . ."

"Well . . ."

"I should be going."

I smiled. "Yes, you should."

Her voice lowered to a lusty hum. "What I'd really like to do is make love."

"Me, too."

"Right here, right now."

"Me, too."

"Some sort of posttraumatic stress, I guess."

I laughed.

"Well . . ."

"Well . . ."

"See you tomorrow."

"Right."

This time we got the job done.

I drove home on automatic pilot, glad the ambush had worked out, glad Jill was glad, too, glad the police department might be a shade more upright in the months to come, glad I'd helped put Chandelier and Millicent and Violet and Eleanor out of danger. But my reverie was broken when I turned into my street and saw enough red lights to suggest all of the cops in the city were congregating at my doorstep.

I pulled to the curb and stopped, in the grip of the sudden fear that a gang war of sorts had begun, a struggle between good cops and bad for control of the department and in some sense the soul of the city. I took my gun out of its holster and laid it in my lap. Then I waited to see if the remnants of the Triad had come to exorcise me before I could do any more harm to their cause.

But the longer I waited the less sense it made. If they came for me at all, it would be a sneak attack from cover, an anonymous assault in a city that was full of anonymous assaults, not the obvious extravaganza taking place down the street. Something else must have happened; something other than my hunch.

Normally I park in the garage beneath the building, but the way was blocked by an ambulance and a squad car. As I pulled to the curb for the second time, two EMTs emerged from my building shepherding a body on a gurney. The body was entirely draped in blue blankets, and the flashing lights on the ambulance suddenly went dark—sure signs that someone had died under my roof. With a jolt of anger and adrenaline, it occurred to me that the corpse might have been in the way of a weapon that had been targeted at me.

When I opened the door to the building, I came face-to-face with a uniformed cop. He crossed his arms and inspected me as though I were stark naked. "You have business here, sir?"

Because of the events of the evening, I was sure I looked capable of whatever crime had just been committed. "I live here," I explained.

"Where?"

I pointed up. "Apartment three."

"How long have you lived there?"

"Almost twenty years."

"You know the woman in two?"

"Pearl. Pearl Gibson. Did something happen to her?"

"She's dead."

I sighed. "Who did it?"

The cop blinked and stepped back and put his hand on his weapon. "Now why would you say something like that?"

"I don't know. It just came to mind."

"She was an old woman. Seems to me what would come to your mind would be stroke. Or maybe heart attack. Not homicide."

"I saw her two days ago. She seemed as healthy as you do."

"Looks can be deceiving," he said, looking me over even more closely, as if to prove his point.

"I'd like to know what happened to her," I said while the inventory was still in progress.

He ignored me. "Where were you earlier this evening, Mr. . . . ?"

"Tanner."

"Tanner."

I nodded.

Something came to his mind and he voiced it. "You're the guy who killed Sleet."

"Afraid so."

"You were his buddy."

"Yes."

"He forced your hand."

I nodded.

The cop stuck out his hand. "Hollingsworth. Central Station. Charley was the best cop in the city."

"Yes, he was."

"They say you did him a favor."

"I hope so."

In response to some inner rhetoric, the cop made a decision to trust me. "Know anything about the old woman?"

"Not much. She was a little eccentric but she was nice. So it wasn't a violent death?"

He shook his head. "Not according to the ME at this point. Of course it's not official till the PM."

"When you find out for sure, will you let me know?"

"Sure."

He started to turn away but I grabbed his arm. "How come you're here, anyway?"

He shrugged. "All I know is someone called it in as possible foul play."

"Who?"

"Don't know."

"How long has she been dead?"

"Not more than twelve hours."

"How did the caller know about it?"

"Don't know that either. You might talk to dispatch at the station." He touched his hat like someone out of Dickens. "Have a good evening. We should be out of here in a few minutes."

"Take care. And thanks."

He turned away, then turned back. "You still didn't tell me where you were this evening."

"You'll read about it in the morning papers."

chapter 31

I slept late and stayed in bed even later. Although I should have been thinking about Jill Coppelia or Chandelier Wells or any number of other people nearer the core of my life, I spent most of my time thinking about Pearl Gibson.

After Hollingsworth had left the scene, another cop asked me if I knew any of Pearl's next of kin. I told him I didn't. Then he asked if I knew if she had any close friends. Although it occurred to me the mailman might qualify, I told him I didn't know of any. After they hauled her off to the morgue, I calculated my liquid assets with a view toward assuming the expense of her burial, since I seemed to be the only option that could keep her out of potter's field.

Inevitably, thinking about Pearl made me think about age and my birthday. And thinking about age and my birthday made me think about the future. More specifically, it made me wonder whether I could, in good conscience, keep doing what I had done for a living the past twenty years.

I had made plenty of mistakes over that time, but they had not usually turned out fatal, or even often embarrassing, until lately. But then I'd shot Charley Sleet. And in the case before this one— the death of a young woman down near Salinas—I'd made so many miscalls the local sheriff thought I was both nuts and inept. And just this week my unprofessionally romantic impulse to do a favor for Jill Coppelia had cost Wally Briscoe his life, not to mention that my tug-of-war with a gang like the Triad could have put my only child in jeopardy. As if that weren't enough, the woman I loved wanted me to quit my job and move somewhere I could cultivate a nice tan.

There were subjective aspects to the issue as well. Now that Charley was dead and I no longer had a sidekick, I wasn't all that crazy about the job any longer. Plus, other people's problems, particularly those brought on by stupidity or self-indulgence, which in my experience is most of them, seemed to provoke my ire more than my sympathy these days. Also, by any measure of the concept, I could no longer argue, even to my inner self, that I was much of a success at my trade. All of which would seem to resolve the issue except for one thing—I was broke.

I'd always been broke, more or less, but had usually been content to be thus, given the toll of being otherwise. But I was only a few weeks short of fifty. I needed to create some financial security. IRAs; 401(k)s; mutual funds; annuities. I needed all the stuff they prattle on about on CNBC to become part of my life.

Or maybe that was silly. Maybe my retirement plan was already in place. Ruthie had money to burn. She would pay me a handsome wage just to keep Conrad out of the house most of the day or to water her roses or whatever. And if Jill and I stayed together, I could sit back and let her pay the bills while I fished or played checkers or surfed the Web or did any of a number of other things retired people claim are fascinating. Jill seemed willing to participate in such an arrangement, and she certainly had the wherewithal to support me far beyond the style to which I've become accustomed.

All well and good, except if my life meant anything at all, it meant that morally and philosophically such arrangements were taboo. Under the Tanner Tenets, there are certain things a man doesn't do—he doesn't cook anything fancier than tuna sandwiches, he doesn't pay more than ten bucks for a haircut, he doesn't drink herbal tea, he doesn't watch PBS, and he doesn't live off of women.

But if Ruthie and Jill were out, where did that leave me? Looking for another line of work, presumably. But what? I had no particular skills, no particular expertise, no particular passions at this stage of the game. I'm not on-line, I'm not into wine, I'm not long in the stock market, I'm not transported by popular music. I'm neither notably energetic nor productively aggressive, and with fewer and fewer exceptions, I don't care for my fellow citizens a whole lot. I couldn't work with someone who thought he was my boss or with someone who believed I was his. So what the hell could I do? As with most questions I pose in the morning hours, nothing comforting came to mind.

In the nature of a diversion, I called Jill at the office. When she answered, I asked how it had gone at the arraignment.

"They all got bail but Hardy."

"Any of them looking for a deal yet?"

"All of them, almost. Hardy's going to be hit by a ton of adverse testimony. Even Jake Hattie won't get him out of this one."

"Jake's his lawyer?"

"And proud of it, so he says."

"How's Hardy affording Jake's tab?"

"We think Hardy made a fortune from his Triad operation. We're trying to trace his assets, but it's going to be tough. Hardy's not stupid and he can afford to pay someone to help him hide them."

"Do you think the Triad is out of business at this point?"

"Pretty much. Oh. I've been talking with Lark McLaren. I sent one of our computer people over to Ms. Wells's house and he's found stuff under a hidden file named Wally B. that has even more on the Triad than Briscoe gave us at the grand jury. Lots of names; lots of crimes; lots of narrative links. He spilled his guts to the woman for some reason."

"I think the reason was Charley Sleet. I think Wally figured, with his help, the next Chandelier Wells magnum opus could serve as Charley's memorial."

"You know that for a fact?"

"Not to a moral certainty. But Wally was a good guy and he thought Charley was God."

"So did you, you know."

I laughed because I'd just had the same thought myself.

"Want to have lunch?" she asked. "My treat."

"Can't. I've got things to do."

"Like what?"

"Call Cleveland, for one. Oh. Remember Pearl, the lady who lived below me?"

"Sure. She's a sweetheart."

"She died last night."

"Murdered?" Jill blurted.

"My reaction exactly, but apparently not. Probably natural causes, pending the final PM. My question is, what if she has no friends or no next of kin? Who takes care of her stuff and who arranges for burial?"

"The public administrator, if there's no will and no family. The current administrator's a man named Hardesty. Nice guy."

"You know him?"

"A little."

"Would you ask him to look into it for me? Pearl Gibson was her name. I don't want her lying around the morgue any longer than she has to. Tell him if there's a money problem, I'll take care of the funeral."

"I didn't know you were that close to her."

"She was a neighbor."

Jill waited for more, but I didn't have any. "Okay. I'll give Hank a call. You're a good man, Marsh Tanner."

"Only on special occasions."

After I hung up, I called the Cleveland number Millicent Colbert had given me. When I told her it was safe for her and Eleanor to come back to the city, her relief was audible. "Are you sure?"

"Reasonably."

"Is that enough?"

"I think so."

She hesitated. "Stuart called. He's quite upset."

"I don't blame him."

"He wonders if it's a good idea for you to come to the house any longer."

"I don't blame him," I repeated as a tremor swept through my veins. I envisioned Stuart blocking the door to his house the way George Wallace had blocked the door to the university.

"Or see Eleanor at all in the future," Millicent expanded.

My words were desperate and automatic. "I don't blame him. But I'm going to make it all right from now on."

"How?"

"I'm going to quit my job."

"No."

"Yes."

"And do what?"

"No idea."

"I can't see you working nine to five, somehow."

"Maybe I could help Stuart dress the models for the fashion shows."

Millicent wasn't sure I was joking. "I guess we don't need to discuss this now."

"Probably not."

"We'll fly back in the morning."

"Good. I'll meet you at—"

"Stuart can make the arrangements," she said with uncharacteristic primness. "But thank you. I'll call when we get home."

"Good."

"Eleanor's at the grocery with her aunt Margaret, or I'd put her on."

"Tell her hi for me."

"I will. Thanks for calling, Marsh. And for doing whatever you did to make things right."

"Tell Stuart I won't let anything happen. To either of you."

"I will."

"He won't believe it, but it will be true."

In the grip of a wild foreboding that the worst thing that could possibly happen to me might be in danger of actually occurring, I got in the car and drove across the bay to Alta Bates. If the Colberts put Eleanor off limits, the death of Charley Sleet would seem like a tailgate party.

Lark McLaren was where she always was, waiting for her boss's summons. This time she had her laptop whirring and her fingers flying, but above the machinery her lovely face had taken on the exhausted countenance of a refugee.

I took the seat next to her and touched her arm. "How are you?"

Lark started and looked up. "Mr. Tanner. You surprised me." She rubbed her face and closed the cover on her machine. "I'm fine. Just helping Gert put out a publicity release. You can't believe the press—they act like Chandelier's the reincarnation of Princess Di or something."

"You look like you forgot to sleep this month," I said easily.

"Nonsense. I'm up to three hours a night. It's a veritable feast of snooze."

"How's the boss?"

"Better, actually. Even I can see it."

"Can she have visitors?"

"Briefly."

"I'd like to see her for maybe a minute."

"Can I know why?"

"I'd like to give her my final report."

Her eyes grew lively and inquisitive. "You know who planted the bomb?"

I nodded.

"It has something to do with the police, doesn't it? The guy who came to look at the computer and the thing on the news this morning."

"Most of it does," I agreed.

Her eyes grew lively. "Wait a minute. You're the private investigator who was out there, aren't you?"

"Yes."

"Why didn't they give your name?"

"I don't know," I said, but what I thought was that Jill was trying to protect me from recriminations from the members of the Triad still afoot in the general populace. I didn't know if I liked that or not, since I wasn't in a position to protect Jill nearly as well.

"Are Chandelier and Violet out of danger?" Lark was asking fervidly.

"I think so."

"Thank God." She put her laptop aside and stood up. "I'll see what I can do."

She hurried away and returned in two minutes, which was

plenty of time for me to worry that I was being more optimistic than the situation warranted. "You can see her now."

"Thanks."

"Follow me."

She led me down two and a half corridors to the area marked INTENSIVE CARE. A doctor was waiting for us. So was Ruthie Spring.

I pulled Ruthie off to the side. "How's it going?"

"Slow as Sunday. What brings you by?"

"It's pretty much wrapped up, I think. You can take off anytime."

"That business on the news this morning have anything to do with it?"

I nodded.

"Quite a party out there, sounds like."

"Hats and horns."

"You were there?"

"Yep."

"I didn't hear your name mentioned."

"Just as well."

"So the cops Sleet was disposing of the night he got shot were the ones who did the deed to Chandelier?"

"Right. Most of the rest were collared last night."

Ruthie's eyes twinkled. "By your own personal DA, am I right?"

"So she says," I bragged, and felt oddly ecstatic about the sound of it.

I turned Ruthie toward the exit and gave her a little shove. "Go. Make Conrad happy. And send me a bill or I'll sue you."

Ruthie turned away, then back. "Some lady lawyer named Sundstrom was by. She wasn't pleased. With you or with me or with anything."

"People like Ms. Sundstrom are never pleased. It's why they're lawyers. They get paid to be malcontents."

After Ruthie had gone and Lark had introduced me to the young doctor, he gave me some scrubs and a mask to put on, then opened the door. "Second bed to the left. Don't make her laugh; don't make her cry; don't make her sneeze."

"Noted," I said, and entered the room, which, like all hospital rooms, gave me the willies and made me resolve to lose weight.

Chandelier Wells was a sight, and that was putting it mildly. There were tubes running into her and tubes running out. Her flesh was pink in some spots and black in others and swaddled in others with what looked like yards and yards of cheesecloth, as though they were preparing her for the deli case. The only part that looked normal were her eyeballs, and they were so bright they seemed fake. Even the bed was dramatic, with curved bars and ropes and pulleys and little motors that made it look like a car on a thrill ride, one that twists and twirls and makes you wish you'd skipped lunch. I wasn't sure, but I think it was so they could turn her over without touching her.

A nurse was hovering and so was the doctor. I walked to the side of the bed and sat in the chair already beside it. "It's Marsh Tanner, Ms. Wells. The detective. You hired me to learn who sent the notes and set the bomb."

I paused to see if she'd heard me. Only the blinks of her eyes suggested she did. And even that much response seemed agonizing for her.

"In both cases, it was cops," I went on, my voice a buzz through the mask. "Members of a gang called the Triad. The one Wally Briscoe told you about when you talked to him while doing research for your next book."

I got another blink so I went ahead.

"The leader, Vincent Hardy, admitted what he did to you and the DA has it on tape. Hardy's in jail without bail and the rest of the gang is spilling its guts to the DA. I don't think you or your daughter will have any more trouble from them. As far as I'm concerned, I'm off duty. It's been nice working for you. I hope you feel better soon. Oh. They killed Wally Briscoe. It was my fault. It didn't have anything to do with you and your book."

The next blink extruded a tear. Whether it was for Wally or me or herself was left for me to decide.

"If you have questions," I said, "I'll be happy to answer them, but your doctor would probably rather you didn't ask."

When nothing more happened, I stood up and left the ward after shedding the mask and the scrubs. Lark McLaren caught up to me as I was about to leave the hospital. "I want to thank you, Mr. Tanner."

"I was lucky. It happens that way sometimes. I'm just sorry Chandelier got hurt so badly."

"You were awfully nice to work with. People aren't, always. I just wanted to say I appreciate it."

I grabbed her hand and kissed it. "You're easy to be nice to, Ms. McLaren. You ought to give some nice young man the chance to reciprocate."

When I got back to the office, the phone was ringing. When I picked it up, a woman began screaming in my ear like a banshee.

chapter 32

T|he woman was Jill Coppelia and she had five sentences out
of her mouth before I understood a single one of them.

"You're going to have to start at the beginning," I said as
soon as I could get a word in edgewise.

Her breath heaved and wheezed as though she'd just played tag
with someone far more energetic than I am. "Okay. Okay," she
panted. "Just let me take a few breaths. There. Now. Where was I?
Oh. The beginning is, I got a call from Hank Hardesty."

"The public administrator."

"Right. He was calling about your friend Pearl Gibson."

"Has he made the funeral arrangements?"

"Yes. Or almost."

"Good. I just hope he holds down the expenses in case I end up
footing the bill."

Jill's titter was giddy, bordering on hysterical. "You're not going
to believe it, Marsh."

"Believe what?"

"What happened to Pearl."

My pulse started thumping the way it does when the subject
turns grisly. "What? Was she murdered after all? Was someone
after me and got Pearl by mistake?"

"No, I . . . Nothing like that. Calm down. Maybe I should start at
the beginning again."

My heart began to decelerate. "Please do."

She gulped a deep breath. "Last night about three A.M., the
police got a call from a man named Guernsey. Peter Guernsey."

"Like the cow."

"Whatever. Anyway, this Guernsey guy called the cops to report a possible medical problem with a woman named Gibson."

"What kind of problem was he talking about?"

"He didn't know. He just thought something might have happened to her."

"Why?"

"This is where it gets good. Guernsey had talked to Pearl on the phone earlier in the day—around four in the afternoon—and he made an appointment to come by the apartment to see her at eight. But when he got there, she didn't answer the door."

"Maybe she forgot."

"He thought so, too, for a while. But he didn't think Pearl sounded like she had any sort of memory problem on the phone."

"I never saw any sign of it."

"And he also knew this appointment was one she'd definitely want to keep. So he lay awake half the night worrying that Pearl was sick or hurt or something and finally called the cops to have them check it out. To give himself peace of mind, if nothing else."

"Which is where I came in."

"Right. I talked to an officer . . ."

"Hollingsworth."

"Right. Hollingsworth about the situation. He said he got the call a little after three. He and his partner responded right away, found a key under the mat, let themselves in, and found Pearl collapsed on the floor in the middle of the living room. No vital signs; no sign of violence or forced entry. He's pretty sure it was her heart or a stroke. And so is Guernsey."

"What does Guernsey know about it? Is he some kind of doctor?"

Jill paused. "Guernsey didn't tell Pearl precisely why he called, but he could tell she was getting excited so he figured she'd guessed right away. He also figures the excitement is probably what killed her. He feels pretty bad about it, apparently."

"I still don't get it. What excitement is he talking about?"

"Guernsey works for an outfit called the Manumission Corporation," Jill went on, her voice taking on the fullness of parody.

"Never heard of them."

"Neither had I. And for good reason. They publish a magazine called *Balls*."

I laughed. "That sounds like something Pearl would have lying around. She read tons of magazines. Or subscribed to them, at least. She got them because she thought they would . . ." A light came on somewhere in the vicinity of my frontal lobes. "Wait a minute. You're not going to tell me Pearl *won* something, are you?"

Jill could barely contain herself. "That's *exactly* what I'm telling you."

"This guy Guernsey made an appointment to give her the prize."

"Right. Which he knew she would want to accept. Which is why he thought there might be a problem when she didn't answer the door."

"Makes sense."

"Yes, it definitely does," Jill said somberly, as though we'd solved the riddle of the Sphinx.

"So I guess this means she can pay for her funeral," I joked, just because it hurt to think of Pearl lying dead in her little apartment for hours on end. And to think she finally won a prize that would capture some attention, but she wouldn't be around to enjoy it.

"That's not going to be a problem," Jill was saying. "Pearl's final expenses will be easily covered out of the assets in her estate."

"So I'm off the hook."

"Right."

"Did they find any family?"

"No. Hardesty is sure there isn't any."

"Too bad. How much did she win, do you know?"

"I'm glad you asked that question." Jill was practically bursting with news. "Are you ready?"

"Sure."

"Six million dollars."

"What?"

"Six million."

"For a *magazine?*"

"This Manumission Corporation is new on the scene in this country. They're owned by a huge Dutch publishing conglomerate that's trying to get a foothold in our market. They're trying to make *Balls* the new *GQ* or *Maxim* or something. And they hoped to make their first big splash with this sweepstakes deal."

I laughed. "Which was won by an eighty-four-year-old widow, not some swinging young stud."

"Right."

"Life does get good once in a while."

"It's going to get even better. Believe me."

"So Pearl was worth six million dollars when she died."

"Right as rain, Sherlock."

I still didn't like it when she called me Sherlock. "Too bad Pearl isn't around to enjoy it," I mused, my mind on the fortress of magazines.

"There's something else." Jill's tone of voice seemed tentative all of a sudden.

"What?"

"It seems Pearl left a will. Holographic. Written a few days before she died. Signed and dated. Completely valid in the state of California."

"And?"

"She left her real property to a man named Larson."

"What real property?"

"She owned an apartment house, apparently. Out on California Street somewhere. Do you know anything about this Larson person?"

"Not much." I laughed. "I think he's our mailman."

"You're kidding."

"I'm pretty sure that's the guy. He and Pearl were buddies."

"Well, he's a richer man today than he was yesterday." Jill paused long enough to take a sip of something. "But he's not as rich as you are."

"Then that apartment house must be a major slum."

"Not really. Because Pearl Gibson's residual heir is you. Marsh Tanner. Apartment three. Which means you're worth at least *six million dollars*. Before estate and inheritance taxes, of course."

When I didn't say anything, Jill laughed. "Did you hear me?"

"I'm afraid so."

She laughed yet again. "Marsh?"

"What?"

"Maybe I'd better come over and help you get through this."

epilogue

aster. Come on, Tanner. Floor it! We're going to miss the
beginning."

"It's only a movie. Which you've seen twenty times."

"But the beginning's the best part."

I increased my speed to forty-five, hoping the cops who patrolled
Van Ness during the workweek were bowling or boozing on Sat-
urday night instead of looking for scofflaws like me.

When I pressed the pedal, my Buick groaned at the abuse. A
woman on the corner shook her fist as my rusty muffler frightened her dog. And Jill punched me in the arm with her fist. All so
we could make it to Jill's place in time for her to see her favorite
actress, Katharine Hepburn, and her favorite actor, Cary Grant, in
her favorite movie, *The Philadelphia Story*, on Channel 27. We had
to get to Jill's house because I don't get Channel 27. I don't get
Channel 27 because it costs extra. But as people keep reminding
me ad nauseam these days, I don't have to live like that anymore.

I took a left on Lombard and another on Broderick and wound
my way to the cozy nook that was Jill Coppelia's handsome home.
I was surprised we arrived on schedule, actually, since my mind
had been even more wayward and undone than usual ever since Jill
had told me about Pearl Gibson's winnings and her will. As it
turned out, everything Jill had said on the phone was true and then
some—for reasons known only to her, Pearl had made me a rich
man. I'd barely ventured out of my apartment since hearing the
news, which Jill thinks means I haven't come to terms with it yet. I
think it means I'm determined not to let my windfall make me flagrant and crude and ubiquitous.

I parked at the curb, went around to open Jill's door, took her hand to help her out, and wrapped my arm around her waist as we strolled up the walk toward her house. "Nice night," I said absently, meaning, I imagine, that it wasn't raining.

"I hope so," she said, and dug her elbow in my side. There'd been a lot of that lately—jokes and pokes and tickles. I'm not sure it's a compliment to either of us to say that Jill was happier about my good fortune than I was.

When we reached the stoop, she handed me her key and I unlocked the door. When we were inside, I handed the key back to her, but in the crepuscular gloom of the foyer, she dropped it. "Just a minute," she said. "I'll get the lights." Whereupon she bumped into things and banged into other things, making enough noise to wake the neighbors.

I stayed put till the lights came on, then fished the key from under an antique church pew that served as a coatrack, and handed it over. Jill dropped it in her purse, checked her hair and makeup in the mirror above the antique commode, then tugged me toward the center of the house. "Come on," she urged. "We'll barely make it."

Like a child being towed toward the potty, I followed her down the hall and into the pitch-dark of the den. "A bulb must have burned out," Jill said, and fumbled for the switch on the wall. An instant later the room filled with light. An instant after that, a chorus of voices yelled, *"Surprise!"*

There were thirty or more of them, emerging from a variety of hiding places, smiling broadly and bellowing my name, toasting me with various forms of libation, and reveling in my dismay and embarrassment. The celebrants included virtually everyone I knew in the city, almost everyone I considered a friend but for two: a mother and a daughter, and the mother was still mad at me.

I looked at Jill, who was grinning as if this were a beauty pageant and she was Miss Congeniality. "I suppose you're to blame for this," I muttered.

"Ruthie, too."

I surveyed the throng. "I'm not sure the name tags were necessary."

"We didn't want people to take it too seriously. Plus with you about to turn fifty, some of us got concerned about your powers of recollection."

I stuck out my tongue. "So what's the occasion?"

"Your good fortune, of course. And your birthday. These people are happy as clams for you."

"Good for them."

The grin dropped off her face the way spoons drop off a table. "If you're going to be a grump about this, I'm going to be royally pissed."

"We wouldn't want that."

"No, we wouldn't."

I took a deep breath. "I'll be good. And thanks."

"Don't mention it." She goosed me in the side again and gave me a quick kiss. "Till later, that is. Now mingle."

Jill moved off toward the crowd clustered like minnows near the buffet table, leaving me vulnerable to attack from all sides. The first to venture forth was Zorba, proprietor of my favorite restaurant. His HI, I'M ZORBA tag almost put me in stitches.

"I got to get back to the café," he said in his still slightly broken English. "I want to say I'm happy like punch for you."

"Thanks, Zorba."

"I name a breakfast after you, next time I redo the menu."

"You don't have to—"

"Marsh Madness, I'm calling it. Bacon, Cheddar, and onion scramble, just like you like. What you think?"

"Sounds great."

"Good. See you in morning."

"I'll be there."

"Good. Old ways are best ways. Money not same as happiness. Is true?"

"I'll let you know."

Zorba left, to be replaced by the triple divorcée from Guido's who had brought me tons of food when I was laid up after Charley had shot me. Her smile seemed a little less than pure, but maybe that was projection. Even after all the casseroles, I still didn't know her name.

"So you hit the jackpot," she said after a sip of straight bourbon from a Waterford glass that she gripped with both hands.

"Looks that way."

"Guess you won't be needing any more tuna casseroles."

"I'd eat tuna casserole three nights a week if I could."

"Your girlfriend might not like it if I dropped by that often."

"My girlfriend may need to broaden her gustatory horizons."

A glance at Jill and then at her glass made her decide not to pursue the flirtation. "You going to keep coming to Guido's?"

"Sure."

"Guido says hi, by the way."

"He does not."

She grinned. "Well, he thinks it, at least."

I laughed and she waved good-bye and drifted back toward the pack. Jill swept past, handed me a highball, but kept moving. "Blink twice when you need a refill," she said over her shoulder, then headed off toward the kitchen. She was replaced by Al Goldsberry, pathologist and charter member of the poker group.

As usual, Al was a man of few words. "Hey, Marsh."

"Al."

"Heard the big news."

"Miracles actually happen, apparently."

"I see them every day in the hospital."

"This is a little different."

"Not really."

Not for the first time, I declined to debate him. "Thanks for coming down," I said instead.

"Glad to. We got a game Friday night?"

"My place at eight."

"Great." Al looked left and right. "Marsh?"

"What?"

"Your friend. Jill." He leaned closer. "She's more of a treasure than the money."

"Thanks for confirming my suspicion."

Al hurried off when he saw Ruthie Spring lingering and waiting a turn. "Now you and me got *two* things in common, Sugar Bear," she began with her usual bluster.

"What's that?"

"One, we loved the hell out of my late husband. Two, when we weren't looking, a big bag of money fell right on our heads."

"Right on both counts, Ruthie."

She lowered her voice. "The thing you need to know is, I made my peace with both of them. It took time, and it was damned hard work, but eventually I found a way to be happy."

"I know you did."

"So don't let this money business drag you down like I know it is now."

"I'll try."

"Hell, it's all serendipity anyway. Some people are allergic to lobster; some people strike it rich."

"But rich people usually earn it."

"Bullshit. Rich is random, Marsh. Was, is, and always will be. It'll help if you keep it in mind."

Ruthie moved off toward the bar, and Tommy Milano replaced her. "I brought some of that ravioli you like. Want me to bring you a plate?"

"Maybe later, Tommy."

"We playing cards next week?"

I nodded. "My place."

"Great. Well, I got garlic bread in the oven. I better keep track of it."

"Thanks for bringing the food, Tommy."

"No problem. You come to the restaurant some night next week. I got a nice Chianti Classico put back for you. We drink to your *buona fortuna.*"

"I'll be there."

After Tommy left, Jill brought me a fresh drink. "How are you holding up?"

"Fine."

"These are really good people, Marsh."

"I know."

"And every one of them adores you. You should be proud of that."

"I am," I said. "Except when I'm afraid I haven't kept up my end."

"Gangway," Clay Oerter directed before Jill could instruct me further in matters of group dynamics. He sidled up to her and planted a kiss on her cheek as naturally as a dog licks a bone, then shook my hand with vigor. Clay was a stockbroker. He was used to making the most out of parties. "So the big guy finally hit the jackpot," he said to Jill.

"Big time."

Clay regarded me with the glint of a guy who works on commission. "We should talk."

Jill excused herself and Clay edged closer. "Sooner or later your uncle back in Washington will try to take a big bite out of your money. We need to get together with Andy and figure out how to turn the bite into a nibble."

"Probably so."

"Plus we should put the funds to work right away. There are some diversified futures programs I'd like to put you into. Any idea when you'll get the first check?"

"Not for several more months."

"Good. Because people are going to be coming out of the woodwork with bright ideas about what you should do with your money. I'd like you to run them past me even if they sound good to you."

"Will do," I said without knowing if I meant it.

When Clay motioned for him to do so, Andy Potter joined us. "Between the two of us, we should be able to keep you solvent for a few years," Andy said after we exchanged pleasantries.

"So far that's been a tough task."

"But now we've got something to work with. I'll have our trust and estates guy make me a memo on your options."

"Okay. But let's wait till the money shows up."

"Sometimes it's better to have things in place beforehand."

I shrugged. "Whatever's right. As long as the bill is contingent on actual money being in an actual account having my actual name on it."

"I'll talk to you, Marsh," Andy said. "Nice party."

"Thanks."

Clay and Andy moved away to huddle in private just as a commotion sounded from somewhere back near the foyer. A moment later, Jake Hattie swept into the room, complete with a blonde on his arm and a cape down his back. *"Tanner,"* he boomed with his usual bluster. "I hear now I'm only ten times as rich as you."

"Conservatively."

"Shit, the only conservative thing about me is my Rolls. Now you got money, you should get in the horse business. I got a three-thousand-dollar claimer would be perfect to start a small stable."

"I don't think I'm going down that road, Jake. Thanks anyway."

"You see your colors cross the line in front, it's better than sex." He squeezed the blonde closer to him. "Course there's always the chance someone will prove me wrong."

The blonde tittered and jiggled and scolded, then Jake swept her off toward the door, having given me my quota of his valuable time.

By the time the perpetual whirlwind that was Jake Hattie had calmed down, Ruthie was back at my side. "There's someone in the sunroom," she said in a near whisper. "Wants to talk to you privately."

"Who is it?"

She shook her head. "Check it out; I'll stand guard." Ruthie shoved me toward the door at the end of the room.

The lights were out, so when I slid the door to the sunroom open, I couldn't see anyone amid the furnishings and drapes and wall hangings and the shadows formed by the spotlight shining from a post in the garden outside. Then a figure rose off the couch and moved into the pool of light to make sure I saw her. "Hello, Marsh." Her voice was warm and unmistakable.

"I'll be damned," I managed.

"I hope you don't mind. Ruthie called to tell me the news and . . . I wanted to be here."

"I'm glad," I said, amid rushes of memory from the ocean of time during which Peggy Nettleton had become my secretary, and then my lover, and then a comparative stranger until I had gone to Seattle to help her solve a delicate problem with her stepdaughter, which was the last time we'd talked.

I walked to where she was and we hugged, isolated in the bright light of memory and sentiment. "You look great," I said, because she did.

"You do, too," she said, because she was kind.

"How are things in Seattle?"

"Fine."

"Ted?"

"Fine."

"Nina?"

"Fine as well. Thanks to you. They send their love."

"Good."

She grasped my hand in both of hers. "So you won the lottery."

"The equivalent, at least."

"That's so great. You've been poor long enough."

"I was never poor, Peggy." For some reason, at this place and time, the declaration seemed important.

Peggy hurried on. "You know what I mean. Now tell me about your personal life. Ruthie hinted at developments."

"I seem to be in love. With the woman who owns this house."

"How wonderful."

"Yeah."

"Have you set the date?"

"Not yet."

Her expression made me take her next question seriously. "But it's real?"

"I think so. Yes."

"What's her name?"

"Jill Coppelia. She's an assistant DA."

Peggy smiled. "When I worked for you, you weren't so kindly disposed toward DAs."

"I guess I'm a changed man."

"I hope not. And I hope you're eternally happy, Marsh," she added as I colored from what I regarded as praise. "I really do."

"I know you do," I said, trying not to be disappointed that the news of my romantic entanglement didn't seem to faze her.

"Which doesn't mean I still won't think of you every day," she was saying, which let me think that maybe she was fazed after all.

"I'm glad."

"And wonder what it would have been like if we'd worked things out ourselves."

"I know."

"But that's life."

"That's something, all right."

We looked at each other for a long time, then kissed as chastely as siblings. "I'd like to meet your girl now," Peggy said when she backed away.

"Sure."

"Does she know about me?"

"Everything. Almost."

"That will make it easier."

"That was the idea."

She took my arm and we went into the living room. I caught Jill's eye and motioned for her to join us. After I introduced them and they hugged the way women do, they went off to chat at Jill's insistence and undoubtedly at my expense. To keep from getting more confused than I needed to be, I wandered the room like a good guest of honor, greeting latecomers like Carson James and Betty Fontaine, feeding my face on the fly, and feeling only a little less foolish than I had after the lights had come on and people had started yelling.

Several minutes later, Ruthie began clapping her hands. "Attention, please. Listen up. It's time to present the guest with his gift."

She reached for my hand and pulled me to her side. "Not that he needs it or anything, but we wanted to get Marsh something to remember this by. So we gave him something he craves."

Ruthie pointed to a huge round ball of something that was sitting on the coffee table, wrapped in red paper and tied with a big bow. "Open it, Marsh. So these folks can get back to the booze."

I tore off the paper. Beneath the wrapping was a magnificent cut-glass bowl, twice the size of a basketball, etched with smoky scenes of the city and filled to overflowing with Oreos. The only way to stop grinning was to eat one. "Perfect," I said around a mouthful of crumbs. "Thanks to all. And thanks for coming. And thanks to Ruthie and Jill for putting it together."

I should have stopped talking, but I raised my glass. "A toast to absent friends. Harry Spring. Charley Sleet. Pearl Gibson. All of them changed my life for the better. As have all of you. Thanks for sticking with me all these years. And for giving me the best times of my life. I appreciate it more than you know."

To keep from breaking down, I drained my glass in tribute. "I'll try to spend the money in ways that will make you proud of me."

Lots of people clapped; a few people even started crying.

I was one of the latter, and that was before they started singing "Happy Birthday."

Stephen Greenleaf is the award-winning author of thirteen previous John Marshall Tanner novels, most recently *Strawberry Sunday*, for which he was nominated for an Edgar Allan Poe Award, and *Past Tense*. A graduate of Carleton College in Minnesota, he received his law degree from the University of California at Berkeley and attended the Iowa Writers' Workshop. He lives with his wife, Ann, in northern California.